ABDUL KUNDI

Legacy of the Third Way

A novel

First edition

ISBN: 979-8-9897642-0-4

Cover art by Ali Jamali
Illustration by Flaticon.com

This book was professionally typeset on Reedsy.
Find out more at reedsy.com

Dedicated to my mother, Hukum Jana; she was the best storyteller.

One

Prologue

I t was raining more than usual this February in Fresno. The lawn outside looked lush green and soothing to the eyes. It was late afternoon, a few hours to sunset, but an overcast sky with clouds slowly descending, casting early darkness on the city. Sher Shah was standing at the window, looking out, lost in his thoughts. He was donning khaki pants and a blue-striped shirt with his signature mandarin collar. The clothes fitted loosely on his over six-foot-tall frame, suggesting recent weight loss. His wrist sported an automatic watch, considered antique in these times of smart everything. He stood motionless, with one hand in his pocket and the other on his chin, hardly covering his beard that was thinner near the temples and thicker at the chin. His snow-white hair hinted at a wealth of experience, and a well-worn wedding ring had formed a groove on his finger.

He was in a small room with beige-colored walls and a white

roof, featuring a wooden floor adorned by a Persian area rug with white, green, and red floral motifs. The room had only one door, and a tall window looked out to the backyard. To the right of the window was a small wooden writing table with just one drawer in the front. There were three full letter-sized notebooks lying on the table with a denim-style cover.

Sher Shah had bought these in the morning while passing through an antique shop on the street in the old town, intending to record his thoughts on them. They looked primitive, as paper notebooks were no longer in use. The use of paper was deemed environmentally harmful, given the vital lung function of trees essential for purifying polluted air. Fresno, surrounded on three sides by mountains, encountered unique challenges as the Pacific Ocean breeze transported polluted air into the Central Valley from the industrial centers of Southern and Northern California. In response to these environmental considerations, the law required the recording of almost all personal notes and writings on digital devices, that were seamlessly connected to remote servers. Access to these digital contents remained consistently available through a secure encryption key assigned to each citizen by the federal government.

Sher Shah had more than just a mistrust of the state as a reason for recording his life story in paper notebooks. He saw humanity as being in a perpetual state of war, with civilizations constantly destroying each other throughout history. From the Roman and Persian empires, in antiquity, decimating each other to the twenty-year war between Europe and Russia in the 2030s, warfare has been a constant to resolve contests for geopolitical power between regions. The Russo-European war included cyber and weaponized warfare, which led to the destruction of the digital and physical infrastructure of these countries, taking them fifty years backward. These wars had not just caused economic losses but inflicted intellectual destruction as well, with many works of art and manuscripts being lost in the fog of war.

Having visited museums in Egypt, Europe, and the Americas, Sher Shah had seen how written words had survived over time, preserving the stories and knowledge of past generations. He believed that entrusting his life story to digital bits and bytes on a distant server was too precarious, as it could disappear with the flick of a switch. Instead, he chose to take a chance on paper notebooks, wanting to ensure that some part of himself would survive for future generations, even after his body returned to the earth and dissolved into it.

One of the walls in the room displayed a digital picture frame cycling through a collection of family and other pictures. Now, it was showing a family group photo. In the picture, Sher Shah stood in the center alongside a petite woman with gray hair, a light brown complexion, brown eyes, and a full curvaceous figure. Surrounding them were young men and women, accompanied by over half a dozen children seated on the ground. Adjacent to the picture frame hung his electrical engineering degree in a nice wooden frame.

There was a bookshelf in one corner. One of the shelves displayed book covers, showcasing the reading interests of the occupant. The books represented a wide array of topics, from non-fiction works of history, arts, psychology, philosophy, and politics to novels about life and its drama. The books were authored by contemporary and classical-era writers from the early 20th century. One of the bottom shelves had artifacts from Africa, Asia, and the Americas. It appeared that Sher

Shah was a well-read and well-traveled person. The bookshelf was not just a piece of decor but also a great conversation starter for his close friends who occasionally visited him in the study room. The room had a two-seat brown leather sofa beside the bookshelf and a small round coffee table to facilitate these conversations.

The small room was his sacred place to hide from the world. The room was always kept cozy, with a light spring-style breeze filling the space through invisible pores in the walls. He would spend many hours of the day, especially early morning and late afternoon, reading, writing letters, meditating, receiving important calls, just like the one he had today with his oncologist, or taking occasional naps.

No one was allowed to enter the study room except his wife, Nour. She could enter anytime without knocking. Whenever she came, they would sit on the brown loveseat to talk about family matters, gossip about friends, or make vacation plans, as both loved to travel. One of their favorite pastimes was watching comedy movies or short clips on their synchronized artificial reality headsets. Whenever they sat, they never failed to hold hands as if to create a connection for the current of life to flow between the south and north poles of a magnet. The usual disagreement between them would be about music. He liked music playing in the background, but as soon as she entered it had to be stopped. His music taste varied from classical to modern. Despite his efforts to find a genre of music to her liking, it never worked, and the only option left was to stop it whenever she was there.

Sher Shah walked away from the window and started pacing the room, still deep in thought. The room was beginning to fill with darkness from the outside. He uttered in a loud

4

voice, "Lights and Mozart Symphony 40." His command lit the room with soft yellow light, and music started streaming as if emanating from the walls.

Having paced for a few minutes, Sher Shah came to a halt at the table. While standing, he began to flip through the empty pages of the notebooks he had purchased earlier that day. Lost in thought, he absentmindedly voiced, "I don't have time. I don't have time. I don't trust the government. Why should they be privy to my inner thoughts on life and my feelings about various events? I need to narrate my life story and share the lessons I've learned. I don't want the probing eyes of the state to intrude on my personal reflections. I don't have time. I must commence writing without delay." Contemplating, he questioned whether three notebooks would suffice to encapsulate the experiences of a seventy-year lifespan. Perhaps he should have procured more.

Two

Birth

⁓⚬⚭⚬⁓

Sher Shah entered the study room still in his pajamas and a nightgown. He held a mug filled with hot black tea made with milk and sugar. Steam still rose from the cup, creating interesting patterns in the cool morning air. He had inherited the morning tea habit from his Asian father, while his American-born mother preferred black coffee, like most fellow Americans. It was his way of staying connected with his father, who was often absent from his life during early childhood and teenage years. Whenever his father was home, he would make tea for both of them in the morning. They would sit, talk, and enjoy their tea at the kitchen table while his mother prepared breakfast. His father favored a hearty breakfast with an omelet, jam, bread, and fruits. This was another habit he had acquired from his father. He could skip lunch or dinner, but a good breakfast was a must-have to start his day.

Sher Shah gazed out the window to check the weather. The sky remained overcast with clouds, but the rain had ceased. Droplets of water and dew were tenaciously clinging to plants and trees. He spotted a hummingbird flitting from flower to flower, sipping nectar to nourish its dynamic small body. Honeybees were competing with the hummingbird for the nectar. The weather was gradually warming as it was nearing the end of winter paving the way for the upcoming spring as it approached the end of February. Fresno was getting ready to welcome spring.

Sher Shah sat in his study, gazing out of the window with a distant look in his eyes. The familiar hum of the news channel that usually filled the room with the latest updates was conspicuously absent. His cup of tea sat untouched, slowly cooling on the side table.

As he stared into the distance, it became evident that something weighed heavily on Sher Shah's mind. The routine that had grounded him for as long as he could remember was disrupted, and the absence of the news ritual spoke volumes about the shift in his priorities.

Perhaps he had reached a point where the constant influx of global events no longer held the same significance. It could be that personal matters had taken precedence, required attention, and overshadowed the importance of world affairs. Or maybe, he had grown weary of the relentless stream of information, needing to detach momentarily from the external chaos.

His decision to break away from the routine hinted at a deeper contemplation. In this departure from his daily ritual, Sher Shah's study transformed from a hub of current affairs to a sanctuary of reflection. The digital screen remained dark, the newspapers unread, and the outside world temporarily pushed to the periphery. It was a momentary retreat, a pause in the ceaseless flow of information, allowing Sher Shah to navigate the currents of his own thoughts and emotions.

Sher Shah's mind wandered back to the previous day's conversation with the oncologist. The oncologist had explained the gravity of the situation, detailing the aggressive nature of the colon cancer that had resurfaced for the third time.

As he sipped his tea, Sher Shah couldn't help but feel a mix of emotions—resignation, frustration, and a tinge of fear. The ergonomic chair, designed for comfort, seemed almost out of place in the heaviness of the moment. His wife's thoughtful gift, aimed at providing relief from his recurrent back pain, contrasted sharply with the emotional and mental challenges he now faced.

Reflecting on his health journey, Sher Shah pondered the role of genetics in his condition. Was the recurrence of colon cancer an inevitable outcome, written in his DNA? He thought about his family history, wondering if there were symptoms or patterns that he might have overlooked when it appeared the first time.

Despite the gravity of the situation, Sher Shah found solace in the routine of his favorite chair, the familiar surroundings of his writing desk, and the warmth of the tea. Perhaps these small comforts provided a temporary escape from the harsh reality of his ongoing health struggles.

Lost in thought, he contemplated the road ahead. The battle against a relentless illness was not new to him, the prospect of facing it once again required a different kind of resilience. Sher Shah knew he needed to draw strength from within, leaning on the support of his loved ones and the lessons learned from previous encounters with illness.

Over the course of three months, he had lost nearly twenty pounds of body weight. His doctor had suggested looking into his health charts to consider replacing his colon with a 3D-printed organ compatible with his DNA. Sher Shah had hoped his healthy lifestyle and determination to live would enable him to conquer the illness for the third time, but it was not meant to be. During the holographic phone call, his oncologist had shown him that many other organs in his body were now infected with cancerous cells, and replacing the colon was no longer an option.

Although Sher Shah had been prepared for the worst, the news still shook him. He asked his doctor how much time he had left, but as with any professional doctor, no definitive timeframe was provided for him. It seems doctors felt hope can add to a person's lifespan. He was told he could live anywhere from a few weeks to a year.

Still contemplating how much time he had left on this earth; Sher Shah opened the notebook and retrieved a ballpoint pen from the mug holder on the table. He wanted to write about his life—lessons from a life well-lived that could guide others in facing the vagaries of existence, rather than making the same mistakes he made through trial and error. He remembered the emotions of dealing with the uncertainties of making choices, but there had been no one to guide him as he reached adulthood without a father.

Sher Shah ran his hand over the blank pages of the notebook, feeling the grainy surface of the paper. He recalled how his father had taught him to flip the pen on his fingers and catch it before it fell. It had been many decades since he held a pen in hand. He was well acquainted with the law prohibiting writing on a piece of paper, even personal, private thoughts. However, nearing the end of his life, he no longer cared about the state's iron fist imposing laws and punishments. He believed freedom of expression should encompass the medium and method of expressing oneself.

Staring at the blankness of the notebook, Sher Shah pondered, "Where do I start? Does it hold any value? What should I include from my life?" Gripping the pen, he carefully scrawled the date, "April 8th, 2020." Writing those simple three words proved challenging because he hadn't held a pen in hand for over three decades. His fingers seemed to struggle to grasp the slippery surface of the ballpoint pen, and his handwriting was so poor that he worried no one would be able to read it. Nevertheless, he decided to press on and complete what he had set out to do. It was better than idly waiting for death.

* * *

April 8th, 2020

I should not be alive today. I was supposed to be a stillborn, destined for death upon arrival. Whenever I felt sad or depressed, my mother would remind me to be grateful for every day of life and to face life's challenges with a smile. It was easier said than done.

I arrived in this world on Wednesday, April 8th, 2020, on a sunny day at noon, at a local community hospital. My birth was far from easy; in fact, it was a perilous affair from the start. I nearly lost my life in my mother's womb when the umbilical cord wrapped tightly around my neck. It hindered the flow of blood to my brain. It seems through this struggle for life in the womb of my mother, I learned to survive even before being born. It was as if I had decided not to embrace life and was on the brink of surrendering to being prevented from experiencing it. Fortunately for my parents, who had attempted for years to conceive a child, the doctors intervened just in time to perform a procedure that brought me into this world alive, kicking and screaming.

Of course, I was too young to remember the events of my birth. I learned all these facts from the collection of family videos and my parents' endless reminders of it. My mother liked to record every event on her smartphone. One of my cherished childhood memories is watching the video of my father rushing into the hospital room, his face beaming with joy, as he took me into his arms. He gently placed his index finger on my lower lip, playfully plucking it like the strings of a guitar, all the while speaking to me in his heavy Punjabi accent.

"My Sher has defeated death. Look at these strong arms and legs," he would exclaim, using the term for a lion in his native language.

"Shah, come here, give me the baby to feed him," my mother called from her hospital bed, using his first name—an unconventional practice in South Asian conservative families, where women typically referred to their husbands by their last names or with a respectable nickname. Women were expected to show deference towards their male spouses.

A friend of my father, who was recording the event, turned the camera toward my mother as she called out to my father. She appeared tired but in good spirits, having delivered a living baby, sparing herself the tragedy of yet another failed pregnancy. The thought of carrying a fully formed child within her womb, only to lose it, would have inflicted a deep and enduring pain, one she might have carried with her throughout her life.

"Balbala, I'm going to call our son Sher Shah. What do you think?" Shah Zaman, my father, asked, using the nickname he had chosen for her. It took me a long time to discover that my mother's real name was Zarqa.

"Whatever you like, Shah Zamana. I'm just happy we have a living son," my mother replied, playfully altering his name Shah Zaman, to sound like Pashtun, her parents' native language.

They quickly agreed on the name, but I would bear the brunt of the slurs that came with it throughout my school years. My friends would mockingly call me an animal, referring to the "Sher" part of my name; my football coach would taunt me for my poor performance by suggesting I change my name from Sher Shah to Sowar Shah, using the Urdu term for a pig—an American symbol of laziness. I was grateful my father never heard this slur from the coach because being called a pig was an unforgivable offense in his culture. In my father's native country, you can call a person anything, but calling someone a pig would certainly result in a fistfight. He would have most definitely complained to the principal to reprimand the coach.

Shah Zaman, my father, was a tall, brown-skinned man with a lanky stature hailing from Khushab, a district in the Punjab province of Pakistan. He belonged to a well-to-do family with substantial agricultural lands. He was forced to seek asylum in the United States in the late 1990s after a deadly land dispute erupted between my grandfather and his brothers. He was just nineteen at the time of migration and had recently completed high school. Fortunately, he arrived in the USA when immigration laws were not as stringent as

12

they would become in the aftermath of the terrorist attacks on the New York Twin Towers. While he eventually obtained citizenship, the difficulties faced by Muslims post-9/11 left deep scars on his psyche. He would panic if the doorbell rang after nine o'clock at night or when police stopped him for a traffic violation. I never asked him if he faced interrogation from law enforcement that induced these episodes or if was it just a fear derived from the stories of others.

Lack of education and language barriers pushed my father into physical labor. He worked odd jobs to survive and eventually obtained a truck driver's license, providing a steady income for the family but taking him away from home for most days of the month. He would jokingly tell me that the only difference between him and a pilot is that pilots are too scared of the chaotic traffic on the roads to drive on land.

Zarqa, my mother, was a stark contrast to my father. She had a fair complexion, beautiful green eyes, medium stature, and a soft curvaceous figure. My favorite hiding place, when tired or anxious, was curling up in her lap and resting my head on her arm. She was born into a conservative Pashtun family in New Jersey, where her father worked at a gas station throughout his life. They lived in the USA but maintained a lifestyle as if they were still in northern Pakistan. My mother never wore Western attire; at home, she preferred to dress in traditional shalwar kameez, a South Asian dress made of long shirt and baggy trousers. When she ventured outside, she donned a long shirt and wide-bottom pants. I never saw her leave the house without wearing a hijab.

My parents' unlikely union was orchestrated by the imam of a New Jersey Mosque that my father frequented during his long-haul trips. It was an arranged marriage, but they fell deeply in love. Theirs was a match between two lonely souls craving love and affection. I never witnessed them engage in heated arguments, perhaps because my father was away most of the time, and they cherished the few moments they spent together. Some days, I would find my father sleeping on the living room couch. It was the only indication that they had fought the previous night, leading my mother to banish him from their bedroom. On such occasions, I would lie down with my father, and he would put his arm around me.

When he woke up, he would start brewing tea for us and talk to me.

"Sher Shah, every day is a new day. Forget about what happened yesterday. Plan for today and tomorrow," he would often say. He practiced what he preached. When my mother emerged from the bedroom to prepare breakfast, he would crack a few jokes, and they would swiftly return to being the loving couple they were.

I eagerly awaited my father's return from his work trips for a reason – he never came back empty-handed. Without fail, he always brought gifts for me and my mother. On various occasions, I received my first stuffed toy, a tricycle, my first tablet, and a mechanical watch, which I received on my eighteenth birthday. That watch was of such exceptional quality that I still wear it today whenever I need to feel emotionally connected to my father during moments of distress and anxiety.

I was the product of this culturally and ethnically diverse couple, a blend of their genes. I inherited my father's height and had a complexion that fell somewhere between his and my mother's. It was neither too light nor too brown. My hazel brown eyes earned me a nickname from my mother who used to call me her "almond-eyed son". My jet-black hair was inherited from my father, but it had a hint of curls from my mother. I had my father's narrow chin and my mother's high cheekbones. My lips seemed to be a fusion of both, with a full upper lip like my father's and a gently curved lower lip like my mother's.

Trucking was a demanding but well-paying profession, allowing my mother to stay home and take care of the family. She was an ambitious woman and started a food catering business to keep herself occupied during the long periods of my father's absence.

My birth was not the only challenging event; it occurred during a period of severe financial hardship for everyone. Four months before my arrival, in December 2019, a COVID-19 pandemic swept across the world, leading to complete lockdowns in most cities.

Humanity often forgets that social interactions are akin to blood flowing through our bodies; they keep us emotionally and psychologically healthy. The immediate response by the government to the COVID-19 pandemic was to enforce a complete lockdown. Families were forcibly separated from their neighbors, colleagues, and even strangers whom you would greet in a store or mall in normal circumstances. Initially, people were euphoric about working or staying at home, not realizing the impact of this isolation, from other humans, on their mental health. However, it eventually led to incidents of depression and loneliness. Financial worries became the least of their concerns, partly due to government-funded welfare programs, but social anxiety became unbearable.

There was also an emotional price to pay. Children and

grandchildren could not meet, hug, or hold hands with their parents or grandparents who were infected with the virus and died. Funerals remained unattended due to the lockdown, leaving an open emotional wound of not being able to bid farewell that couldn't be cured. We all need closure to an emotional wound because failure to do so means it keeps hurting all our lives.

Despite these hardships, human resilience could not be defeated by the virus. In a short span, scientists developed vaccines to contain the spread of the virus. These vaccines were approved without the usual lengthy human trials because there was no time to lose. A cure was needed post haste. Humanity remembered the devastation of the Spanish Flu pandemic in the twentieth century. The vaccine was based on genetic changes in white blood cells to fight the virus. It worked but resulted in a permanent change in human behavior for some people. Some experienced changes in sleep patterns, while others complained about the onset of asthma. Some even talked about changes in their food preferences.

For the four months preceding my birth, my father had been unable to work because there was no cargo to transport in his truck due to the lockdown. He was rapidly depleting his meager savings. While the government had announced some financial assistance, it was insufficient to cover all expenses. In addition, the family had to shoulder out-of-pocket hospital expenses related to my birth, that were not covered by health insurance.

At that time in April 2020, there were discussions about the possibility of a year-long shutting down of all businesses. Governments around the world were in a state of panic. My father later told me that an elderly couple living on the same apartment floor had contracted the virus and passed away within days. In the video recorded at the hospital, my father appeared joyful, but a deep worry line marked his forehead. He had a newborn son to provide for, and there was no end in view to the lockdown and his chances of returning to work. It felt like walking in a dark tunnel leading nowhere.

While Americans are known for their compassion and empathy under normal circumstances, emergencies often bring out the same greed and insecurity inherent in human nature. The lockdown had instilled fear in people, prompting them to hoard groceries and household supplies. A lack of fresh supplies strained quantities available for sale on store shelves and heightened people's fears, causing them to hoard even more. News channels showed images of empty store shelves, with the most sought-after item during the pandemic being bathroom tissue. In news footage, people could be seen pushing shopping carts filled to the brim with rolls of bathroom tissue packages.

The situation was deteriorating into civil unrest, forcing the government to allow long-haul trucking operations to resume after six months. This put an end to my father's misery, and he returned to his trucking job. However, those six months without work had wiped out all his savings.

"My son, these Americans should wash themselves instead of just wiping their bottoms with a tissue. How can they be clean with just a piece of paper?" my father used to remark with a hint of sarcasm. Little did he know that the humble bathroom tissue would eventually bring an early end to his financial woes. He never made that comment again after the pandemic.

Despite his lack of formal education and social status, my

father was a man filled with hope and raw wisdom, which he imparted to me.

"Son, you were born at the height of spring when no one expected you to be born alive. Never forget that and shine like the gentle spring sun," he would remind me every now and then. I never forgot my father's words of wisdom. Even during the darkest times, I would hold on to hope for brighter days ahead.

Three

Sibling

S her Shah sat at the writing table, massaging his fingers. It had taken him over three hours to write a few pages in the notebook a day earlier. His handwriting had gradually improved, but his finger joints had been hurting all evening. He took a sip of tea from his cup and continued massaging his fingers. The illness had impacted his taste buds, and the tea didn't taste good. He drank it out of habit rather than enjoyment, and it also caused discomfort in his abdomen afterward. Nevertheless, he refused to give up his tea; he wouldn't let illness dictate how he lived his life.

Bright sunlight streamed in from outside, giving him hope that he might live long enough to complete writing about his life experiences. As Sher Shah reread the pages, he wrote the day before, they sounded mundane and uninteresting. Doubt crept into his mind, questioning whether it held any value or was just another one of those daydreams he was blamed for having all his life. Nour, his wife, would always make fun of him, saying, "You want to go to Mars in your electric car." For every project he had undertaken, he wanted to be the best and unmatched, but most of his life's work could be called average at best by his high standards.

Despite these reservations, Sher Shah was determined to continue. It was another of his lifelong habits: to finish a project, even when it was clear that it wouldn't produce the desired results. Thinking about adding something about his junior and middle school years, he realized he couldn't recall anything particularly significant and of value from that time. He had been an average student who completed his homework on time but wasn't considered bright. Setting aside those years, he decided to write about an event that had allowed him to share the, until then, undivided affection of his parents with another.

* * *

July 27, 2027

I was a happy child. My parents adored me, and I was the focus of their undivided attention. All this changed on July 27th, 2027, when my mother gave birth to a girl. The events of that day are still fresh in my memory. My mother had been preparing me for her arrival by telling me bedtime stories about princesses in fairy tales. As a child, I was curious and excited to meet a princess.

"Ma, when are we going to meet the princess." I would ask her incessantly during the final months of her pregnancy. She would smile and tell me to be patient.

"Shero beta, princess cannot be met that easily. We have to

prepare for it."

I remember entering the hospital room holding the index finger of my father's right hand. He first went to my mother and kissed her on the forehead to congratulate her on successfully ending the ordeal of delivering another baby. Then we went to the cradle, where I could see a tiny little baby tightly held together in white sheets.

"Sher Zamana, you named our son, but now it is my turn to name our girl. I want to call her Zar Wareen," I heard my mother say as we walked towards the newborn.

"Balbala, it is a good name. But I am going to call my princess Bulbul," my father responded with a burst of laughter, suggesting a nickname for the baby. For him, the arrival of a daughter had completed his dream of an ideal family.

It was the first time I felt jealous that my father gave his daughter a nickname but never gave me one. I was still Sher Shah with no nickname.

As we walked to the cradle, I was unsure how to feel or behave with this tiny creature. I was not yet tall enough to touch the baby myself from behind the wooden structure of the cradle, so my father had to take me in his lap. He bent down so I could have a look at that tiny creature. I peeped into the cradle and saw a fair-skinned tiny little baby. I stretched my hand to touch her hand. It was so smooth and soft. I instantly felt a connection with her. It was my first experience of feeling love for a stranger.

When she was brought home from the hospital, initially, it was difficult for me to adjust to sharing and dividing the attention of our parents with the new member. My toys were no longer mine alone. I felt ignored and unimportant. Anytime my sister cried, one of my cherished toys would be given to her to play with. They expected me to hand it to her and not feel bad about it. It made me envious of her in the beginning. Sometimes, I had to throw tantrums, for no apparent reason, to attract the attention of my parents and regain their undivided affection, even if it was for the briefest moment. But all this changed as my sister grew older. She was fun to be around—playful, witty and had infectious laughter.

I adjusted to her presence in the house until we entered our teen years. We lived in a small house with only two bathrooms—one in my parent's bedroom and the other outside that I shared with my sister. As we grew older, it became increasingly irritating to have only one bathroom shared between us. First irritant, she liked long baths, using the excuse that she had to untangle her long curly hair. Second, I started dealing with feminine items that were none of my business. I wished so much at the time to have my own separate bathroom.

Despite the competition for attention and the typical sibling conflicts that became frequent growing up together, my sister would become the center of my attention. I was her fall guy. Everything she broke was somehow my fault. Every excuse she needed to go out with her friends, I would be her alibi and chaperone, even when I did not even accompany her. Even her love marriage had to be arranged by me. She was a duplicate copy of my mother. Whenever they would go out, people thought they were sisters. The only difference between them was that she refused to be a compliant housewife and pursued her ambitions with gusto.

She was an intelligent and high-performing student in school, unlike me who struggled to keep his grades sufficiently high to enter college. She became a successful human rights lawyer. Perhaps she should have been the one writing about her experiences instead of me.

She would play a significant role in my life when a tragedy struck later in life, leading to a midlife crisis of identity and purpose. Her experience as a human rights lawyer was an asset, always my first point of contact.

Four

Tragedy

S her Shah was feeling sad today without any apparent reason. Illness could have taken hold of his emotions or possibly the impending end of his life. He never understood whether it was chemical changes in the body that occurred first to create an emotion or whether it was the emotion that triggered the chemical changes in the body. He would joke with his doctor friends that they diagnose based on chemicals rather than the cell. If they could communicate with cells, then a cure could have been possible with more accuracy. After all, the illness was a sickness of human cells.

His downcast mood triggered the insecurity that was an integral part of his persona. He read the notebook pages from yesterday and wondered if anyone could even read his handwriting. Gen Gamma was trained in school and at home to read typed text on their tablets, computers, and smartphones. They had no exposure to handwritten text. He pondered if he should read the notebook to his grandkids during their weekend visit. He decided it was better for them to read his life story when he was long gone. It was better for them to cross this hurdle and read it after he was under six feet of dirt.

Sher Shah opened the notebook and stared at the blank page for a long time, not knowing exactly where to start next. His high school years were uneventful. He could not recall any significant event worth remembering and reporting. His teachers helped him learn the academic subjects, that was all. No other aspect of his interaction with them left a significant impression on him. He was a shy, introverted kid who felt awkward in social interactions. His sporting contributions were limited to the school football team, although he was dropped from the team for lack of performance.

Sher Shah was a street-smart student, good at completing his work but not quite smart enough to earn high grades. He remained in the middle of the class bell curve, neither performing terribly nor exceptionally well. His daily routine during those four years of high school was consistent: go to school, participate in a sport, and spend time with friends and family. His school group of friends all came from middle-class families, and their preferred pastime was watching movies, playing a sport, virtual reality video games, or hanging out at a coffee shop. Occasionally, they would take day trips to nearby mountains or visit resort towns in Southern and Northern California.

His lackluster school performance prompted him to consider giving up on the ambition to go to college and taking the easy route of becoming a truck driver like his father, Sher Zaman. Truck drivers earned a decent income and enjoyed autonomy with a flexible schedule. Best of all, there was no supervisor breathing down a person's neck demanding to do more and more. His father was certainly very happy to hear about him considering trucking as a career choice, his mother, on the other hand, would not have any of it. She pointed out the prolonged absences of his father from home and the inherent insecurity of a day job with minimal benefits for unforeseen circumstances. She wanted him to earn a college degree in any subject of his choice and explore a career in the corporate sector. Eventually, she prevailed over him.

His grades were average, barely enough to qualify for college admission, despite that his street-smart attitude in dealing with competitive exams earned him good scores on his SAT. His active participation in volunteering for community events and youth group activities made his college application substantial. Believing that a person could never succeed if they didn't try. Sher Shah carefully considered colleges that offered a realistic chance of acceptance; these would form the bottom half of his application list. While Ivy League colleges might have seemed out of reach, he still saw no harm in applying. He selected the top five Ivy League schools for the upper half of his application shortlist.

Sher Shah expected that, at least, some of them would find him good enough to consider admitting him. The gamble did pay off, and he was accepted at Stanford and Fresno State, as well as a few others. He recalled that the acceptance by Stanford even surprised him and reaffirmed his faith in his father's advice: "Shera, if God has allowed you to live rather than die in the womb, then there must be a good reason for it. Always try things that seem impossible to achieve. A thing may be difficult, but it's always possible to achieve."

Sher Shah remembered his decision to join Stanford. Only if fortune had favored his choice, would he be crafting an entirely different story, but the facts of a life are not built on speculation but reality. It was time to write about the first real tragedy of his life.

* * *

January 9th, 2039

After my birthdate, January 9th, 2039, was probably the most important day of my life. A child would die that day, and a man was born. It would change the direction of my life in unexpected ways and shatter all my well-thought-out plans for a get-rich-quick future. The memories of that day are as fresh as if it all happened yesterday.

It was an unusually cold winter Sunday. The sun was out with a clear sky, but it was not hot enough to warm the city. I woke up that day considering myself a lucky person. I had dreamt the night before about meeting some technology startup founders at Stanford and joining their team for quick riches. I dreamt of becoming a millionaire before reaching twenty-five. Success and riches seemed to be within my grasp, not just an unfounded daydream.

I applied to three Ivy League colleges as well as a bunch of lower-tier ones, including the local engineering college at Fresno State. When Stanford contacted me for additional information, I was happy but surprised. It turned my fluke into a real possibility.

My father didn't care much about which college I went to. My mother was both happy and sad. She was delighted that I was getting into a top school but saddened by the thought of me going away, possibly never returning. It was too much for her to bear. My father was usually away because of his work, and now I was also going away. She never expressed her sadness to me, but I could feel it in her demeanor and see it in her eyes. Once again, my father came to the rescue; he assured my mother that he would give up his long-haul work and find a local delivery job to stay home with her. This solved the problem and lifted the burden of guilt from my conscience.

Once I had the burden of leaving my mother alone lifted, I responded to Stanford's request for additional information. The letter of admission acceptance arrived a few days after my father left for his latest trucking trip to New York. The acceptance letter required confirmation of my consent to join Stanford by Monday, January 10th. I had already started preparing to move to Northern California by the end of July to start graduate college for the fall semester.

That January, the East Coast was experiencing a severe winter storm breaking historic records of the last one hundred years. Analysts blamed climate change for this record-shattering cold weather. The weather forecast worried my mother, she expressed her concerns when my father was preparing to leave on his work trip a few days ago.

"Shah Zamana, cancel this trip. There is a snowstorm approaching the East Coast," I recalled my mother imploring my father to stay. "Sher is going to leave for college soon. We should be together during this time as much as possible," she made a last-ditched effort to stop him from leaving.

"Balbala, you women always have unnecessary worries," my father responded with his customary cheerfulness. "I've been driving for over twenty-five years and been through snowy winters over a dozen times. I'll be back home in a few days to help our Sher prepare to leave for college." His commitment to work and supporting his family was non-negotiable.

I woke up that Sunday with a plan to respond to Stanford, informing them of my decision to join their engineering program before the deadline of Monday, January 10th. I wanted to celebrate this unexpected success by treating my mother and sister to breakfast and taking them out for lunch at a local restaurant my mother liked.

I was busy preparing breakfast when my mother's phone rang. I could hear her greeting one of her friends. Within a minute, she was crying inconsolably. I rushed to the living room and saw her slumped onto the sofa, still crying. She motioned for me to turn on the living room TV.

A thought crossed my mind that some natural calamity had happened in Northern California, given its earthquake-prone locality. But I was wrong; the calamity had struck closer to home. The news channel was reporting a traffic accident on a major East Coast highway due to bad weather.

"Ma, why are you crying about a traffic accident?" I asked, still annoyed about the disruptions to my breakfast preparations. These traffic pileups were quite common in the East Coast winter. It never crossed my mind until then that these accidents were causing grief to people and giving rise to tragedies. My attitude was insensitive, lacking empathy for others in my youthful exuberance.

"Shireen told me she saw your father's truck flipped on its side in the traffic accident," my mother informed me while still sobbing, referring to the phone call she had just received.

"How can Shireen Auntie be sure it was father's truck?"

"She saw a Pakistan flag sticker on the side of the front window and 'Mashallah' written in the center," my mother responded wiping her tears with her head covering, referring to an Arabic prayer used by some for divine protection. "How many truck drivers do you know in America who would have these two symbols?"

It was my turn to be worried, but I made a herculean effort to keep my hopes high and to console my mother.

"Let's not assume anything until we can confirm it," I told her with as much normalcy in my voice as I could muster.

I called my father's mobile phone, but there was no response. Our inability to reach him deepened our worries. Hearing noises from the living room, Zar Wareen came out of her bedroom to find out the reason for this early morning ruckus. She was a strong girl with nerves made of steel, but the fear of losing her father at such a young age was traumatic for her. We kept trying to reach my father, as well as his friends and colleagues, yet there was no confirmation about his whereabouts or well-being.

We remained in a state of panic until the New York police confirmed that my father had had an accident and succumbed to his injuries before help arrived at the scene. For the first time, my mother's worst fears were realized. The house that was supposed to celebrate my success turned into a house of grief and sorrow.

Everything happened so fast and unexpectedly that I had no time to fully grasp the situation. My immediate concern was to console my mother and sister. My own grief would have to wait for later.

We learned later that my father was right about his driving skills in bad weather, but he forgot that other potentially reckless drivers on the road could cause a fatal accident. A self-driving car in front of my father's truck suddenly stopped because the sensors, covered in snow, misread the information from the road about driving conditions. To avoid a collision, my father instinctively took a steep turn that made the truck flip on its driver's side. The safety window was supposed to smash and not hurt him, but bad luck had it that a piece of rock at the side of the road broke the window glass inward causing a piece of it to pierce his neck and ended his life on the spot. The rider in the self-driving car also lost his life. Our grief was shared by another family not known to us but connected at that moment. It is in the nature of the human condition we rarely experience grief or joy alone. It is almost always shared with others whether we like it or not.

My father's truck had a self-driving feature, but he was an old-school man who did not trust the computer.

"I feel worthless and not doing my job sitting in the cabin if I let the truck drive itself," would be his response whenever I asked him to give it a try. In the end, he was both right and wrong at the same time. Such is the nature of our existence. Life rarely exists in black or white. It is usually gray.

It was not just the untimely death of my father but also the death of my dreams to go to Stanford and join a high-flying startup. My rag-to-riches story ended before starting. It was also the death of a child and the birth of a man. I could not bring myself to act selfishly, to leave my mother and sister alone while they were still grieving and fly off to a university to pursue a degree. I had to stay home to arrange for the burial of my father and take care of my mother. She was too young to be a widow, and my sister was too young to be without a father at home. At nineteen years old, I was biologically an adult but still not ready to carry the heavy burden of the family. But it was a moot point. I had to accept my responsibility as head of the family and do it with a smiling face.

I informed Stanford University about my inability to join their program and sent my acceptance to Fresno State College of Engineering. Despite the tragedy, I could not let my mother's dream die and become a truck driver. She wanted me to be educated and have technical skills.

My father was smart enough to realize his profession had inherent risks. He had bought an insurance policy that provided some financial relief, but still, I had to work two jobs to support my family and pay for my education. They were tough years for sure, but they made a man out of me who was resilient and self-confident.

I lost a friend on January 9th, 2039. It left a void that would remain unfilled most of my life. He left when I needed him the most, but it was not his fault. He had escaped Pakistan to avoid a violent death at the hands of his uncles. He had come to a foreign land, hoping to live until natural death claimed him in old age. But it was not meant to be. He died a violent death at just 50 years old.

It seems there is a higher power that has its plans and can disrupt our best-laid plans just when we feel our path is clear. I was supposed to be dead on arrival, but I was still alive. My father was gone, and with him went my old plans for a future out of the window. I was walking down an unknown path from that day. I would be executing a life plan designed for me by destiny.

I cried at the loss of my father after a month.

Five

Nour, the light

The memories of his father's death in the road accident reignited Sher Shah's daily curiosity about global events. He switched on the wall TV to catch up on the world news and read the two newspapers, as he had done for as long as he could remember. The interruption of the last few days had not made much difference. The world had not changed since he had stopped watching the news. There was the usual war in some corner of the world, hunger and famine in another part, protests about the rights of people in an oppressed country, and election campaigns in another country. The news appeared stale and uninteresting; he turned off the display after watching it for about thirty minutes.

It was Saturday, a day when his children visited them with their kids. He always eagerly waited for their weekend get-together. His children were born and raised in America, but

Nour, his wife, ensured they adhered to Eastern cultural norms. The bright and cheerful faces of his grandkids renewed his zest for life. It was this emotional medicine that had helped him successfully fight colon cancer twice before. He was not sure if it would help the third time around, as the disease had spread, and his body was older.

Sher Shah sat at his desk, staring blankly at his notebook. His thoughts were scattered, and he couldn't focus on anything. He knew he wanted to write, but the fear of interruption loomed over him. His kids would be home soon for weekend lunch, and he didn't want to start something he couldn't finish. As he sat at his writing desk, he could hear the rattle of utensils coming from the adjacent kitchen. It was Saturday, and Nour was cooking meals not just for her family, but for the homeless as well. Sher Shah admired his wife's ethical principles, as she shared the same food with strangers that was served to the family. Nour was an active social worker, contributing significant time to community work. Sher Shah smiled as he remembered how he would jokingly tell her to ask God to let him enter heaven as her manservant. She was a few years younger than him and still in good health, and he couldn't help but feel grateful for her presence in his life.

Still undecided about whether to write or not, he looked out the window to check the weather and saw a package lying on the grass. Apparently, Nour had ordered something from an online retailer, and the delivery was made by a drone drop-off. The package was wrapped with an extra layer of plastic strings and had a digital lock. There was no need for plastic protective strings since the delivery was made in their backyard, but Nour, a cautious person, wanted to create one more hurdle for an aspiring unknown thief who could not contain an urge

34

to steal it. Looking at the package made him wonder if he had forgotten one of his grandkids' birthdays, and his wife had ordered a gift for them. She was always a lifesaver for him in such situations.

Just then, Sher Shah realized that the most significant event in his college life was meeting his future wife. Remembering the excitement of their brief love affair leading to marriage. She was the light of his life, illuminating the dark corners of his soul, as her name Nour literally meant. He decided to capture the moment and write about it before his grandkids arrived for their lunch together.

* * *

December 25, 2042

On a cold Christmas morning, I was sitting on a park bench, engrossed in reading the environmental compliance report of the food processing company's boilers, where I had taken up an internship position during the winter semester break from college. I always preferred studying outdoors whenever I could. I found solace in observing life unfolding around me when tackling a boring academic subject or reading a dry environmental compliance report. In this state of mental boredom, a sound breached my ears, like a melodious tune to wake up my slumbering brain.

"Shero, what's so captivating that you can't hear me calling you?" She used my distorted nickname, a choice usually reserved for my close friends and family.

I looked up and saw her round eyes, resembling decorative glass pebbles with a myriad of colors. At that memorable life-changing moment, her eyes felt like a portal into her soul, and

I got lost in them for a long moment. It took me a while to notice the rest of her: a yellow checkered shirt, a pair of jeans, and jogging shoes. She possessed curves that were hard to conceal in her loose full-sleeved shirt.

"How did you find me?" I asked, puzzled, as I hadn't informed any of my friends about my whereabouts that morning.

"I was out for my morning walk when I spotted you completely absorbed in your computer," she replied. "At first, I thought you must be reading a love letter or something equally intriguing."

That was Nour, one of the three girls in our Fresno State study group, pursuing a master's degree in philosophy.

I often teased her, "Nour, you've chosen the wrong major. How many women philosophers do you know in the history of mankind?" She'd respond by calling me a misogynist, sexist, intolerant, and a woman-hater.

Although I had known her for over two years, that day felt like the first time I saw her soul. She stood close to me, and I felt a strong urge to reach out and hold her hand. Instead, I said, "What philosophical problem are you pondering during your morning walk?"

She completely ignored my question and instead inquired about what I was working on so early in the morning on a Christmas holiday.

"These vacations are meant to have fun and enjoyment. You are a boring man, Shero. What is so important that it cannot wait for a few days?"

"I think I'm falling in love," I blurted out, ignoring her sarcasm. Without wasting a moment, she promptly took a seat on the bench in front of me. I had raised her curiosity.

"Who's the unlucky girl?" she asked playfully while intently looking at my facial expressions.

"I can't tell you because, so far, it's a one-way affair," I replied blushing with anxiety that she could possibly read my mind.

"I can be your messenger if you're too chicken to tell her yourself."

"I'll consider your offer when I have some indication that she's interested too," I said returning her piercing gaze.

"What does she look like? Where did you meet her?" Nour was persistent, not letting me evade her questions.

"She looks like you," I confessed without fully realizing the impact my words would have on her. Probably the expression on my face and my eyes that startled her.

I saw a quick blush spread across her face, making her abruptly get up, "let me know if I can help you. Falling in love is better than failing in love." I watched her walk away and sensed a swagger in her step.

The conversation on that cold December morning ultimately led to a love affair. Gradually, Nour came to realize that I was falling in love with her, and she reciprocated. She was the only daughter of a cardiologist father and a high school teacher, immigrants from Karachi who were considered wealthy by American standards. They owned a paid-off house in a posh area of Fresno, three European luxury cars were parked in their garage, and a wardrobe filled with expensive clothes and jewelry. They owned many rental properties around the city. Despite their visible opulence, the family remained firmly rooted in their conservative Eastern traditions. Nour was a unique blend of American individualism and Eastern family values.

Nour made it clear, early on, that if we were serious about

being together, I would need to meet her parents and seek their approval for our marriage. I had no objections, as I was about to complete my engineering degree in a year. I felt it was the right time to start a family.

I would often tease her, "I had to leave Stanford and the potential to earn millions of dollars to be with you at Fresno State." Recalling my decision to join Stanford before the untimely death of my father.

Nour would respond without fail, "What good would millions of dollars be if you don't have love in your life?" Her perspective was influenced by her own experiences at home. Her father was a good doctor but a cold husband and a distant father.

While one might think that marriage shouldn't be an issue between two consenting adults, it's often a different story in Asian families. It's not just a union between two individuals; it's the merging of two families. My mother was thrilled that I was marrying a Pakistani-origin girl, especially after her daughter had chosen to marry a white American. She had given her approval for our marriage before even meeting her potential daughter-in-law.

However, Nour's father became a stumbling block that had to be removed to pave the way for a union. Dr. Rabbani was a successful doctor but had become intoxicated by his success and wealth. He expected his daughter to marry a surgeon or a specialist, a replica of himself. When he learned that my father was a truck driver, he refused to meet me and rejected the idea outright. Nour's mother Afshan Rabbani, who had suffered from her husband's lack of compassion and empathy, sided with her daughter. She was delighted that her daughter had found an Asian heritage man to marry. It was her nightmare scenario that her daughter might marry someone alien to her culture, so she became an ally to Nour. She was wiser than her husband. Together, they used persuasion, tears, and even threats to convince her father to at least meet us.

The initial meeting got off to a rocky start. As soon as I walked in and shook hands with Dr. Rabbani, who stood at 5-feet 4-inches, I could sense his insecurity because of my 6-foot-tall frame and strong handshake. Doctors tend to be self-assured, and any hint of insecurity is unbearable for them.

"How much does an engineer earn in a year?" he asked with an air of arrogance and contempt, as soon as we were seated in their living room.

I wasn't prepared for such a direct question about my potential income. "On average, around $65,000 in the first year of employment out of college," I replied with a hard-to-hide hint of annoyance.

"The car my daughter drives costs more than twice that amount," he retorted, insulting me in front of my mother and future wife. "Where do you live?" was his next question.

"We live in an apartment on Shepherd and Maple," my mother quickly responded before I could answer. She knew this line of questioning was going to boil my blood pretty soon.

"Where are you from, sister?" Dr. Rabbani continued his interrogation, casting angry glances at his wife and daughter. Immigrants often faced such questions from others, not from their own community.

"I'm from New Jersey," my mother replied calmly with a disarming smile.

"Sorry, I mean, where did your family migrate from to the USA?" Dr. Rabbani became defensive because of his lack of clarity.

"Ah, you mean our ancestral origins. I was born in New Jersey, but my parents migrated from Peshawar. Sher's father migrated from Khushab, Punjab."

"We are from Karachi," Afshan Rabbani, Nour's mother, interjected impatiently, eager to move past this interrogation.

This initial coldness from her father led me to believe that our match was doomed from the start and that our brief and intense love affair would come to an end in tragedy. 'Living happily ever after' is generally reserved for fairy tales, after all. Most couples experience the ups and downs of life. Sometimes they weather the storms together, and at other times, they fall apart and part ways. However, I couldn't have been more wrong about our prospects. Little did I know that Nour was a woman of steel. Once she set her mind to something, nothing, in the world, could stop her from achieving it.

If I took the first step in falling in love, it was Nour who made our marriage happen. We were a perfect match in that regard. I would propose, and she would take charge of delivering. Within a year, we were married, just as I was completing my engineering degree and securing my first job offer from the same company where I had interned a year earlier.

Marrying Nour was the best decision of my life. I used to tell her that she was the woman part of me, and I was the man part of her. Why? Because we were both born on April 8th, though a few years apart.

"God sent me ahead of you, woman, so I could prepare the world for your arrival," I would remind my wife every now and then.

"You did not do a good job. Look at all the wars and misery

around the world," she would tease me. "But I hope our home has love, peace, and comfort. If you could do that then I can call you a success."

We lived in a small apartment after marriage. It was an adjustment for Nour because she moved from a big house to a two-bedroom apartment shared with my mother. As a married man, I had to make some adjustments in my lifestyle too, but they were minor compared to her. My mother and wife quickly developed a comfortable relationship. Nour appreciated her help at home while she got busy completing her PhD in child psychology and establishing her career.

While people often say that opposites attract, we were the same in our temperament and outlook on life, yet different in our genders. She was feminine and respectful, while I was masculine and loving. I was more emotional and impulsive, while she was rational, likely influenced by her education in philosophy. When reflecting on our life together, I feel that she accomplished more than me, taking care of our home, raising our children, engaging with the community, and building a successful career as a child psychology expert. I, on the other hand, contributed by helping at home, working as an engineer, and later getting involved in social and political work. She was the better half of the equation. The light shone brighter as we aged.

Six

Children

〜◦⃝◦〜

Sher Shah felt he had no strength due to frequent visits to the bathroom, and his colon's inability to absorb water from digested food left him dehydrated most of the time. Medical science suggested a healthy human body comprised 60% water; he wondered how much of that was left in his frail body.

A day earlier, as he wrote about Nour, Sher Shah had realized that his wife had lived a fuller life than he had. Even the birth of their children could be credited more to her than to him. While he had played a role in conceiving the children, she had shouldered the burden of pregnancy for nine months and safely delivered healthy babies. After their birth, she had assumed all the primary responsibilities of feeding, clothing, cleaning, and assisting them with homework. He had always been there to support them, but his contributions had been nominal at best.

In contrast to Nour, Sher Shah's life appeared to be a series of decisions that had resulted in highs and lows for his family. He began to contemplate whether his notebook served as a confession of these wild rides, ones he hadn't acknowledged for all those years. Recalling his social science teacher's wisdom, "Failure is the best teacher you can have. Never repeat the same mistake twice; always make a new mistake," he could proudly affirm his compliance with this advice. However, the issue lay in his struggle to learn how to make better decisions that could lead to success and satisfy his ego. Despite his numerous setbacks, he had always seen his ideas through to completion, demonstrating his unwavering persistence and discipline.

As he opened his notebook to make his next entry, he decided to report only the significant events in his life and keep his notes concise rather than sounding long-winded. It was time to write about his children, they enriched his life and provided a meaning to his existence.

* * *

May 20th, 2051

Nour and I were compatible life partners, and we usually quickly reached agreements on most family issues and decisions. However, there was one topic on which we had an irreconcilable disagreement, and I still occasionally expressed my discontent about it. Right after our marriage, I had a deep desire to have many children, and I wanted them soon.

"It would be too much of a risk for me to have just one Nour in my life. I want many little Nours running around the house," I would often playfully suggest to her when we watched a movie together or went out for dinner.

But Nour firmly opposed the idea and would tell me to be patient. She wanted to complete her Ph.D. in philosophy and pursue her career in child psychology for a few years before starting a family. She resolutely conveyed that she didn't want more than two children.

Our first daughter was born on May 20th after seven years of marriage, and I named her Mahnour because it contained "Nour," and she was born on a full-moon night. She was a perfect blend of our genetics; she would grow to be a bit taller than her mother, with hazel-brown eyes, a light brown complexion, and prominent cheekbones.

Mahnour was an ideal daughter who didn't cause us much trouble. She excelled in school and decided to follow in her grandfather Dr. Rabbani's footsteps by pursuing a healthcare career in medicine. When she made that decision right after high school, her grandfather was overjoyed and even encouraged her to move in with them. Their house wasn't far from ours, so I didn't object, and it provided some relief as we lived in a small three-bedroom house with two bathrooms. Our other two children were teenagers by then and needed their own space.

Mahnour went on to become a pediatrician and married one of her classmates. She established a successful healthcare practice in Fresno.

March 23rd, 2054

Our second child was born three years after our first, in the spring of 1954, on March 23rd. My mother named her Gulnour because she saw her as a spring flower, and knew I wanted "Nour" in the name. The pregnancy had complications that deeply affected my wife. After the delivery, when I met her, she declared, "Shero, I'm done with this bearing children business. No more. Two are enough." Seeing her exhaustion written all over her, I decided not to press the issue, but it would not be the end of my desire for more.

Gulnour brought a tremendous amount of energy into our household. She was an adventurous child with a passion for sports and athletics. She could easily be described as a tomboy, with her short hair, sporty attire, and a lack of interest in traditional femininity. Dolls were not her preferred toys; she leaned towards video games and toy cars. Her academic performance was average, much like mine was at her age, and she didn't display much interest in science like her mother. However, later on, she found inspiration through my sister Zar Wareen and decided to pursue a career in law. Her goal was to accumulate wealth, much like her grandfather, choosing the career path of a corporate lawyer, differing from her aunt's choice of social activism and serving the less fortunate to have full rights.

She eventually married the founder of a successful information technology company and settled with him in Silicon Valley.

April 8th, 2056

By April 8th, 2056, I had waited for two years and decided to breach the topic with Nour of having more children during our mutual birthday celebration dinner.

"We need one more. I don't think it's too much to ask for as a birthday gift," I told Nour, looking into her eyes with as much affection as I could muster.

She sipped her fresh-squeezed orange juice and responded, "What do you think we need one more of?"

"A child."

She choked on her juice, spilling some on her dress. "No way! Two are enough, and we don't even have an extra room in the house."

"It's not about the room. You are stubborn about not having one more. Can you at least think about it?" I implored.

She nodded her head in agreement, and that ended our discussion. The next day, my sister Zar Wareen, the human rights lawyer, visited us to wish us a belated birthday and hand us our gifts.

"Sorry for not coming over yesterday. I had an emergency at the office," she defended the delay in wishing us, slumping onto the living room sofa.

"What happened, sis?" I inquired politely to be courteous rather than curious. A crisis was a norm in the office of a human rights lawyer dealing with asylum and refugee cases.

"One of the asylum seekers from Eastern Europe, whom I was representing, passed away due to a heart condition in my office. She left behind a two-year-old boy without any relatives."

"What will happen to the boy?" My curiosity was piqued, remembering how my own father's sudden death had left me to deal with life. I was a teenager at the time so I could deal with it. For a two-year-old child, it was a precarious and frightful situation. I felt empathy and compassion for the kid.

"The boy is currently with social services until we find suitable foster parents or better to be adopted."

Nour's social services instincts took over her rational self. "We can foster the boy until a permanent solution is found." She spoke from the kitchen while fixing tea and snacks for Zar.

"But we don't have an extra room for another child, woman.

Didn't you say that just last night?" I couldn't resist expressing myself with a touch of sarcasm.

"Don't get me started, Shero. It's just temporary, not a permanent commitment," she responded with hard-to-hide annoyance. "What do we need to do to get the child, Zar?"

Within a week, all formalities were completed enabling the boy to join the family. That temporary commitment to care for the little boy turned into a permanent feature within no time. Nour had grown too attached to him to let him go, and he had become equally attached to her. A child needs the shelter of a mother to survive. It is a basic human instinct. At first, I wasn't sure if I could love someone else's child as my own. I feared I might treat him with love and affection or discriminate between him and my biological children. However, my daughters Mahnour and Gulnour, much like their mother, wouldn't have it any other way. They welcomed a little brother with open arms.

The boy's name was Ivan Hakimov, given to him by his biological parents, and we decided not to change it. It was essential for his personality building for him to know that he had different biological parents. We did not want him to have any insecurity or doubts about his identity. Ivan had soft, curly, golden-blonde hair, an oval face with large green eyes. It was quite a sight to see when we ventured out to social events and holidays– four brown individuals accompanied by a blonde boy. We attracted curious looks wherever we went.

Today, that boy has grown into a handsome young man with a degree from Stanford University and is a key member of a technology startup team. It's undeniable that there's a higher power at play in our lives. We may believe we're in control, but sometimes, our paths are directed by forces beyond our understanding. My dream of attending Stanford and joining a startup came true, in a way I could have never predicted – it became a reality for my adopted son, Ivan.

Seven

Mid-life crisis

❧

S her Shah entered the room, appearing shaken, with pockets of sleeplessness hanging under his eyes. His old nightmares had returned, the same ones he had experienced after losing his job over two decades ago. He thought he had gotten over it. In bed last night, he remembered that the next event he was going to write about in the notebook was one of the most painful chapters of his life. While in his mid-40s, his life had attained peace, harmony, and purpose, but it all shattered in the blink of an eye when he lost his job and reputation, for reasons he still felt were unjust. He considered himself a disciplined and responsible person, but this self-image could not prevent him from being labeled as negligent by his supervisors. He had believed he had cured that wound in his soul, but it was still festering deep inside him.

We are made to believe that the dust of time erases past

events. But is it true? Past events are part of our history of existence. They remain alive within crevices of memory, although receded to the subconscious. Like a hunter, they wait for the right moment to pounce back to consciousness. An event or a picture reminds us about their existence, reigniting the old pain or pleasure.

Sher Shah sat down at the table to write about that event. He was aware that he was writing this notebook not just for others but for himself as well. It was his final act of catharsis, a way to close open wounds in his soul and leave this world with no outstanding balance. In a way, it was his final act of completing his "things to do" list. He might have come into the world crying like millions of other babies, but he wanted to leave it calmly and peacefully. He was not afraid of death; how could he be afraid of something that did not kill him in the womb? For him, every day he lived was a bonus, and every day was a credit balance in his life story.

Sher Shah grasped the pen in his fingers, drew in a deep breath, and commenced writing about the roller coaster of emotions he had experienced in midlife. It was an event that had unlocked the hidden chambers of his soul, leading him down a path he had never once considered as an option for himself.

* * *

June 15, 2060

Statistics are just numbers; they do not apply to everyone, or probably anyone. Statistics suggest Americans switch jobs on average 12 times in their lifetime. That probably includes odd jobs they do in college or while transitioning between jobs. Statistics also highlight that a gen alpha, I don't know who created these gen categorizations, stays in a position for an average of three years.

These statistics do not apply to me. I joined the food processing company as an instrumentation engineer right out of college. I was happy with the job, and my managers always appreciated my proactive attitude and discipline. They did not want a laggard or someone who needed to be micro-managed. I was promoted from instrument technician to instrumentation manager over the years. I had a team of five technicians who monitored all the sensors in a control room and routinely inspected instruments in the food processing plant. I was a laid-back manager who believed in delegating work to others, trusting them to execute their function professionally. I had built my team with these qualities. I won many company awards for my team's performance and productivity. They were considered a star team and earned the nickname 'the bulls' for pulling the weight of the company's production targets year after year.

By 2060, I had been with the same company for over 15 years. My friends, who graduated with me, were all over the country, most of them earning three to four times more money than me. I was content with what I got. Between Nour and myself, we were making enough money to lead a decent life. As immigrants, our community was our family. We both considered a family was needed to raise kids as good humans and citizens even if we made a little less income. We believed in the axiom it requires a village to raise a child, and it was validated by the success of our children.

Nour was a meticulous planner and started setting aside

small funds for our three children for their college tuition. The funds were growing, and if everything stayed the same, they would have no problem paying for their college tuition without taking a student loan. Student loans, although helpful, were still a burden for a person to start life with a negative balance. Our house was still under mortgage, and we were contributing a little extra to the mortgage payment to pay it off in fifteen rather than thirty years of the mortgage term sheet. It would pay off in five years.

I enjoyed living in Fresno. It was an ideal place to raise a family. Fresno was small enough to save time commuting to work, shopping, or entertainment, yet big enough to offer a city lifestyle. The southern part of the city was home to blue-collar workers who toiled in the agricultural fields of the Central Valley farms or packaged food distributor warehouses. To the north, you'd find well-to-do families, white-collar office workers, doctors, and engineers. While this class divide sometimes gave rise to resentment, it never escalated into civil unrest. Probably because the system offered equal opportunity to all. The South reflected the Wild West with its gang activity while the North represented the prosperity of the modern knowledge economy.

A variety of restaurants, grocery stores, and places of worship catered to the ethnically diverse community of Asians, Hispanics, African Americans, and Caucasian Americans. The tower district had evolved into an entertainment center with restaurants playing live music, Broadway-style musicals, and concerts of contemporary artists.

The complaint I had about living in Fresno was its unbearable air quality. It was hard to breathe despite the local and state governments' claims to have improved significantly over decades of efforts, it sure did not feel like it. Some of my friends complained of asthma and other respiratory issues caused by this air pollution.

For Nour, Fresno and its twin city Clovis, was the best place to call home because it had been consistently rated as the top school district in the country. Not just that, most people were inclined towards religious practices and conservative. Plenty of churches, synagogues, mandirs, gurdwaras, pagodas, and mosques served these people of faith to practice their religion. We all lived in harmony, and no one bothered the other.

Little did I know that the smallness of Fresno would become too big a problem for me and my family to handle. In a big city, a person can disappear among the multitude of people if something significant happens in one's life. But in a smaller city, there is no place to hide. Everyone knows everyone else and their life drama. In a big city, a person could have six degrees of separation from any other person which is reduced to a degree of two or three in a smaller city.

June 15th in the year 2060 was just like any other June day. It was officially not yet summer, but the heat was already sweltering. When I was born in the 2020s, the average temperature in June was in the low 90s degrees Fahrenheit. That had gradually increased to the low 100s over the last forty years. All because consumption has been on the rise as the world population exponentially increased from 7 billion in the 2020s to over 10 billion at the start of 2060. Renewable sources of solar, wind, geothermal, hydrogen, and water energy have kept carbon emissions low to some degree, but the sum of heat generated by consumer gadgets has increased exponentially. Every person was using an increasing number of electronic devices that generated heat. Life without these gadgets was unimaginable. Even in the small room where I am writing this, there are over ten items that emit heat. The air conditioning had to work harder to keep the room cool, but that extra work by the HVAC system meant heat added to the outside environment. The heat signature of all of us has risen to an uncomfortable level.

That simmering hot day, as I was leaving for work, Nour told me to pick up Ivan from school and drop him at the dentist's office for his routine deep cleaning appointment. She would pick him up from there to bring him home. I checked my calendar to ensure there was no meeting planned for that time of the day. I confirmed to her I would be able to take Ivan to the dentist. I had nothing to worry about in discharging family responsibility, my team was well-qualified, and I did not have to micromanage them. Each team member knew what to do without being told how and when to do it. I had good working relations with my manager. He was comfortable with me and allowed me the flexibility to manage my own time and job function. I did not imagine my two-hour absence would cause any issues or disruptions in the workflow.

The morning session at work was business as usual. Before I left to pick up Ivan, I sent an email reminder to my manager regarding the approaching once in three years maintenance of process instruments to be calibrated or replaced, to be compliant with state and city safety regulations. We needed to get the budget approved and order their replacements in time. I instructed my most trusted technician, Smith, to perform a visual inspection of the instruments, with a particular focus on those installed for boiler management.

I left the plant around 1:30 pm to pick up my son Ivan at 2:00. I brought the laptop to work on some reports while the self-driving car handled the drive. Although I could have simply instructed my car to pick up and drop off Ivan at school, my wife's concerns were insurmountable. Nour still did not trust technology, especially when it concerned the safety and security of her kids. She insisted I be there to ensure his safe arrival at the dentist's office. I planned to grab a quick bite with my son at his favorite fast-food joint and return to the plant by 3:00 pm. My phone typically remained on silent vibrate mode because I disliked it ringing at inopportune times. Additionally, I seldom used the car's phone connectivity system, as I wanted to avoid embarrassment if a friend or colleague were to call and use inappropriate language in front of my family.

I went to the school, picked up my son, had lunch with him at the fast-food joint as planned, dropped him off at the dentist, and while driving back to the plant, I commanded the car radio to tune in to the local news channel. The news announcer sounded alarmed and emotional, reporting an accident at a local plant. I was so engrossed in my work on the laptop that the news didn't register with me until the reporter mentioned that a plant technician named Smith was seriously injured in the accident. The mention of that name jolted me to pay attention to the news. I took a few moments to realize that the accident had occurred at my plant, possibly involving the technician I had instructed to visually inspect the instruments.

In a state of shock and disbelief, I remained frozen, taking a few minutes to grasp the gravity of the situation. I checked my phone and saw half a dozen missed calls from my manager. I didn't know what to do. Should I call my manager and inform him that I was on my way? But then he could ask where I was during this time and why I couldn't answer his phone calls.

I hadn't bothered to inform him earlier about going out for two hours because I didn't see the need for it. It had been our preferred modus operandi. I decided to face him at the plant since I was already on my way and just a mile away from it.

The remainder of the drive felt like the longest mile of my life. The car seemed to be moving at a snail's pace due to the high traffic on the busy road while my mind was racing at the speed of light. I was overwhelmed with fear, anxiety, and worry all at the same time. My brain subconsciously reviewed the entire morning's activities multiple times, trying desperately to identify any sign or indication of an impending accident I might have missed. Did I overlook any instrument readings? Was there anything we could have done differently to prevent the accident?

Back at the plant, I learned that the boiler had exploded, and the later investigation revealed that rusted plates in the boiler were the root cause of the accident. This meant that neither my team nor I could be held responsible. However, I couldn't overcome the feeling of guilt, especially regarding Smith's injuries. I contacted his family to offer my sympathies and any support I could provide. A few days after the accident, I visited him in the hospital and apologized, even though he assured me that he didn't blame me for what had happened during his inspection of boiler instruments. Despite his kindness, my sense of guilt persisted.

My manager, someone I considered a friend, betrayed me by blaming me for negligence when the pressure from his superiors intensified. To protect himself, he chose to scape-goat me, deeming my absence from the plant as inexcusable. Despite my fifteen years of flawless performance, the stain of the boiler explosion, an incident beyond my control, loomed large enough to overshadow my otherwise impeccable career. This stark realization underscored the harsh truth that loyalty and dedication in the workplace held little value. Workplace acquaintances remain superficial and break as soon as that threadbare connection is broken.

The incident highlighted a systemic issue, revealing that in a capitalist system, the pursuit of ever-increasing profits often took precedence over recognizing long-term commitment and personal integrity. Refusing to resign to maintain my innocence ultimately led to my termination on grounds of negligence, depriving me of the severance package that would have provided financial support for the next fifteen months. The experience was a jarring revelation about the harsh realities of corporate priorities and the sacrifices that can be demanded in the pursuit of profit.

I didn't just lose a job; it was the end of my engineering career. The incident was widely reported by local and national newspapers, and my name became associated with it. I became damaged goods in the job market, and no employer was willing to hire me or give me a second chance. While I always believed that everyone deserved a second chance, it appeared that no one was willing to provide me with one. I managed to survive on unemployment insurance for a year, but once it was consumed, it became very difficult to maintain our family's lifestyle on a single income. Nour also felt guilty for asking me to pick up Ivan that fateful day. She was incredibly supportive and considerate during the entire ordeal. She was reminded by her father that he was opposed to our marriage from the start. She would side with me and tell her father our lives were none of his business. She declined to accept any financial help from him.

My sister, Zar Wareen, offered her legal help to file a case against my employer for wrongful termination, seeking financial compensation on my behalf. She believed that her expertise as a human rights lawyer, combined with the facts of the case, was in our favor. She argued that I may have been away from the plant without informing my supervisor, but there were no procedural errors or willful negligence committed by me. Process monitoring instruments and technicians were in place to handle any adverse situation. She argued the accident could have happened during my off hours so it could not be a cause for termination.

"Big brother, you can't let an injustice remain an open wound. It needs closure, or it will hound you all your life," Zar made a last-ditch effort to convince me. Her words were prophetic and would be proven right, as I learned too late. I had judged myself convicted of a crime that I had not committed.

"Thanks for your concern, sis. I am not ready to face the scrutiny. I have no strength to deal with it. Maybe some other time."

I refused to pursue the legal path because I felt responsible for my absence from the plant when I was supposed to be there. I didn't want to endure further humiliation.

Those were the toughest years of my life. Everywhere I went, I felt as though people were blaming me for the accident. I would feel they were looking at me with contempt in their eyes. I became scared to go out and spent most of my time at home. In my state of helplessness, I would sometimes look up and talk to myself, "Why did you let me live if I had to go through this pain? Was it not better to hang me in the womb?". I would even talk to my dead father and tell him,

"Baba, you were wrong. Your son is not a spring sunshine. I am an embarrassment to myself and my family."

I don't know if the passage of time allowed the wound on my soul to begin healing as it receded into the subconscious from consciousness or if it was my hopeful nature. After a year of grappling with depression and relying on unemployment benefits, I slowly started to recover. An engineering job was no longer possible. It was the only skill I had that could appeal to an employer. I began applying for various other jobs that were even entry-level as a junior engineer. I was willing and ready for a new start, but unfortunately, I didn't receive any responses. The world appeared too narrow to provide me with a passage. I even contemplated pursuing a career as a truck driver, following in my father's footsteps, but Nour vehemently opposed that idea.

"Shero, I can manage with a lower income, but I cannot handle three growing kids while also working full-time with an absent husband," would be her resolute response. "I don't want to be a single mom while married in name only." She would find my mother and mother-in-law as willing allies. It was an army of three against one.

After three years of enduring emotional hardships and self-doubt, not only that, but my body deteriorated as well, I gained weight losing my prized six-pack abdominal muscles replaced by a pot belly. After prolonged suffering the stalemate was finally broken, and I secured a job teaching math to inmates at a local correctional facility. When I received the appointment message, Nour was standing beside me.

"Woman, it seems like fate believes I should atone for my past negligence by spending some time in 'jail'," I remarked with a grin, gesturing quote unquote with my fingers. Nour encouraged me to accept the position. She believed stepping out of the house would do me some good. She was right. It did help me regain my lost self-confidence enabling me, to slowly but gradually, get rid of some of my belly fat.

The income wasn't as substantial as what I had earned in my previous job, but I was content to be back in full-time employment and contributing to our family's finances. Little did I know that this job was the key to revealing a hidden chamber in my soul pushing me onto a path that I could never have imagined was possible.

Eight

Inmates

S itting at his writing desk, Sher Shah vividly remembered his fear on the first day he entered the correction facility to teach math. Surprisingly, it took only a week for his anxiety to dissipate.

Sher Shah opened the notebook to narrate his encounter with Alex, one of his best students. That two-minute conversation uprooted his old self and launched him into developing a new personality. It was almost like a reincarnation to have a second life.

* * *

December 15th, 2065

I accepted the teaching job at the correction facility as a stop-gap arrangement until I found a better-paying job that could restart my stalled career in engineering. I was skeptical from the start, questioning whether I was doing something that could have a meaningful impact on my students' futures. Will society allow convicted criminals with academic degrees to have a better future? Was this education a face-saving for society not to feel guilty about letting down these citizens? However, all this changed when the best student in my second-term class posed a thought-provoking question to address the issue of having a second chance. It was one of those chance encounters that profoundly impacted one's life. Such events made one feel that the river of life was flowing with such uncontrollable power that a person had no free will and was compelled to just swim with it.

For my first day at work, I naively picked my finest suit in the wardrobe, not realizing that I would be teaching inmates within a prison, where one's attire mattered the least. Wearing nice clothes was meant to convey to the students that I took my job seriously and anticipated the same level of commitment from them. However, the choice of clothes proved to be misguided as it made me stand out conspicuously among the sea of orange jumpsuits of my students, as that was the standard jail uniform. I stood out as someone alien that was untouchable and unapproachable. I instantly became conscious that this frivolous symbol of my freedom could create an insurmountable divide between us and hinder my effectiveness as a teacher. From then on, I chose to wear an informal outfit usually matching the color of inmates' jail uniform.

In terms of amenities available at the facility, it resembled more of a hostel than a typical prison. The rooms, although small, were clean and comfortable. Inmates had access to the internet and entertainment that was only limited by time restrictions. They had a library with tablets and computers to access digital books. They received adequate meals and changed their attire every two weeks, with access to communal showers. Despite the decent living conditions, the inmates still grappled with feelings of incarceration and separation from society as outcasts. I observed a deep-seated anger in their eyes, etched on their faces, and reflected in their body language. It appeared that they held society responsible for their predicament, even though their actions had caused them to be behind bars.

My classroom, in its architecture, resembled a conference room equipped with audio-visual capabilities. Each student's desk had a computer.

The program participants spanned a wide range of ages, the majority were in their late teens but there were a handful in their late 30s, 40s, and 50s. Among them, some exhibited high levels of motivation and dedication to their studies, while others seemed more inclined to seek relaxation rather than fully engage in rigorous academic pursuits.

The students were enrolled in the program based on their academic profiles, expressed their desire by applying to be admitted to it, and were being prepared for an exam that would qualify them as high school graduates. In theory, this could potentially lead to college admission and open access to various job opportunities for them. However, the reality was more complex.

By 2065, I had been teaching math at the correction facility for two years. December 15th marked the last day of my second term. My third term was scheduled to start on January 15th after a four-week break between terms. I had already planned a two-week trip to Europe with Nour and

Ivan. Our itinerary was to celebrate the New Year in the ancient city of Athens by listening to an orchestra in front of the ruins of the old metropolis. While I had provided the funds for the trip, all the arrangements were handled by Nour. She had a knack for planning, and I trusted her judgment more than my own in such matters. Besides, I wasn't in the mood to be held responsible for choosing the wrong hotel or overlooking essential amenities, which might lead her to blame me. Men are generally held responsible by women whenever something goes wrong, while they are always blameless. I never understood the psyche of a woman. Nevertheless, I wanted to rest and enjoy the trip.

As I gathered my papers and contemplated the upcoming trip, I heard someone calling out to me from the back of the classroom, "Professor." It sounded strange because no one had addressed me that way in two years. They usually addressed me by my first name.

I turned around and saw Alex Campbell, one of my best students, approaching my desk. Alex was a striking example of how first impressions can be misleading. He was an eighteen or nineteen-year-old tall, muscular stout body, blonde kid with luminous green eyes. Looking at him often reminded me of my son, Ivan. I would sometimes wonder if Ivan would have ended up in a correction facility if we hadn't adopted him. Alex's body was covered in tattoos, visible even on his upper torso, arms, and neck. They were gradually encroaching on his face. It appeared, as though, he was using tattoos as a shield to hide from society. He was serving time for selling drugs to an underage student and was due to be released in the next few months. Despite his intimidating appearance, Alex was the top student in the class, boasting a flawless 4.0 GPA. It was a clear reminder that judging a person solely based on their looks could be misleading.

"What can I do for you, Alex?" I asked, still gathering papers in my hurry to leave.

"Do you have a few minutes?"

"Yes, sure, please sit down," I said, feeling guilty for giving him the impression that I had no time for him.

"I wanted to ask you a small favor. Actually, two favors," Alex said, hesitating and clasping his hands signaling his unease in requesting assistance.

"Go ahead. I am here to help you, Alex. Please speak freely," I assured him, imagining I was talking to Ivan.

"I am planning to apply for college and need two reference letters."

"That's not a problem. When do you need them? I could write one, and I'll ask my wife to write the second one."

"By the end of January," he replied.

"What's the other favor you need?"

"I need some guidance. How will I finance my college tuition? I mean to say, who will give a job or scholarship to a convicted criminal? Will I be able to get a job after I graduate?" Alex's concerns reopened my still-fresh wound. I remembered that I hadn't been found guilty of fault in the boiler explosion accident, yet no one wanted to give me a second chance. I became a persona-non-grate in the engineering world.

I sat there in silence for a long moment until Alex addressed me, "Professor, are you alright?"

"Yes, sorry, Alex. I am fine," I finally said. "I don't know what to tell you about finding a job and financing your tuition. I'll have to research your options and get back to you."

"Thank you, Professor," Alex said, his face softening, and

a slight smile appeared on his lips. The mere promise of researching a solution gave him hope. I felt a sense of responsibility to help this young man get a second chance. We were connected by destiny.

As the car drove me home, I opened my computer to research how long a criminal record remained on a person's profile. Unfortunately, I couldn't find a clear answer, so I called my sister for guidance.

"Zar, how long does a person's criminal record stay on their profile?"

"Legally, it's three years, but effectively, it lingers for their entire life," my sister responded without even thinking.

"What does that mean?" I asked, not sure what she meant.

"Well, legally, a company shouldn't refuse employment three years after the completion of a jail term," she explained. "But in reality, no company wants to hire someone with a criminal record. Convicted criminals aren't even invited to interviews, let alone seriously considered for a job."

She paused and then drove her point home. "Have you forgotten what happened to you?"

"I understand, sis. What can be done about it? Give me a solution."

"Run for the office," she said, and I could sense a smile in her voice.

"What?" I was taken aback, "I am not a politician. Nor do I want to be a politician."

"Yes, big brother. We need legislation to compel employers to give a second chance to convicted criminals, especially those with minor offenses."

"Okay, then we can start a signature campaign to pressure both Republican and Democratic parties to work on this legislation," I suggested, determined to act.

"You can try, but I'm not very hopeful," she replied. "That's why my first response was for you to run for office."

"Why wouldn't they legislate for this? There are millions of people impacted by it," I insisted. The US was one of the top five countries in the world for most people behind bars.

"They're afraid of appearing soft on crime, and they can't afford to lose the support of big corporations." She highlighted the influence of big business on the two political parties. "I've got to go, big brother. I'll let you know if I can think of something else."

She hung up, but my mind remained fixated on the issue. I had a personal reason to pursue justice to compensate for the injustice I experienced. I felt a deep connection and empathy for Alex and countless others. I did not want them to face injustice and deserve a second chance.

I couldn't sleep that night and kept tossing and turning in bed. Even the anticipation of our upcoming vacation and the beauty of Athens couldn't dispel the restlessness I felt inside.

For me, it felt like the vacation was over before it had even begun. My mind and soul remained preoccupied throughout the trip pondering over the injustices in society that couldn't be rectified by any court of law because there was no apparent illegality involved. Holding a company accountable for discrimination in a court of law, when all hiring records were maintained to show compliance with the law, was nearly impossible. Initial screenings of job candidates were done by artificial intelligence-powered facial analysis tools, but the final hiring decisions were made by humans. Detecting human prejudices was challenging, especially in a society that harbored apprehensions about crime and criminals. How could anyone truly determine if a convicted criminal had reformed?

I considered various options to address this social issue. I could provide personal assurances to employers to hire my students like Alex and others. I could also help them access support from civic organizations working to rehabilitate past criminals. While this would resolve the issue for those I knew, the larger societal problem of unresolved injustice would remain unaddressed. These options did not help me to regain peace of mind and close the wound. If charity could not solve the problem, I would have no choice but to turn to politics.

I became curious about my political prospects. Upon our return from vacation, I immediately began gathering information and researching the congressional districts in Fresno. Two congressional districts, 22 and 23, were assigned to the city based on the population. I lived in District 23. It had a diverse population, with nearly evenly divided demographics among Hispanics, Asians, African Americans, and White Americans. The incumbent was a Democrat named Kevin Johnson, in his late 60s. He had been representing this district in Congress for the past twenty years, all research showed that his support had gradually eroded, and his age could be a factor in the upcoming 2066 midterm elections. District 22 was heavily populated by Hispanic voters, with over 73% of registered voters from that community, and it had not elected a non-Hispanic representative in the last sixty years. It was evident out of the two, District 23 could be considered as a possibility. I am still amazed I even contemplated the option without knowledge of elections or politics.

Next, I researched the qualifications required to become

a candidate for the U.S. congressional district. The person had to be a resident of the district, have a voter registration, have no pending unpaid federal income tax, or tax penalties in the last five years, and file a petition with the county clerk, to become a candidate, signed by at least 2% of registered voters in the district. This last requirement threw a wrench into my plans, making me hesitant to proceed. The congressional district had 285,450 registered voters (roughly half the population of Wyoming), and 2% of that meant I would require 5,709 signatures. How and where would I gather these signatures? I had no answer to this question.

Even if I could gather the required signatures, there were additional hurdles, including my lack of political experience, knowledge of the legislative process, and the need for a team and resources for the election campaign. I could provide the energy, commitment, and dedication, but these alone were insufficient for the task at hand. I had to also shed my introverted shy nature by transforming myself into a different person. I decided to talk to my family and friends about my political plans before taking concrete steps.

Nine

Wife first

~ ❧ ~

Sher Shah could feel the boost of adrenaline in his blood flowing through his body just thinking about his past adventure. He remembered the courage he had mustered to talk to Nour about his decision to pursue election for the U.S. Congress.

Sher Shah picked up his notebook and turned to a fresh page, ready to write about his meetings with friends and family as he sought support for his election plans.

* * *

January 10th, 2066

I knew that the first step in any political contest was to win over the support of friends and family. If they remain unconvinced, it is difficult to persuade others to support or vote for me. I prepared my case with solid arguments to convince them. I did my research and considered all the possible concerns that could be raised by them.

The relationship between a husband and wife is unique. Two complete strangers come together to form one unit, maintaining personality differences but walking hand in hand in synchronized motion. They may disagree on which path to take in life, but they must agree on the destination. If they don't, they eventually reach a fork in the journey and part ways. There has to be a compromise, even if they agree to walk together towards a shared destination. These compromises could be small, like changing a habit, or big, involving giving up a career, and sometimes even a country.

Every family has a unique story to tell, generally hidden from the public view. The entire family may portray a substantially different picture in their public appearances when the reality at home could be very different. Hiding the ugly side of family affairs is a shared responsibility of all members, and painting a rosy picture works for all, as well as society. Dirty linen should only be washed in the laundry washing machine at home.

When it was time to tell Nour about my plans, I wasn't entirely sure if she would agree. Her focus was on family, community, and work. However, her involvement in social work gave me some confidence that she might support my political aspirations. She always encouraged me to find a good cause to work on.

Navigating the decision to engage in politics brought forth a heightened awareness of potential challenges. The impact on our children's relationships at school and overall lifestyles loomed large, and the fear of irreversibly disrupting their lives was palpable. Politics, with its divisive nature, not only fractures societies but can create schisms within families. Social, economic, and political debates can polarize communities, making it nearly impossible for a political figure to shield their family from the repercussions of their work. Media scrutiny becomes relentless, probing into every detail, sometimes with the intention of applying pressure to compromise on legislation, even against personal convictions. The intricate balance of family life amid such challenges becomes a daunting task.

I had contemplated what would happen if Nour opposed my plans and remained steadfast in her opposition. I had never confided in anyone until today, I was resolute to pursue the political path even if it meant risking my family life. I needed to find inner peace and untie a knot in my soul.

I had been searching for the perfect moment to talk to Nour about my plans. I considered talking to her in the morning, but she always rushed to leave for work and was usually in a hurry. I thought about arranging a dinner date to discuss my plans with her. I imagined her reaction, "So, this dinner is an attempt to buy my support for your crazy idea." I wondered if she would walk out of our dinner date to express her displeasure. The risk was too much in that approach, so I abandoned the idea. After considerable thought, I settled on talking to her after our Sunday dinner at home. I imagined her sipping green tea, relaxed and ready for the upcoming work week. It would be the perfect setting to discuss an outlandish idea.

We usually had dinner at 7:00 pm, and my evening cup of black tea with milk and sugar would follow. I also liked to have cookies or snacks with my tea in the evening. Nour had made several attempts to convince me to change this habit because she believed that having tea that late in the evening could interfere with my sleep. However, I adamantly refused to accept her advice and reassured her that tea didn't affect my sleep. It was indeed true as I rarely experienced insomnia even though I was a light sleeper, despite the fact she never accepted my stance and would repeat her advice every few months. Some women, in their nurturing nature, tend to treat spouses like adult children, attempting to regulate various aspects of their behavior—an inclination deeply ingrained in the female psyche.

Finally, the moment arrived on Sunday, January 10th, 2066, as I had anticipated the dinner went well, and we engaged in our usual small talk about friends, family, and community. I complimented her cooking to prepare the mood for telling her about the bombshell of the news. Kids were already in their rooms, immersed in their schoolwork or social media. Nour appeared relaxed, which gave me some confidence. It felt like the perfect time to broach the subject.

"I'm thinking of running for elections," I mentioned casually, holding the hot teacup in my hands to feel the warmth and avoiding making eye contact with her.

"What kind of elections? School district?" she asked, her tone not registering the seriousness of my statement.

"Elections to the US Congress, representing District 23."

"Is this some kind of joke, Shero?" She turned her head to look at me, sipping her green tea.

"I'm completely serious," I replied looking back into her eyes. Eyes are considered portals to the soul. I wished that eyes could do the talking for me. The seriousness of my tone and the expression in my eyes made her move uneasily in the chair. I could not figure out what she could be thinking.

"If you're going through a midlife crisis, I can suggest

a community service project," she proposed, clearly not comprehending why I would entertain such a crazy idea.

"No, I thought about it. I want to run for the US Congress from District 23. You know me. I never leave any project unfinished."

"Right, like you couldn't even keep your job," she retorted angrily, immediately realizing that her words might have hurt my feelings and reminded me of the identity crisis I went through. Apparently, the feeling of guilt softened her tone.

"And why do you want to do this?" She shifted to a more genuinely curious tone, trying to understand the motivations behind my seemingly irrational idea.

I shared with her the story of Alex Campbell asking for a favor and my subsequent conversation with Zar Wareen, about providing second chances to convicted criminals.

"Shero, I appreciate your desire to help others. There are other practical ways to help, you have no knowledge or experience of politics, and you've never delivered a public speech. How are you supposed to run for elections? And where will the money come from? Don't even think about using our family savings for your crazy idea," she bombarded me with questions.

"I can learn to make public speeches. Even if I don't excel at it, I can have face-to-face meetings with voters. To generate resources, I plan to discuss it with my friends tomorrow. I wanted to talk to you first before approaching them."

"Who are you meeting tomorrow?" she asked with indifference.

"The usual gang. Ashraf, Ranbir, and Jimmy"

"None of them have any knowledge of politics to provide good advice." She had raised a good point.

"Yes, I agree. But they have helped candidates in the past elections and contributed to campaign funds." I was defensive but knew she was right. I needed political advice from someone with a domain knowledge. I made a mental note to look for someone with experience in politics.

"You have zero chance of winning. If, by some divine intervention, you do win, don't expect me to move to Washington and disrupt our children's lives. It could hurt their grades. You'll be on your own." After issuing this effective threat, she got up and left.

To be fair to her, deep down inside, I knew my chances of winning were slim to none. Because of that, I hadn't even considered the implications of moving to Washington DC, and how it might affect my family life. That night, the bed felt colder than it ever had in our entire married life.

Ten

Friends

⟨ᖇᑎᕼᑫᖇᑎ⟩

S her Shah entered the room with the aid of a walking stick, a gift from his son Ivan. Ivan was concerned about his weakening body which needed support while walking. Sher Shah accepted this as a reality of life, understanding a fall could result in a hip injury that could be fatal at his age.

Seated at his writing table, Sher Shah accessed past communications on his device instead of opening his notebook to write. He punched his communication ID and encryption key to access it.

The communication ID was considered a utility provided by the State, much like water or electricity. At birth, every citizen received a social security number, a communication ID, and an encryption key. It was a legal requirement for citizens to use this government-assigned communication ID for all forms of communication, encompassing personal, social media community, and government-related matters. The communication ID was never changed, but an encryption key could be requested if a citizen felt it was compromised.

Citizens had complete control of their communication IDs. No one could access them without express permission from the ID owner; all forms of correspondence, whether voice, video, or text were done using the same ID. A person could rescind these permissions at any time. All thoughts and notes were stored on government servers through the ID and encrypted using the unique key provided by the State. All these thoughts and notes were considered the intellectual property of the citizen. They could grant these rights to their family, friends, or business associates, and transfer them as per the will of the citizens. All such communications stored on government servers could be used as credible evidence in a court of law if necessary.

Sher Shah remembered when the legislation was initially proposed for the State to offer communication IDs to replace email, there was significant opposition from privacy advocates, internet service providers, and civil rights organizations. However, people were fed up with spam messages, incessant marketing from brands, fake news, and online fraud. The proposed platform promised citizens to cut down on the waste of millions of hours and money wasted on unsolicited marketing calls, messages, and social media marketing that were the norm in the 2020s. Impulsive buying resulting from these marketing efforts was another cost that was never measured. Needs and wants remained blurred concepts because of these psychological marketing techniques. People bought things that they hardly ever used. They faced a choice: entrust their communications to commercial entities that profited from their private data while making dubious privacy assurances, or let the government oversee the email service and be accountable to the citizens. They rejected the former and chose the latter.

In a rare turn of events, the majority opted to repose their trust in the elected government rather than profit-driven corporations. As an added safeguard, the government committed to encrypting all communications, assigning a unique encryption key to each citizen. Crucially, this key remained inaccessible without the explicit consent of the citizens and was subject to judicial oversight. These concerted efforts aimed not only to prioritize citizens' privacy but also to establish a system of checks and balances, ensuring that the power inherent in encryption remained firmly in the hands of the people and their elected representatives.

Sher Shah wanted to revisit his communications to refresh his memory about the key events of his election campaign before writing them in his notebook. He found the email he had sent to his closest friends on the afternoon of January 10th, 2066. It read:

"Guys, good afternoon,

Let's meet tomorrow at lunch. I have something to discuss. Be prepared for a proposal that may sound crazy to you.

Regards, Sher"

He read the acknowledgments from his three closest friends with nostalgia, and each of his friends responded with an emoji expressing their emotions. If a picture is considered worth a thousand words, an emoji is worth a million. It could make you smile, irritated, or downright angry. As technology evolved emoji evolved with it. They were now three-dimensional with sound and facial expressions.

After reading his messages from the distant past, Sher Shah was ready to record his thoughts and opened his notebook to begin narrating the details of the meeting with his friends that began his journey of life on an uncommon path.

*** *** ***

January 11th, 2066

After receiving confirmation from my friends, I instructed my car in the morning to make a lunch reservation at a local restaurant that was conveniently located for all of us. The artificial intelligence powered system knew our food preferences and could calculate an approximate dining location that would suit everyone.

I chose to wear my signature mandarin collar shirt with blue stripes, khaki pants, and a light brown jacket. The weather that day was perfect for an outdoor lunch. Clear sky with no clouds on the horizon, the deep blue sky felt like a canopy covering as far as a person could see, and warm sunshine felt good to reduce the chilliness of the winter air. It was a good break before the rainy season would start mid-February.

My three friends were an intriguing mix of individuals from diverse backgrounds. Jimmy Dean attended Fresno State with me and graduated as an electrical engineer. He was part of our close-knit group of friends who hung out and studied together. He was a mutual friend of mine and Nour. I was the best man at his wedding, and he performed a Bhangra dance during the traditional mehendi ceremony planned by Nour's friends for our wedding. It was hard to believe his transformation into a devout person of faith. Two years after graduation, he underwent a significant personality transformation. Jimmy resigned from his job and became a Protestant priest at a church in Fresno. I anticipated that he might be the least surprised when I informed them of my plans. At the time, I felt his life experiences made him perfectly suited to be my guide and mentor in my own transformation from a shy and introverted person to a politician. His presence was reassuring and confidence-building.

Ranbir Singh was the son of a Fresno farmer who migrated from Indian Eastern Punjab. His father was a close friend of my father Shah Zaman. I practically grew up with him because my father liked to spend most of our weekends at their farm. Ranbir and his brothers had inherited the farm from their father. They expanded the operation to include food processing and dairy farming. Ranbir was kind enough to offer me a job at their food processing business after the boiler accident, but I declined it. I wasn't comfortable with the suggestion of turning my childhood friend into my boss. I accepted the offer to provide consultations to help them improve their plant efficiency and make it environmentally friendly. It was a per diem arrangement and augmented my meager unemployment benefits after being terminated.

Ashraf Ul Islam, on the other hand, was a Bangladeshi American cardiologist. Our friendship had formed because he didn't particularly like my father-in-law. He was the polar opposite of my father-in-law, contributed generously to community centers in the city and organized charity events. In fact, his contributions practically sustained many of these centers. His organization held two free medical camps every year to help uninsured blue-collar farm workers in Central Valley. Unlike most successful doctors, he was humble, had a broad smile that never left his face, and had an excellent sense of humor. As I waited for them at the restaurant, I mentally prepared myself to be the target of his jokes.

They all arrived within ten minutes of the appointed time. Ashraf Ul Islam was usually the last to reach, and his usual excuse was, "There is no set time for death and a patient's condition to change." We had no choice but to accept his excuses.

After exchanging pleasantries and ordering our food, I decided to get straight to the purpose of our meeting.

"I am planning to contest elections."

"We just had city council elections. Isn't it too early to talk about it now?" Jimmy was the first to respond.

"I am going to contest for the U.S. Congressional District 23. What do you all think?" As soon as I uttered those words, they all shifted in their chairs.

Ashraf Ul Islam's response was clear and straightforward. "If you want to run on your own, the answer is yes, go for it. But if you're looking for some kind of involvement from us, then I say no to this crazy idea," he declared with his customary smile. "I squeeze a lot of dollars from the sick hearts of people. I have to spend it for good causes using common sense. My patients gladly pay the hefty medical bill because of my charitable causes."

His sense of humor hadn't deserted him even in this serious discussion, and we all chuckled at his remark.

I turned to Ranbir Singh. "I don't know what to say. I've given campaign donations to some candidates, but that's all I know about politics." Ranbir Singh sounded uncertain about whether to encourage or discourage me.

"Nour said that the same thing last night, Ranbir." I wondered whether Nour had talked to them behind my back to tell them to dissuade me.

"Why do you want to contest elections?" Jimmy asked, wanting to understand my motivations and conclude the discussion.

I proceeded to narrate, once again, the story of Alex Campbell, my conversation with my sister, and my own sense of injustice committed by society that had led to the end of my engineering career. They all listened attentively, but their expressions told me they thought I was ridiculous.

"Have you ever made a public speech?" Jimmy inquired.

"No," I replied uneasily and shifted in my chair knowing full well that there would be more questions.

"Have you ever participated in student politics?"

"No."

"Have you ever served on the board of a community organization?"

"No."

"Have you ever participated in any political campaign as a volunteer?"

"No."

"Have you even voted in the last congressional election?" Jimmy asked rather desperately, seemingly to get at least some positive response to give them a reason to agree with me.

Tiny beads of sweat formed on my forehead. "I was visiting the East Coast during the last congressional elections, so no, I didn't vote. But I did vote in the city council elections."

"Who is your political advisor?"

"Three of you."

"We have no experience in politics and election campaigns," all three of them spoke in unison shaking their heads in disbelief.

These revelations were too much for my three friends to bear.

"Get out of this crazy idea," they all said almost in unison.

I was not one to easily abandon an idea even if it failed on all levels of rationality. "How can I prove to you, my friends, that I can be a good candidate? Give me a test or a challenge."

I thought my resolve to pursue and prove my capability was a good milestone to cross to convince them to support me.

"Which party do you want to use as a platform?" Jimmy took the lead again in questioning and exploring.

"None."

"Sher Shah, I thought you were crazy, but now I think you're mad," Ashraf Ul Islam said half-jokingly. "Let me call the local mental health hospital before it's too late."

"Hear him out, please," Ranbir Singh came to my aid. "What is your plan, Shah Sahib?" Addressing me with a South Asian salutation.

"I have looked at the ideological and policy positions of both parties," I began, deciding to make my first political stump speech to my three closest friends. "They are not serving the people but vested interests. I cannot agree with their politics. I will contest on local issues and election promise to serve the interests of my constituents, not some rich vested interest."

To my surprise, this small speech piqued Jimmy's interest. Shaking his head in agreement, "I agree with that." He expressed frustration with the two-party system labeling them two sides of the same coin, one that served narrow special interests rather than the people. This small alignment of thought changed his approach in my favor.

"Have you looked at the requirements to become a candidate?" Jimmy asked, getting down to the business.

"I have, and I meet most of the criteria. But to qualify, I need signatures from about 5,709 registered voters to be precise."

"When is the deadline?" Dr. Ashraf became serious for the first time in the whole conversation.

"February 28th, in seven weeks."

"What is your plan, and what do you need to get these signatures?" Ranbir inquired. It seemed the challenge inspired all of them to want to feel young and adventurous again. It would be like old times when we would pitch outlandish ideas to challenge each other. All of us need some challenge to make our lives meaningful and useful. Pursuing a larger cause beyond self-interest is integral for inner contentment. Age has nothing to do with it.

"I would need a team of five volunteers, marketing materials, and a social media campaign to collect these signatures outside malls and online."

"What sort of marketing material?" Ranbir continued.

"Some posters, holographic displays, and handouts for this stage to gather signatures."

"I will get you five volunteers from my staff and get your materials printed," Ranbir Singh announced, coming to my side and turning the table on the other two.

At that moment, I remembered the age-old axiom "A friend in need is a friend indeed."

"I will share the printing cost with you, Ranbir," Dr. Ashraf chimed in. "If you cross this hurdle, you can count on me to contribute to your campaign funds."

"I am here to provide moral support. I am always available to provide advice," Jimmy stated. "But we have to get together again once this hurdle is crossed. We don't have a campaign yet."

As soon as I got home, I began working on the budget for the first phase. I didn't want to burden my friends too much and decided to contribute equally towards printing the marketing materials. I looked at the past campaign slogans and materials of Democratic and Republican candidates. Democrats traditionally used blue, while Republicans used red. I decided to use purple for my campaign, a color produced by mixing red and blue. My slogan would be "Local First." I sent all this information to Ranbir Singh so that he could get the design work started. I also set up an appointment for the next day to record my five-minute video message for holographic presentations to be displayed at five different locations in the constituency, which would help volunteers secure signatures from the public.

"Did your friends put an end to your craziness?" Nour asked as soon as she walked into the house from work.

"We agreed on a plan."

"Was Jimmy there?" She sounded both surprised and disappointed.

"Yes."

"And he agreed to the plan?" It appeared; she was hoping he hadn't.

"Let's just say he was outvoted," I replied with a smile. I was certain Nour had spoken to Jimmy to dissuade me from pursuing it.

I had achieved my first small political victory at home. Considering her annoyance and opposition, I was afraid my wife would vote against me in the elections and embarrass me, I needed to win her support.

Eleven

James McCoy

Sipping from a hot cup of tea, Sher Shah watched the promotional video recorded at the start of his election campaign. It was used as a holographic presentation at the five locations assigned to the volunteers to gather signatures.

Sitting at his writing table and looking out at the beautiful scenery of the backyard where squirrels were scavenging for food, he vividly recalled those challenging days of his election campaign and the emotions that accompanied them. He opened his notebook, ready to write about the pivotal event that would ultimately turn the tide in his campaign.

* * *

February 5th, 2066

The next day after meeting my friends, I recorded the video at a local studio arranged by Ranbir. The five-minute video took me six hours to record. It was my first-ever performance in front of the camera. There were three cameras in the studio, arranged in a manner to record a 360-degree view of my speech. The videographer kept asking for a retake. I struggled to satisfy his professional quality standards. Sometimes my body language was off; other times, I moved my hands too much, and then my eye contact was not good enough. Sometimes, I spoke too slowly or too fast. A few times, I forgot the lines and stammered. It would take twenty takes before the cameraman was satisfied with it.

In the promotional video, I wore a black pin-striped suit and an off-white shirt with a mandarin collar. I made an extra effort to get perfect shine for black Oxford shoes. I believe the character of a man could be judged from his shoes. Everyone could fake a facial expression, but it was hard to hide shoes. The style and cleanliness of the shoes revealed the character.

Jimmy had helped me prepare the script for the video. We decided I should be presented as a candidate who had local roots, being born and raised in the city. My election slogan would be "Local First, Everything Else Comes Second." In the video, I talked about a lifelong commitment to the city and being familiar with its issues. I pledged to help legislation that provided a prosperous future to all citizens without discrimination. Securing better funding for improving the climate, especially air and water quality, and gaining support for the agricultural sector would be my roadmap to prosperity. Jimmy, Ranbir, and Ashraf reviewed the video and gave it two thumbs up.

After recording the video and while driving home, I logged in to my laptop to download and read ethical compliance material from the county clerk's website. I took notes from the material and prepared a training module for the five volunteers. Ranbir had sent me the communication IDs for these volunteers in the morning. That same evening, I shared it with them in a virtual reality meeting room. We also performed role plays to prepare for possible questions from the voters to secure their signatures.

I helped each volunteer download the mobile app from the county clerk's website. The app provided them with a code that had to be used by the registered voter to submit their signature to my candidature petition. Every evening at 5 pm, the county clerk's office would update its stats to inform us about the signatures secured so far. Candidates could also request a digital copy of the signatories for their records. There was a pie chart that would give them visual information about how far they were from the goal. It would remain red until they crossed the hurdle of 5709 signatures and turn green signifying the candidature has been qualified. The team tested the system by submitting their signatures. That evening, I had six done 5703 more to go.

The day after training volunteers, I identified the six most visited locations in the city and assigned one spot to each of them, keeping the sixth one for himself. The team agreed to work at each location from 2 pm to 8 pm as it was the most trafficked time of the day. We would start as soon as the campaign material was delivered.

It took seven days for the printed materials and holographic equipment to arrive. While waiting, we couldn't start our signature campaign. I didn't want to waste any time, so I decided to reach out to my friends and family and requested Ranbir, Jimmy, and Ashraf to do the same. With over 200 names in my communication device contact list, I expected most of them to be registered voters. I expected similar numbers for my three friends. If all these people signed the petition, I would have a good head start.

However, when I contacted people to request a signature, they sounded enthusiastic and assured me of their support. Yet, when I would check the election office mobile app, there would only be a handful of new signatures. I couldn't understand why people would promise support but then not follow through. This aspect of human behavior puzzled me. Was being polite more important than creating false expectations? I considered whether I had the same attitude as others. Why couldn't they just tell me they didn't support me?

Despite these initial signs of trouble, my euphoria and enthusiasm blinded me to face reality. I was excited when the election materials arrived on January 18th. I delivered it to all five team members on the same day. I held a virtual reality meeting in the evening to go over and finalize the execution plan. With 38 days left to collect 5,659 signatures (having already secured 50), we needed 149 signatures a day. We projected to interact with a total of 3,000+ people every day at the six locations, which meant a conversion rate of 5%. It seemed like a straightforward task to convert 5 out of every 100 people we met with.

February is typically expected to bring cooler weather, but Fresno's climate is known for its peculiarities. Even in February, standing in the sun can feel scorching, while the shade offers a contrasting chill. Even donning lighter winter attire provides warmth in the sun but proves insufficient when in the shade. The temperature undergoes a wide swing within twelve hours. In the morning, it hovers around 66 degrees Fahrenheit, only to climb as high as 90 degrees by 5 pm, before returning to 66 degrees by 8 pm. I encountered these weather fluctuations during my two-week election campaign.

On the first day of campaigning, I set up a small tent in the mall parking lot, approximately a hundred yards from the entrance. The tent provided some relief from the sun, but I often had to step out to greet people with handshakes, so its shade offered limited respite.

I chose the city's busiest mall as my primary location to collect signatures from the public. I arrived around 1:00 pm, earlier than my team, working at other locations. I wanted to engage with mall shoppers until the closing time of 8:00 pm. The first few days were the most challenging. I grappled with approaching people and initiating conversations. Shyness would overcome me when it came to shaking hands with strangers and starting a conversation. It felt like an insurmountable high hurdle. I remained in this state of hesitation until an elderly woman approached me.

She inquired, "What are you asking people to do?"

I responded like a trained parrot, "Hi, my name is Sher Shah. I need your support to become a candidate for the US Congress District 23," as I handed her my campaign material.

She examined the material and asked, "Which party do you belong to?"

"None. I don't believe the two parties are addressing our problems." I saw this as my opportunity to secure my first voter signature.

She nodded and asked, "You are right about that. What do I have to do?"

I handed her the device and guided her through the process. This encounter bolstered my confidence, helping me overcome my initial shyness by the day's end.

However, while the math was simple, the real-life execution proved to be much harsher. On January 19th, our first day, we could only secure 25 signatures at all six locations, most of them coming from where I worked. The second day saw similar results. On the third day, I decided to change locations for the volunteers, and they managed to collect 75 signatures, a significant improvement but still short of our daily target to reach the threshold.

Despite growing despondency in the team and a decline in my morale, I remained resolute in my decision not to give up on the campaign and to see it through to the end.

As the days passed, the required average number of signatures we needed each day increased exponentially, and with that rising number, my motivation started to wane. Nour kept track of the numbers and was convinced that the experiment would end on February 28th. I didn't blame her, as she made it clear repeatedly that her top priority was our home and children, and she didn't want to risk it for what she saw as an irrational attempt to do petty politics. I only wished for her support in his endeavor.

While making some progress and collecting several signatures, we remained significantly short of the required numbers. We had been at it for over two weeks, yet our total signatures had barely crossed the 1500 mark. To meet the February 28th deadline, we needed an additional 4200 signatures in the next 23 days, equating to an average of 183 signatures per day. Falling short on any given day meant having to collect even more signatures the next day. As each day passed, my hopes dwindled, and my friends prepared to console me to handle the expected failure and move on. They even made a list of possible community projects that I could work on.

My hopes were indeed dwindling, but my energy remained unflagging. I still greeted everyone with enthusiasm.

"Hi, I'm Sher. Can I count on your support for the US congressional election?" I approached every passerby with a smile and energy, although at times, I felt like a robot that was devoid of any emotions.

The responses from people varied widely. Most would scrutinize me from head to toe and then shake their heads in refusal. Others extended a handshake and offered words of encouragement, promising to submit their signature later when they reached home. Some, however, reacted with apprehension, worried as if I might be seeking a donation for some charitable cause. A few were annoyed, shooting me an irritated glare for interrupting their thoughts, others seemed to resent the idea of being reminded about politics, which they felt was intruding on their enjoyment of spending money. Nonetheless, a small number of individuals readily agreed to support me, and that's how we managed to accumulate 1500 signatures.

On February 5th, 2066, I enthusiastically approached a tall Caucasian man with a reddish beard and hair. As we shook hands, he unexpectedly asked, "Why should I support you?" I was not prepared for such a serious inquiry.

"I was born and raised here. I know the city's issues," I replied with my usual thoughtless monologue.

Before I could finish my sentence, he probed further asking, "I know the issues too. But do you have a solution?"

I fumbled for an answer. "I've posted our policy plans and manifesto on social media. The links are in the hand-out," I failed to offer an explanation with a list of policy options, as I handed him our campaign material.

He continued, "Which party are you contesting from?"

"None. I'm an independent candidate," I replied with confidence.

"How will you, as a lone congressman, defeat the two behemoths and pass legislation?" he challenged.

"I'm sure there are people in both parties who can support a good policy proposal," I responded, but even to myself, the answer sounded shallow.

"Good luck," he said as he began to walk away. This brief but serious conversation left me feeling like a political novice, and I started to wonder if everyone was right, and I was wrong about my election idea.

As I watched him get into an expensive European self-driving sports car powered by solar energy, I couldn't help but feel that he symbolized the deep pockets and influence that were often associated with politics.

You might think I should have given up at this point, but that's not who I am. I had resolved to persist until the very last day and accept whatever fate had in store. I refused to give up without giving it my all.

Two days later, I encountered the same person again. This time, he approached me rather than pass me by.

"You're still here," he remarked with a chuckle.

"I'm still here," I replied, extending my hand for a handshake.

"How many signatures have you collected so far?" he inquired.

"1704, to be precise, and it'll be updated at 5 pm today," I answered with a cheerful tone hiding my disappointment with it.

"How many do you need?" he asked.

"5709."

"In how much time?"

"Exactly twenty-one days from today."

He continued condescendingly, "If you understood politics, you wouldn't be standing here. And your presence here makes me feel like I'd be wasting my signature endorsing you."

"I do need your signature endorsement. What else can I do to convince you?" I wanted to demonstrate my perseverance and resolve like a child.

"That's a long conversation. Give me your contact information. Let me think about what I can do for you."

I quickly transferred my contact information to his device, and then, caught up in the whirlwind of shaking hands and seeking endorsements, I temporarily forgot about him.

The next morning, I received a message from someone named James McCoy, requesting a lunch appointment on the same day. At first, I was puzzled about who this person might be. The name did not ring a bell. I thought it could be someone I had encountered during my election campaign handshakes. The proposed meeting time clashed with my scheduled campaign activities at the mall. Initially, I contemplated turning down the request. Upon second thought, I realized that sacrificing an hour of campaign time wouldn't hurt, given our struggle to gather the required signatures. I decided to accept the lunch invitation and instructed my car to schedule the trip accordingly.

The restaurant chosen for our meeting was an upscale diner, frequently patronized by the city's elites. I had shared many family lunches and dinners there with Dr. Rabbani and my friend Dr. Ashraf Ul Islam. When I mentioned that I was a guest of James McCoy at the check-in counter, the usher promptly escorted me to his table. As I approached, I saw the tall, red-bearded man I had encountered at the mall already seated, and he stood up to greet me.

"Thank you for accepting my lunch invitation during your busy election campaign," he said as we both took seats.

"You're welcome, and I appreciate your interest in my campaign."

We placed our orders. I settled for the soup on the menu. Interestingly, the waiter didn't even ask for his order, implying he might have placed it in advance, likely a regular or a familiar face here.

"Tell me everything about your election campaign," he inquired after the waiter left.

I proceeded to recount my journey, from my initial meeting with Alex to my personal experience as the fall guy for the boiler accident. I shared details about my research on the constituency, conversations with friends, and the strategies we'd adopted to gather signatures.

"Malls are not the ideal place to seek political support," he commented as soon as I had finished. "People go there to have a good time and enjoy the experience of buying new things, often things they don't even need. They're least interested in being reminded of problems or thinking about politics. You are messing up their leisure time." He concluded with a smirky smile.

I shifted uncomfortably in my seat. "What should we do then?" Recalling Nour had advised me to consult someone experienced in politics.

"You'll need to do a lot, and you'll need to do it quickly," he replied, sounding like someone with a plan. "You effectively have nineteen days left to collect the required signatures."

We paused for the waiter to serve our food before continuing our conversation.

"I can help you, but I have two conditions," he said as he picked up his knife and fork.

"First, I will be your campaign manager."

I was intrigued by this stranger's surprising pronouncement, and eager to know the second condition. "And what is the second condition?"

"You will do exactly as I tell you. You won't overthink it. You'll just do what I tell you to do."

While I was comfortable with the first condition because I desperately needed help, the second condition gave me a pause. How could I agree to become a puppet for someone I didn't even know?

"I'm comfortable with the first condition, but the second condition makes me feel like I'd be your puppet," I confessed, opting for frankness.

"I understand," he replied, calmly savoring his lobster. "I'm referring to executing your campaign strategy. I will design and execute the election strategy."

Curiosity got the better of me. "Why do you want to help me, if I may ask?"

"I despise the stranglehold of the two parties on our politics. They've failed the people, and they need to be challenged," he replied, his tone and eyes reflecting a hint of anger.

"How much time do I have to make a decision?"

"Until we finish our lunch."

It wasn't much time, but as I ate and engaged in small talk

with James, my mind raced to debate and arrive at a quick decision. I considered the current state of my campaign, and the reality was that I was failing to gather the required signatures. Without those, I wouldn't even qualify to contest the elections. I had nothing to lose and everything to gain.

"We have a deal," I finally said as we finished our meal, extending my hand to seal the agreement.

"Good. Gather your volunteer team for a breakfast meeting tomorrow morning. We'll discuss our new campaign strategy," he replied, shaking my hand firmly.

As a political novice, it would turn out to be undoubtedly the best political decision I made.

James McCoy, a graduate in political science from Harvard University, had previously worked as a staff member for a Democratic Party congressman in Washington, D.C. His exposure to politics in the nation's capital had transformed him into a vocal critic of the two-party political system. Subsequently, he chose to leave his position with the congressman and transitioned into the world of investment banking. More recently, he had taken early retirement and relocated to sunny California to escape the chilly, gray winters of New York.

He would later tell me, "Sher Shah, I don't know if you can win the election. But I certainly plan to give these two monsters, who are eating away at the future of this nation, a run for their money."

I needed a partner who shared my determination to pursue what seemed like an impossible path to political victory, and in James, I had found that partner. After two weeks of campaigning with lackluster performance and anxiety, I finally had a good night's sleep on the day I had lunch with him to strike a deal and bring him on board. I appreciated the wisdom of Nour. She was the first to ask if I had consulted a domain expert with knowledge of politics and campaigning. I went a step further and found one as a campaign manager.

Twelve

A small win

⚜

Flipping through pictures, Sher Shah stopped and gazed at the images capturing the first meeting between James and his election volunteers on the wall display. It was a moment frozen in time that had completely altered the course of his election campaign. Without James, he believed his political journey would have likely ended in failure. There would be no inspiring story to recount today if their paths hadn't crossed and if James hadn't stepped up to take on the role of his campaign manager.

With gratitude in his heart, Sher Shah opened his notebook to narrate the events of that pivotal day when James had met his election team, forever changing the trajectory of his political journey.

* * *

February 6th, 2066

Nour may not have been fully committed to my election project, but she was a warm and courteous host. She prepared a breakfast feast that could have fed an army. It was a heartwarming gesture. She woke up earlier than her routine on a weekend day to prepare an elaborate menu with two types of omelets, an array of eggs boiled or fried, a variety of bread, and an assortment of condiments and beverages adorning the table. It made me hopeful that she might eventually lend her active support to my election campaign rather than remain passive or indifferent.

"It seems your chances of winning the election have improved from zero to 5%," Nour commented as she left to do her weekend chores of buying groceries and other essentials for the family.

James contributed an invaluable wealth of experience, resources, unwavering commitment, and boundless energy to the team. He was a true multi-tasker, an expert at optimizing every moment, and his infectious energy uplifted everyone around him. He arrived punctually at 8:00 am. I greeted him at the door. He was accompanied by a woman in her mid-20s.

"Hello, Sher, meet Gina Alderman," James presented his companion as I welcomed them at the door. Gina, a woman in her late 20s, possessed a petite frame, short hair, and round glasses, radiating a geeky charm in her ensemble of a checkered skirt and a snug, dark green sweater. She would become a cornerstone in our election campaign. In the realm of effective strategy, it's not just about crafting plans; it's about cultivating a proficient team for execution.

"Thank you and welcome to the team, Gina." I ushered them into the living room, where everyone else was gathered.

The five team members were already seated. After helping ourselves to breakfast, we gathered in a circle to dive into the day's agenda. James took the floor, introducing himself and sharing his political background, emphasizing his prior role as a staff member for a congressman. His presence and extensive experience were evident, instilling confidence in everyone present.

Following his introduction, James turned to Gina, inviting her to introduce herself. Gina, too, brought a wealth of experience in political work, having previously been engaged in the election campaign of the incumbent Democrat Congressman Kevin Johnson. Despite her Democratic Party background, Gina made a pivotal decision a couple of years ago to join James at his investment bank. Her disillusionment with the Democratic Party stemmed from its failure to fulfill election promises and meet voter expectations. This disappointment fueled her belief in the necessity of a third force in politics, becoming a key motivation for her involvement with our team.

When she finished, James explained, "Gina will be responsible for managing our social media campaign, voter surveys, and overall strategy implementation." It was evident that he did not want to waste time taking on the role of campaign manager.

James continued by asking each of the five volunteers to introduce themselves and share how they had come to know me. After the introductions, he surprised us with a question that left me somewhat uneasy: "Will you all vote for Sher on Election Day?" It seemed to be prompted by the fact that all my team members were compensated for their work.

As the five volunteers hesitated in their response, I began to realize they might have signed up for the campaign more as part of their day job than out of genuine support. I wondered if that was the reason for their lackluster performance in collecting signatures from voters. I had expected an enthusiastic "yes", instead there was silence and a lack of immediate commitment.

One of them finally mustered the courage to speak up, "I guess we could vote for him," but the response clearly lacked enthusiasm.

I could see a chuckle appear on James's face. He didn't let the hesitant affirmation slide and pointed out, "You don't sound too excited or convinced. The point I wanted to make is that you can't convince others to support your candidate if you're not convinced yourselves." Confirming my earlier suspicion.

To further challenge me and ensure my team's dedication, James asked me to make a five-minute speech to persuade these non-supportive team members to become committed voters. It was an unexpected and nerve-wracking request, as I had never delivered a public speech before. I felt unprepared and nervous, my forehead moist with sweat, and my thoughts scattered.

"A politician should be ready to make a speech at any moment," James insisted, putting an additional burden on me that felt heavy to carry.

With trembling nerves, I stood up and delivered a speech that lacked fluency and coherence, leaving me embarrassed and uncomfortable.

"It's alright, Sher. You did well. We're here to help you improve," James applauded to boost my morale, despite my apparent struggle to make a speech.

Following my speech, James encouraged them to ask me as many questions as they wished. Although shaken by my earlier speech disaster, I gradually regained my composure and began to respond to their questions more confidently. My experiences during the two weeks of campaigning in front of the mall had prepared me to handle some of the questions that came my way.

At the end of these questions, James went to the far corner of the kitchen and placed his digital device and pen on the counter. He then asked the team members to cast their vote in a contest between me and the incumbent Democratic Party congressman Kevin Johnson. He assured them that the voting system would not ask for their names, ensuring an anonymous vote. They took their turns to cast votes. I observed them closely, trying to discern from their body language whether they would support me or not. Some of them paused for a moment before making their choice.

Once the voting was completed, James retrieved his digital device and stood up to announce the results of this mini election, resembling a referee in a boxing match. Despite being aware it was just a sample and not a judgment of my ability, I still felt nervous about the outcome. Looking me straight in the eyes James announced the result playfully: Incumbent Kevin Johnson 2, and challenger Sher Shah 3.

"Congratulations, Mr. Shah, you have won your first election," James declared with a mischievous smile. It would not be the last time he would put me on the spot during the election campaign. I breathed a sigh of relief, even though it was a mock election, it significantly boosted my confidence.

James then outlined our election strategy to gather the remaining 3,856 signatures needed to cross the 5709-signature hurdle. At that point, we had 1853 signatures and 22 days left, requiring an average of 176 signatures per day.

James demonstrated a keen understanding of human psychology. To garner support, we needed to connect with people when they were in a receptive state of mind. The next day, which was Sunday, James assigned each volunteer to visit a church and set up a display at the entrance. He emphasized the importance of dressing appropriately to respect the sanctity of the place. He told them that those coming out of religious services were often contemplative and concerned about the challenges people face in pursuit of their lives. They were more likely to support an underdog candidate who needed their help. This common-sense idea never occurred to me. It was an indication of my inexperience and a reminder that I had to learn much to be an effective politician.

In addition to churches, James instructed us to carry out similar activities at synagogues, mosques, temples (mandirs), and pagodas. Fortunately, each faith community had a separate day of the week for their ritual events, making it possible for us to reach out to them effectively.

James also instructed us to set up holographic displays near walking trails in the constituency, as those who used these trails were interested in self-improvement and were more open to ideas to improve society.

He provided a list of retirement and old-age residential complexes and asked Gina to set up appointments for my presentations and handshakes with the residents. We were also to engage in door-to-door canvassing every weekday between 5 pm and 7 pm.

James's strategy was not just about collecting signatures but also about building a connection with voters who could relate to our cause. It was a thoughtful approach that played to the emotional and empathetic aspects of human nature, it reflected his deep understanding of politics and psychology.

James introduced a digital aspect to our campaign strategy that I had never considered. He informed us about federal and state laws that allowed candidates to reach potential voters through unsolicited email. This revelation surprised me, as I was unaware of this opportunity.

He assigned Gina to prepare a communication campaign targeting voters who were undecided and not aligned with any political party. The goal was to reach out to those who were disgruntled with the two-party system and might be open to supporting an independent candidate like me. To kick-start this initiative, he instructed Gina to obtain a list of communication IDs from the county clerk's office.

Injecting a note of optimism, Gina highlighted the increasing number of disgruntled voters in recent years. This revelation buoyed our campaign, affirming that a substantial portion of the population sought alternatives. The responsibility now rested on our shoulders to adeptly communicate our message, enticing them to endorse me as a candidate to meet the minimum requirement to qualify to be on the ballot paper.

James went a step further by committing his own funds to set up a social media advertising campaign. His willingness to invest his money in my campaign demonstrated his dedication and belief in our common cause.

As our strategy meeting concluded, James checked his smartwatch and reminded us to reconvene the following Saturday.

As he prepared to leave, I couldn't help but express my appreciation for his contributions. I told him that he should be the candidate instead of me, given his knowledge and commitment to the cause. However, his response left me speechless. He stated bluntly, "I hate politics." This unexpected statement made me question my decision to pursue politics, but it also reinforced the idea that James was genuinely dedicated to challenging the status quo. We had a common goal, and he was willing to work tirelessly to achieve it.

With renewed energy and determination, we all set out to implement James's strategies. On Sunday evening, the county clerk's app reported that we had accumulated 2,367 signatures, an increase of 514 in one day from the previous Saturday evening.

On Sunday night as I lay down in bed feeling hyped-up because of the higher-than-expected number of signatures gathered, I turned to Nour and asked, "Would you be willing to bet I will gather the necessary number of signatures by February 28th."

"The bet is on." She was not one to refuse a game. "What are the stakes."

"Whatever you say."

She thought for a long moment, "You will cook dinner for a month."

"Fine. What do I get if I win."

"I will become part of your campaign."

"You got a deal woman."

The numbers continued to rise with each passing day, bolstering my hope of crossing the signature requirement. On the evening of February 27th, just a day before the deadline, we were only 101 signatures shy of meeting the requirement. Our hard work and James's strategic guidance had brought us to the brink of crossing the milestone to start the journey.

Thirteen

The milestone

February 28th, 2066

I had a good sleep the night before the deadline to submit signatures. I overslept because the room was still dark, making me believe it was still too early. When I finally looked at the clock, it was 7:30 am, and I had overslept by two hours. I jumped out of bed, wondering why the room was still dark. I pushed the curtain to the side, and it felt like a bucket of cold water fell over my head.

The backyard was inundated by water due to a heavy downpour, and thick, dark clouds were covering the entire sky. I had slept with confidence that the last day to get signatures, being a church service Sunday, would help us easily reach the required number of signatures. In the last three weeks, Sundays had been our best-performing days. It felt like the one controlling this universe did not want me to become the candidate.

I loved rainy days, but it was destroying my chances today. I looked up at the sky and said to myself, "Why? Why such heavy rain today?" The weather service forecast had suggested periodic light rain for the weekend. But the stormy conditions outside were defying that forecast, drowning my chances to do electioneering on this final day to cross the hurdle of acquiring the required number of signatures.

Still depressed about my endangered chances of success, I went to the kitchen and made a cup of tea. Nour was working in the kitchen, preparing food for the results-watching party we had organized to celebrate finally becoming a US congressional candidate. She saw the expression of depression written all over my face.

"Give me your device; let me put my signature on your petition," she said to cheer me up and lend me her support. "Now you only have to worry about 100 more."

I smiled and gave her my device. When she was completing the voting procedure, there was a message from Jimmy.

"You have my signature. How many more do we need?" He knew I would be in a state of disbelief and shock.

"99," I sent him a short reply.

It did uplift my mood a little, prompting me to check the weather forecast for the day on my handheld device. A storm system, forming for the last few days off the Pacific coast, had gained strength, and the earlier forecast was adjusted accordingly. Unfortunately, it wasn't in my favor. It predicted continuous heavy downpours throughout the day, with flood warnings in some areas. The little hope I had felt earlier was washed away as I read the weather report.

I received messages from three of my five teammates, informing me of flood warnings in their areas and that it wasn't safe for them to go out. I told them to stay home and join the evening party if the flood warning was lifted. The memory of Smith getting injured when checking boiler instruments on my instructions was permanently etched in my memory. I had promised myself never again I would ask anyone to do a task if there was any chance of a risk of physical injury.

Next, I received a message from the person who had made the seemingly impossible possible. Before I opened James's message, I anticipated that he would be as devastated as I was. However, I couldn't have been more wrong.

"I just posted my signature for you. It's not over until it's over. We are going to try until the last minute," read the message from James. "Let's ask all our team members to reach out to their contacts." I wondered if he would be good at being a sports coach.

James put me to shame. I was the candidate, and he was the strategist. I should have been encouraging people and not frozen in fear of failure.

"I am sending one last email to the voters asking for their help. Requesting them to act as we can't let the two parties own our future by being short of a few signatures," Gina informed me in a message on my communication ID. I felt proud of my team members. They were not going to let the force of nature dictate our destiny. It is this never-say-die attitude that makes humans superior to other creatures, using intellect to improvise and overcome impossible hurdles to achieve something bigger than life.

Our daily average had been around 200 signatures since we adopted the strategy designed by James. We needed just half of our daily average number of signatures; we could make it happen by being creative and active. I took a quick shower and got into action.

I sent a text reminder to my contacts list on the device, informing them that today was the last day, and we were only short of ninety-eight signatures. I told them that a friend who couldn't believe in me was not a friend of mine. It may have sounded like a desperate appeal, but I was done with being nice. It seemed I had struck a chord with them, as I received more positive responses than expected. The lesson I learned from that experience; desperation invokes empathy in others. When I checked my device after taking a shower, I had confirmation screenshots from twenty-five of my friends enabling us to get closer to crossing the threshold. We needed seventy-three more signatures, and the rain could still wash away our chances of getting it done.

By 9:00 am that day, I got dressed and went out to install my campaign tent in front of the largest church in the area. The attendance at the church was only a quarter of their average, I could see an expression of compassion and empathy in the eyes of the people. They were apparently impressed with my resolve and commitment. Many came up to me and granted their signatures while braving the rain under my tent that could hardly contain the rain. Others promised to do it when they got home. The expression on their faces told me I could trust their promise after all these were God-fearing people. No God can tolerate a false promise.

I returned home by noon to help Nour prepare for the evening. I felt a certain calmness, and my worries were lifted. I had done my best, if it was not meant to be, then so be it. We had invited all who had helped us with the campaign: James and his wife, Gina, my five team members, my in-laws, and my three friends - Ranbir Singh, Jimmy Dean, and Ashraf Ul Islam - with their families. Gina brought her sister to share the excitement. Alex would be there too, as he had completed his term at the correctional facility a few days earlier.

Nour is a good host and loves parties. She prepared a sumptuous four-course menu: Bar B Q lamb chops, Pakistani lamb curry and chicken biryani, lentil soup, salad, two types of desserts, and fresh fruit juices. We had moved the living room sofa to make space for tables and chairs. The living room display device would be where we would watch the result posted by the county clerk's office at exactly five pm.

At 3:00, I went up to our bedroom to take a shower and get ready to receive guests. I decided to dress in black pants and a light purple shirt. Purple is not my favorite color, but I had picked it as our campaign color, so I had to wear it on that important day.

We had asked everyone to arrive at 4 so we could eat before the results. I expected the mood to be either wildly happy or somber after the result. A failure could impact their appetite. I wanted them to enjoy Nour's cooking before I could potentially destroy their hunger for food if I failed to cross the milestone of 5709 required signatures.

Guests started arriving on time, and we had food. I thanked everyone individually for their support and tried to sound as energetic as I could, although the anxiety of failure lingered in my mind. At 4:45 pm, Ivan took control of the device to be ready to refresh the app to display the result, and everyone took a seat. Those fifteen minutes moved with the speed of a slumbering snail. I thought they would never end.

When the clock struck 5:00, Ivan promptly refreshed the page. The only thing I remember seeing in that instant was a green checkmark. That is all that mattered to me. I would be happy with 5709, which was needed, but we got 5795 signatures. In an instant, the whole room erupted in a loud shout of exhilaration, and everyone jumped from their chairs. There was too much pent-up energy in them that needed a release. I was happy about crossing a milestone that looked impossible to achieve just two weeks ago. Everyone came to me one by one to shake hands and congratulate me. I thanked them in return for their support.

Alex congratulated and thanked me for taking this initiative.

"I want to help you in the election campaign." He asked with hesitation unsure if I would accept his help as a convicted criminal."

"I need all the help I can get Alex. You are welcome to join, and I thank you for this contribution."

James was the last one. "Alright, buddy, we are in play."

"Yes, we are, and it is all because of your plan and execution."

"Thanks. But it is always the candidate that wins or loses an election." James did not forget to remind me that the burden was on me. "We should have a brief meeting tonight to chart the future course of action."

James was not one to waste time. I nodded in affirmation. We decided to hold a meeting when everyone left. I told my three friends to stay back for our brief meeting and send their spouses and kids home. All six of us, myself, James, Gina, Ranbir, Jimmy, and Ashraf, gathered in the living room after everyone left.

"We have crossed a milestone to start a journey," James opened the discussion. "It will be tiring, demanding, and sometimes frustrating. Are we ready for it? We still have time to back down."

"I am not backing down," I declared. The euphoria of crossing the hurdle was still high for me to rationally analyze and evaluate the situation. The enormity of the task would dawn on me a little later.

"Okay then. Here is the first hurdle. We would need, at a minimum, a million and a half to fund the campaign." He was good at throwing bombshells at the start. Everyone shifted uneasily in their chairs.

"Here is the good news. I can help and also bring in some funds too," he assured the gathering. "But we would need a lot of donors."

"I can help with fundraising," Ashraf may have felt that if James was willing to help, then my friends should not be far behind.

"I will help too," Ranbir wanted to add more to the contribution he had already made to kick-start my campaign by funding the election material.

"Alright. Ranbir and Ashraf, you will be co-chairs of the finance committee. I will help and guide," said the campaign manager in action.

"I can help provide some volunteers from my church organization," Jimmy did not want to be left behind.

"Great. We will need a lot of volunteers to reach out to voters."

"What do I do?" I was feeling as if I was not needed in all this.

"For the next two months," James began listing my tasks. "Read all about legislation done in the last three years. Get to know your competition from the Democratic and Republican Parties. Read everything you can find about them. Watch videos of their speeches. Relax and spend time with your family. Attend campaign fundraising dinners and lunches. Work on your public speaking skills. And please, avoid a scandal." As he concluded the long list, I nodded like an obedient student responding to a professor's homework task.

Later that night, when I lay down in bed, Nour looked at me with affection and love pouring out of her eyes, "Congrats on winning the bet. What do you want me to do for your campaign?"

"Keeping me happy is your first task." The coldness of the bed that I had felt on the night, when I told her about my election plans, was gone. I enjoyed my small victories because life is easier that way. Those who ignore such moments of happiness remain unhappy most of their lives.

The county clerk's office released the roster of candidates set to appear on the November election ballot. Detailed biographies of Democratic and Republican Party candidates were featured in the newspapers reporting the list of candidates. However, my qualifications and introduction as a candidate for the US congressional elections were noticeably absent in the news articles. They briefly mentioned my candidacy at the end of their reports in just one line, making it clear that they did not view me as a serious contender capable of challenging the two-party monopoly. Instead of dampening my motivation, this unequivocal dismissal inspired me even more to prove them wrong. My determination surged as I set out to change their perception and demonstrate my viability as a candidate.

"Have you seen the papers?" I sent a message to James the next morning after reading the newspapers.

"Yes."

"They are not going to give us space in their election

coverage," I continued.

"No. It is going to be one of many of our hurdles to cross."

Fourteen

The talking mind

S her Shah woke up feeling exhausted, weariness etched across his face from a restless night plagued by old nightmares. The weakness in his body caused by the progressing illness was playing games with his emotions during sleep. As he entered the study room, he instinctively checked the weather through the window. The sky was overcast with clouds, but there was no rain, much like the day after he had met the requirements to become a candidate.

He settled down at the table to continue writing his story. The first notebook was completely consumed, and he contemplated getting two more, as there was much more to tell after the elections. He affixed sticker #1 to both the front cover and the side of the notebook. While the inside of the notebook contained the dates, ensuring readers could identify it as the first one, Sher Shah wanted the sequence clearly visible on the exterior to assist readers in selecting the correct volume from the series.

Opening the second notebook to write about the day after the confirmation of his candidature, Sher couldn't help but reflect on the heavy burden he had felt weighing on his soul and the relentless chatter of his mind when he went to bed that night.

Still rattled by the emotions from the nightmares, Sher Shah grabbed the pen in his fingers and opened his notebook to write.

* * *

March 1st, 2066

The mind is a ceaseless chatterbox. It never ceases its discourse. Sometimes, it assumes the role of a friendly companion, while at other times, it becomes a harsh critic. In certain instances, it transforms into an outright adversary. It can shout at you as if you are hard of hearing or whisper as though your thoughts are audible to others. The mind continues its narrative during prayer, work, leisure, or play. It persists even when you strive to meditate and clear your mind of all thoughts. It doesn't stop when you sleep, it morphs into a storyteller, producing countless movies to entertain or fascinate like a science fiction movie or scaring you as in a horror movie that haunts you when you wake up.

Post-traumatic stress disorder (PTSD) is not limited to soldiers returning from war, it can be experienced by anyone who undergoes a traumatic event. The mind typically disconnects from distressing memories during sleep, allowing individuals to rest peacefully. However, in some PTSD cases, particularly severe ones, the mind refuses to disengage from these memories, causing the traumatic event to replay in one's consciousness even during sleep. This can become unbearable and result in self-induced insomnia. This deprivation of sleep then produces hallucinations.

I vividly remember experiencing this condition when I was declared as a candidate. Instead of feeling happy and relieved by my success, although small, it had the opposite effect, giving rise to anxiety and disbelief. As I lay in bed on the night of February 28th, after everyone had left, my mind had been relentless. I tossed and turned for what felt like an eternity before finally drifting off to sleep. However, my slumber was interrupted abruptly by a nightmare: I was falling from a great height, suspended between two towering buildings. My friends and family tried to reach out to me with their outstretched hands beseeching me to grab it to save me, but I couldn't grasp anyone's hand. The fear of falling to death had gripped me in that dream, and I woke up abruptly, sitting upright in bed just before hitting the ground in the nightmare. I could not sleep after that. It was a night filled with restless thoughts and fears that refused to relent.

I woke up the next day, on March 1st, feeling utterly exhausted due to the lack of sleep. I had been tossing and turning in bed for many hours, trapped in a fitful slumber plagued by unsettling nightmares. My mind, it seemed, had become a relentless interrogator, bombarding me with questions for which I had no answers. It was as if I were carrying an immense burden upon my shoulders.

First and foremost, there was the weight of my family's expectations. They yearned for my success, but their hope was tinged with fear for their own future, which was intricately tied to the outcome of my political journey.

Then there was the burden of those strangers who had entrusted their faith in my candidacy, expecting me to fulfill the promises I'd made if I were to win in the general elections. In a sense, my failure would also be their failure, and the mere thought of failure was a heavy burden. After all, every one of us aspires to triumph and wants to bask in the glow of success and be happy.

As if these two burdens weren't enough, James had placed upon me the Herculean task of raising a staggering million and a half funds from friends, family, and even unfamiliar donors. I would have to approach them, hat in hand, and request them to contribute their hard-earned money to fund my election campaign. Yet, these very funds could have been used for vital purposes such as paying for their children's education, feeding the hungry, clothing the homeless, or acquiring the essentials they had been deferring due to financial constraints. It meant that each donor would have to sacrifice something to support my cause. But what could I offer them in return, and what if I were to lose the election? The weight of their wasted contributions would undoubtedly haunt my conscience, regardless of the election's outcome.

All these burdens seemed to be piling up, becoming increasingly difficult for me to carry. And to compound matters, my mind had become my adversary, relentlessly reminding me of past failures and regrets. I couldn't simply silence it, nor would it be ethical to proceed without resolving this inner conflict. A half-hearted campaign had no chance of achieving anything and would most likely end in embarrassment. It would be unethical to continue in such a state of mind.

Over the past six weeks, I had been consumed by work and campaigning, leaving no time for introspection. But the day after qualifying, I felt an urgent need for a conversation with myself. With this on my mind, I took a long, steaming shower, put on warm clothing, and meticulously prepared a backpack filled with essentials—a flask of water, a thermos of hot tea, and sandwiches made with mango jam and butter, alongside two boiled eggs with salt and black pepper. My hiking shoes, hat, and stick were already in the trunk of the car. With everything ready, I set my course for the nearby mountains, a place that had always served as my sanctuary for contemplation and self-reflection.

"Woman, I'll be back after lunch, so don't wait for me," I informed Nour as she prepared to leave for work.

"Where are you going?" she inquired a little surprised seeing the serious countenance of my appearance.

"To the mountain," I replied, closing the door behind me.

The spot I frequented was roughly an hour's drive from home, nestled at an altitude of around 4000 feet. It saw minimal foot traffic, especially on weekdays. It was a place where a person could hike for a mile or two to find a tranquil spot overlooking the valley, perfect for meditation. Sometimes, I visited to release pent-up frustration by screaming at the top of my lungs—a cathartic release not feasible in the bustling city, where such an act would likely earn a person raised eyebrows and judgmental stares. Even a simple act of releasing inner stress is not possible among people.

Having hiked for two miles, I arrived at the spot around 9:30 am, ensuring I was adequately hydrated and had a bite to eat before settling on a sizable boulder. This over-sized rock provided a comfortable vantage point, allowing me to gaze at the valley below. The presence of such large boulders scattered across the Central Valley Mountain range always intrigued me. I couldn't help but wonder if they were remnants from the ice age. Many of these boulders exhibited smooth, round surfaces, hinting at a history of carving by the flow of water.

I sat facing the valley, the sun hiding behind a sequoia tree, its rays reaching me to keep me warm at such an altitude. It was a scene of utter tranquility and quietude. The towering, unwavering sequoia trees stood sentinel, their lofty forms immobile. They had witnessed countless generations come and go, yet they remained resolute and unflinching. A carpet of wild yellow and purple flowers graced the ground around the boulder where I sat, adding a splash of color to the serene landscape. An irrational thought occurred to me as I surveyed the scenery: would we have liked it if the grass were purple and the sky yellow instead of green and blue? I reprimanded myself for pondering frivolous things when serious questions needed answers.

The air hung motionless, devoid of even the faintest whisper of a breeze. The only sound that permeated the stillness was the ceaseless chatter of my mind, occasionally punctuated by the rhythmic strikes of a woodpecker hammering away at a towering sequoia tree. At that moment, I couldn't help but draw a parallel between myself and that small bird, both of us endeavoring to make a mark, however modest, within the grander system.

"Why are you subjecting everyone to your quest for ego gratification?" my inner voice probed.

"I'm not seeking ego gratification," I countered.

"Yes, you are," it persisted. "Ever since the boiler accident, you've carried a lingering sense of failure, and you're using this endeavor to prove your self-worth."

"It wasn't my fault," I defended.

"But you were dismissed for negligence, and the whole world knows," it struck at my vulnerability.

"I wasn't negligent, and the boiler explosion wasn't our team's fault."

"Why then carry this burden of guilt? What do you hope to achieve?" my inner voice pressed.

"I want to make sure society offers people a second chance," I replied.

"Six weeks, and you've secured the support of a mere 2% of the populace. You're deluding yourself if you think you can challenge seasoned politicians," my mind retorted, playing tricks on me.

"Should I just give up, then?" I wondered aloud.

"Yes, you should," my inner voice urged.

"Why am I even alive? Wouldn't it have been simpler to never exist at all?" I contemplated going back to the event of my unlikely birth, searching for meaning. "Would the world be any different if I'd never been born?"

"You are raising two daughters and adopted a son that would have been an orphan without you. Isn't that reason enough for living?" it pointed out.

"Is that the entirety of existence? To have a family, live with them, and eventually die?" I questioned, still grappling with the purpose of life.

"What more do you want from life?" my inner voice inquired.

"If my house is well-kept, my fridge stocked with food, and my closet filled with clothing for all seasons, yet others lack these basic necessities, shouldn't it matter to me?" I challenged the rationale myself. "What purpose does life serve if I don't make a difference?"

"Do you think you have solutions to all problems?" Another trick question popped into my mind.

"I don't have solutions to all problems, but I can solve some."

"But why politics?" my mind continued its relentless questioning.

"Should I focus on charity rather than politics?" I pondered.

"You can," my inner voice conceded as well as nudging me towards what Nour had proposed many times.

"Would people be willing to donate a million and a half dollars to feed the hungry?" I mused.

"If you can't ask them to donate to a noble cause, how can you ask them to invest in an inexperienced politician's election campaign?" my inner conversation persisted challenging the rationale of my endeavor.

"I don't know," I confessed.

Deep within, I must confess that I had harbored doubts about becoming a candidate and successfully collecting the required number of signatures. Crossing that milestone shocked me in an almost traumatic fashion.

I spent nearly an hour and a half on that boulder, engaging in a heartfelt conversation with myself. Although I remained unsure about the path forward, I felt a sense of relief after this inner dialogue.

As I made my way back to the car, I sent a message to James: "We need to talk. Can we meet for lunch tomorrow?"

He responded with a yes. I started contemplating what to say in our impending conversation.

Fifteen

To be or not to be

Sher Shah flipped through the pictures on the wall display until he found one that captured a moment of him shaking hands with James, both of them wearing smiles as if they were celebrating a significant achievement. The caption below the photo read, "Election Day - Tuesday, November 2nd, 2066." Despite the challenges and the burdens of that time, they remained good friends until this day and continued to consult with each other. James once told him that meeting Sher Shah had changed his life. He also felt a deep sense of mutual appreciation for their enduring friendship.

As Sher Shah sat down with the pen in hand, memories flooded his mind, transporting him back to that pivotal lunch meeting with James. He began to recount the story of a moment that had shaped not only his career but also his perspective on friendship and self-doubt. The lunch meeting with James had become a turning point, a chapter in his life that spoke of friendship's ability to dispel self-doubt and provide the support needed to navigate the complexities of life.

* * *

March 2nd, 2066

I woke up that day with the heavy weight of doubt lingering on my mind like a leech sucking blood. I was determined not to continue down the path of politics unless I was genuinely convinced it was the right thing to do. However, I couldn't make this decision on my own. James had invested his time and resources in helping me become a candidate. I felt the need to share my fears and uncertainties with him before making any final choices. I had decided to rely on his political experience to guide me.

I had chosen not to share my anxieties with Nour until I was sure what path to pursue. I had a hunch that her advice would be to have a swift withdrawal from the realm of politics. She was a wonderful life partner but had no desire or eagerness to expose the family to the harsh glare of public scrutiny. Her comfort zone resided within the narrow boundaries of family, friends, and community service. She viewed politics as a realm of theory, often too detached from the tangible and immediate problems faced by the people. For her, long-winded debates in Congress were a demonstration of politician's egos rather than serious consideration of the merits of an issue. The votes were decided based on party loyalties rather than the weight of the arguments or the interests of the constituents.

Nour's perspective remained steadfastly anchored in the belief that the forefront of any political endeavor should be practical, immediate solutions to people's everyday challenges. She would remind me that most people were preoccupied with the provision of basic necessities: finding stable employment to have food at the dinner table; ensuring a roof over their heads to sleep without worry; and safeguarding their family's well-being through affordable education and healthcare. Matters such as climate change, fiscal policy, foreign policy, and social justice, though vital for the long term, were often deemed philosophical concerns that seemed distant from the pressing needs of a homeless person seeking sustenance or a vulnerable individual seeking warmth against the biting cold.

When I would counter her to defend the importance of these policy matters.

She would say, "Shero, if we are funding government through debt, why did we spend trillion dollars on foreign wars. Wars that were later found to be based on lies. This debt has to be eventually paid by our taxes. We don't pay the mortgage for our neighbors, but we gladly pay the mortgage for the politicians. It is this social injustice that has to be fixed."

She viewed politics as a domain often better suited for the wealthy who needed to feel important and sought purpose in their lives to feel relevant. While I respected her perspective and understood her concerns, I wrestled with my convictions regarding the potential for political change to effectively address the very issues she deemed paramount. Even though the journey ahead was fraught with uncertainty and self-doubt, I couldn't shake the belief that it was worth pursuing.

I had not shared these thoughts with my three friends – Jimmy, Ranbir, and Ashraf as none of them had the knowledge and expertise to make sense of it and provide guidance. James was the only one on whose judgment I could rely on to arrive at a decision.

I had to discuss my anxieties and concerns with James because of his political experience and understanding of the emotional dynamics involved. I sought reassurance through his insights, knowing that his experience could help me carry the heavy burden that would be otherwise unbearable without conviction and inner satisfaction.

As I began my day, I drove to work, ready to teach mathematics to my third-term students at the correctional facility. The weight of responsibility hung heavy on my shoulders as I entered the facility. These young curious minds, although incarcerated for a time, looked to me for guidance and education. The thought of disappointing them by giving up on my mission to bring about legislative change for their benefit filled me with guilt.

In the classroom, engaging with my inmate students revealed eager faces and a palpable thirst for knowledge, an expression of a stark reminder of the untapped potential within each of them. The weight of responsibility pressed upon me; I couldn't afford to let them down, nor could I allow the system to fail them. The task ahead seemed daunting, almost overwhelming. Yet, it was a critical mission—one that held the potential to provide a second chance and a new beginning for these young individuals.

After the class, I found myself buried in grading a stack of quizzes, preoccupied with finishing this overdue task, and lost in an inner struggle about being undecided whether to contest or not to contest the elections. Amid the frenzy, I forgot about the lunch appointment, my car's computer played its part, seamlessly orchestrating a lunch appointment at the Mediterranean restaurant I favored, even sharing the details with James's vehicle. Technology had become an integral part of my life, reminding me of commitments I might have overlooked. Reliance on memory in such matters was unreliable.

As I received a timely reminder on my handheld device from my car, it snapped me back to the present moment. The reminder ensured that I didn't miss the lunch appointment. I arrived slightly ahead of schedule as planned.

When I greeted James at the restaurant, he couldn't help but notice the fatigue etched on my face. In my absent-mindedness, I had worn a t-shirt that had wrinkles and an unkempt beard presenting a disheveled appearance. He extended his hand for a handshake, visibly concerned about my well-being.

"I am fine," I replied sheepishly, aware that my emotions were written all over my face.

We sat down and ordered our food. I didn't waste any time in expressing my doubts.

"I'm having second thoughts," I admitted, wanting to be honest and forthright.

"Why?" James asked.

"Why should my friends and family invest a million and a half to fund my election campaign?" I decided to open the discussion with what felt like the heaviest burden on my shoulders.

James didn't answer directly but instead asked me, "What is your favorite sport?"

"Soccer."

"Alright. Why do people spend time and money to watch 22 men kick a ball around?" James responded with a riddle. It was apparent this was not the first time he had had such a discussion. Experiences in life provide us a benchmark to evaluate the risk of future events but they are no guarantee to provide assurances of success.

"Fun. Being part of the community. Gamble." I presented my list of reasons for people to watch soccer.

"Right. People have various reasons to spend their money. They want to be part of the action, and there's a price for that."

I pressed further, wanting to understand, " Why people would donate to a political novice like me?"

"Everyone has a different reason," James explained patiently. "Some will support you because they want to encourage you, like your family and friends. Some will do it out of frustration with the two main parties. Like me and my friends. Some are gamblers and want to bet on the underdog because they relate to being underdogs themselves. Betting on your success is their way of betting on their success as an underdog. Society will decline if there is no fresh induction of ideas and infusion of new energy. You are a symbol of newness."

My next question revolved around our chances of winning, and James estimated them at a modest 5%.

"Why should we spend a million and a half on an election campaign with just a 5% chance of winning? Why not use that money to feed the poor?" I challenged.

"Our chances will and should improve as we progress. Were you expecting your chances to be 50% with no political experience and track record?" It was a valid argument.

James went on to explain the fundamental difference between charity and politics. Charity, he said, addresses immediate problems affecting a segment of society, and politics aims to create a better society for everyone. Politics, he believed, was the ultimate form of charity, as it could benefit both the rich and the poor without discrimination.

I couldn't help but bring up James's apparent dislike for politics, to which he clarified that it was the way politics was currently practiced that he detested. His support for me stemmed from the fact that I wasn't a typical politician, at least not yet.

During our discussion about the campaign, I proposed a more frugal budget, emphasizing the importance of responsible spending that aligned with a middle-class perspective. I suggested that to augment the perception of being a middle-class candidate, we limit our campaign budget to no more than 500,000 coins, which was roughly a third of the average campaign cost from past election campaigns. This figure was chosen to ensure that our campaign reflected the financial realities of the average American, who earns around 50,000 coins a year.

I wanted our campaign to send a clear message that we were responsible stewards of the contributions we received from the people. By keeping our spending in check and avoiding excessive costs, we could demonstrate our commitment to representing middle-class values and share similar concerns about social justice that were at the heart of our campaign. It was a practical approach that I believed would resonate with voters and show that we were focused on their needs and financial well-being.

James, initially cautious, recognized the value of this approach. I felt a sense of calm wash over me as my internal conflict began to resolve and my deep convictions replaced doubts.

"If democracy is truly for the people and by the people, then our election win should be, in part, the responsibility of the people," I asserted.

Intrigued, James asked me to elaborate. I explained that we should avoid hiring all paid staff, seek volunteers from the community, spend less on advertising, and focus more on grassroots networking. We needed to discard the old rulebook and innovate to set a new example.

A broad smile spread across James's face, and his enthusiasm and energy were reignited. He extended his hand, "we have a deal," he declared.

The next step was to inform my team and convince them that this unconventional approach would succeed.

Sixteen

The team

March 6th, 2066

I waited until our weekly core group meeting to share the details of my conversation with James. To complete our campaign committee, I decided to invite Alex to join the meeting. We scheduled it for 3:00 pm, just after lunch, and allocated two hours for our discussions.

Recognizing the gravity of unveiling an unconventional campaign strategy. The choice of attire was a deliberate element in setting the tone for the discourse. A black suit with thin white stripes exuded a sense of professionalism, while a blue mandarin collar shirt added a touch of distinction. Completing the ensemble were black Oxford shoes, a testament to the gravity of the occasion.

It was a conventional dress code, carefully selected to unveil an unconventional campaign strategy. I wanted to convey a sense of seriousness, a commitment to our cause that would resonate even as our new approach stirred uncertainty in the minds of those present. The balancing act between tradition and innovation, though uncertain in its outcome, was a risk I was willing to take.

Nour, a steadfast supporter of my idealistic approach, was appreciative of the bold move. Her encouragement served as a catalyst, urging me to embrace the path less traveled. "Be different," she said, "and in doing so, you'll have the opportunity to truly serve the people."

As we gathered around the table for our core committee meeting, I took the lead and wasted no time in laying out the conversation I had with James and the decisions we had made. I scanned their faces to gauge their reactions. Ranbir and Ashraf seemed visibly relieved; they were responsible for securing funds from donors. Jimmy appeared nonchalant but curious, Alex was indifferent, while Gina wore a worried expression.

Gina was the first to voice her concern. "How can we run a successful campaign with just 30% of the budget?" she questioned, leading the discussion. "We will be outspent by our two deep-pocket adversaries."

Considering the complexities of our democratic process, one glaring flaw stood out - the insurmountable financial barrier that hindered the aspirations of the middle class from actively participating in politics. In an age where election success seemed synonymous with a hefty campaign budget, the dreams of many were stifled by the weight of financial constraints.

Candidates found themselves in a paradoxical situation. Theoretically, they could seek support from the people and wealthy donors alike, but the reality was far from ideal.

The arduous task of fundraising consumed valuable time and effort, creating a high hurdle that only the financially privileged could effortlessly leap over. This, in turn, raised the question of whether our elected representatives were reflective of the diverse voices within our society.

The election outcome seemed predetermined, with success for a candidate hinging not on qualifications, ideas, commitment, or dedication, but on financial figures detailed in quarterly reports filed with the county clerk. Media projections of possible winners were primarily based on the money candidates had raised, resembling more of a horse race where handicaps were announced each quarter upon the public release of financial reports. It presented a cruel irony, considering that the essence of democracy should be rooted in the representation of the people's will.

The system perpetuated a cycle where the inability to appease donors almost translated to disqualification from the race, reinforcing a scenario where only those adept at navigating financial landscapes could contend for public office. This money-centric approach seemed to overshadow the democratic ideals that should prioritize the genuine representation of the people and their interests.

This inherent flaw led many qualified individuals to seek positions of authority through non-elected offices. Yet, even in these roles, loyalty often veered towards the benefactor rather than the public. The system, it seemed, had created a subtle dichotomy between serving the people and serving those who held the purse strings.

I turned to James, seeking his perspective on Gina's concern to achieve success with a reduced campaign budget. "It will undoubtedly be challenging, but not insurmountable," he responded with his customary optimism. We became two pillars of the whole effort.

Gina's agitation persisted. "Are we in this to lose?" she pressed, "James, you know from experience that we have to persistently bombard the voters with campaign messages to overcome their inertia to act. How are we going to achieve it with no funds?

James replied firmly, "No, we're in this to win. It is difficult but not impossible." His response left me pondering whether he viewed politics as a kind of sport, a game to be won.

"I want to emphasize that we won't accept donations from corporations," I interjected expecting this idealistic approach will inspire them. "Our goal is to secure at least 50% of our funding from the citizens. This reflects the democratic values and ideology we aim to embody."

Gina leaned back in her chair and remarked, "Now I'm quite certain we don't want to win."

James lightened the mood with an announcement: "To lift your spirits, I have secured a space for our campaign office from a friend. It will be his contribution to our campaign"

Excitement rippled through the room. I couldn't help but ask, "That's great news! Where is it?"

"It's an empty storefront located in one of the shopping malls north of the city," James pointed to the map of the city shown on the display. "We have access to it until the elections."

Turning to Gina, James asked, "Gina, what can you do to assist us with our reduced budget?"

She replied, "I can reduce my consultation fee by 25%, but only if I'm convinced this is a winning strategy."

We went on to explain our plan to work with a larger number of volunteers to market the message and operate on a reduced advertising budget. The subsequent discussion allowed everyone to scrutinize whether we had thoroughly thought through our campaign strategy. They bombarded us with their questions, and we tried to answer them.

"Let's leave it at that, and we will reevaluate our strategy after a month," James concluded.

"Gina, you have to conduct polls to find out where we stand among the voters and identify the five key issues on their minds." He moved on to start assigning tasks to the team.

"Alex and Jimmy, your task is to set up online and offline campaigns to recruit volunteers, train, and lead them."

"Ranbir and Ashraf, your focus should be on arranging donor meetings, and I'll assist with that."

"I'm going to reach out to a friend in the media to develop an advertising campaign. Encouraging people to donate and recruit volunteers for the campaign. We'll ask for donations of 50 coins. To reach our target of 250,000 coins, we'll need 5,000 donors. If we can achieve this, our campaign will have a real shot at winning," James assigned tasks to each of us. "Right now, we need 25,000 coins to fund this advertising campaign."

Ashraf assured him, "I'll send you some today."

Ranbir chimed in, "Count me in too."

"As for me, I'm going to focus on honing my public speaking skills, studying legislation, and researching our opponents." I really needed to work on it.

With our assignments in hand, we dispersed, I couldn't help but notice the lingering uncertainty about whether this bold new approach, leaning on the strength of ordinary citizens, would prove successful. My vision for our election campaign was clear – it needed to be a contest between the power of the people and the power of money. It was a challenge to determine whether democracy truly belonged to the people or if it had been co-opted by big business. I was determined to pose a challenge to our community: either seize political power and control it for themselves or cease complaining about the ineffectiveness of democracy on their behalf. It was a call to action, an invitation to reclaim agency and actively shape the future of our society.

As we parted ways, I knew that one of my primary responsibilities would be to keep the team motivated and optimistic. We were embarking on a path less traveled, one that required unwavering faith in the ideals we were championing and in the collective strength of the citizens who believed in our cause.

Seventeen

Political understudy

March 7th to 12th, 2066

I spent an entire week honing my public speaking skills. My first step was to watch videos of politicians active in parliament and government at that time. I scrutinized every detail – their attire, posture, hand gestures, body language, and especially their oratory skills, paying close attention to how they emphasized certain words and used pauses for effect. Next, I delved into the best speeches of the 20th and 21st centuries, watching those videos repeatedly.

As I pondered over the components of a politician's charisma, I found myself entangled in a web of possibilities. Was it the resonance of their vocal cords, the eloquence that captivated audiences? Or perhaps, the expressiveness of their body language, the ability to convey sincerity and conviction? The attitude they projected toward others, or the genuine depth of emotion and empathy for the people they served –

all seemed like pieces of a complex puzzle.

Throughout history, many philosophers have grappled with this conundrum. Was it the leader who molded their times, shaping the narrative and influencing the course of events? Or was it the era itself, with its challenges and opportunities, that carved a leader, giving rise to individuals who could meet the demands of their time?

In my reflections, I couldn't escape the realization that it was likely a combination of both. The leader and the era were intertwined, each influencing and shaping the other in an inseparable dance. A charismatic leader was not merely a product of their innate qualities but a response to the needs and aspirations of the times. Likewise, the era found its expression through the leaders it produced, creating a symbiotic relationship.

As I delved deeper into this intricate dance, it became clear that the charisma of a politician was a dynamic force, an amalgamation of personal attributes and the demands of the moment. The ability to connect with people, to inspire and lead, required an astute understanding of the prevailing circumstances and an authentic response to the collective emotions of the people.

The research aspect was relatively straightforward, but applying these skills proved to be quite challenging. I had installed a full-length mirror in my study room for practice. Setting up my device on a stand, I recorded my practice sessions for review. To ensure I stayed on track, I scripted a speech aimed at potential donors.

Speaking to your own reflection in a mirror is undoubtedly a peculiar experience. The person staring back at me appeared almost unrecognizable. I couldn't help but notice a small pot belly, the presence of graying and receding hair, my own awkward body movements, and a gaze that lacked its usual sparkle. My beard, which Nour and my daughters loved, gave me an unkempt appearance. I decided to get it trimmed before my first donor meeting. These were flaws in my personality that, perhaps, I hadn't fully acknowledged before. Overcoming this initial self-critique took some time, but I knew it was essential before shifting to perfecting my speech.

I diligently completed ten practice sessions, carefully reviewing the video recording after each one. As the day drew to a close, I felt significantly more confident in my ability to deliver a compelling speech. However, I couldn't ignore the fact that while practice was essential, the real test would be the actual delivery – an area where I currently lacked experience.

My focus shifted to collecting information about the Democratic incumbent, Kevin Johnson, a towering figure in the technology industry and a billionaire in his own right. He was in his late 60s, a family man with three grown children. Renowned for pioneering air taxi services that transformed urban transportation, he had left an indelible mark on the landscape of major cities in the USA and Europe. What intrigued me was his strategic relocation to Central Valley Fresno from the Bay Area, a move seemingly timed to meet the residency requirements for candidacy.

Despite maintaining a house in the constituency, it became apparent that his presence there was sparse. Kevin's wealth, derived from the technology industry, translated into a substantial campaign war chest, primarily fueled by generous contributions from tech companies. This financial backing, coupled with his status as a billionaire, painted a picture of formidable electoral machinery.

As I collected data about his voting record, a consistent pattern emerged. Kevin Johnson displayed unwavering support for technology companies, often at the expense of pressing concerns related to climate change. The stark contrast between his priorities and the urgent environmental issues facing the constituency left me with a lingering impression of disloyalty to his constituents.

Despite Kevin Johnson's prolonged tenure in office, an intriguing question lingered in my mind like a persistent echo: had he become complacent in his position? Shielded by the vast financial resources at his disposal and the absence of formidable opposition, it seemed plausible that the landscape of his political career had fostered an environment of comfort. Prolonged periods without facing serious challenges can create a sense of invincibility. The lack of formidable opposition might have contributed to a perceived immunity from scrutiny. The very nature of democracy thrives on the healthy exchange of ideas, the clash of diverse perspectives, and the constant accountability that challenges bring.

Without a robust challenge, the dynamics of representation can become skewed. A leader, shielded by financial prowess and a lack of opposition, may inadvertently lose touch with the evolving needs and aspirations of the people. The absence of accountability could erode the very essence of democratic governance.

While Kevin Johnson's financial resources and influence may have paved the way for a seemingly unchallenged political career, I recognized an opportunity – an opportunity to present a formidable opposition, to bring fresh ideas, and to reinvigorate the democratic process in our constituency. The upcoming election would be more than a clash of candidates;

it would be a test of the resilience of our democratic ideals.

On the Republican side, Roberto Gonzalez emerged as a prominent figure—a lawyer who had amassed wealth through personal injury litigation. His political journey had been a steady climb within the Republican Party, starting from the school board, progressing through the city council, and eventually reaching the state congress.

In his early 50s, Roberto Gonzalez was a family man, married with two children. His legislative record revealed a focus on farm reforms, a critical issue for the local farming community. It became evident that his political stance was aligned with the interests of the agricultural sector which had the lion's share of the local economy. Most notably, Roberto Gonzalez's campaign funding derived primarily from the farming community. This financial backing underscored his commitment to addressing the concerns of local farmers and signaled a strategic alignment between his legislative priorities and the financial support he garnered.

As I analyzed the landscape of my opponents, it became clear that each had carved a distinct path in their political careers, with strategic alliances reflecting their priorities. Understanding the intricacies of their backgrounds, sources of support, and legislative focuses would be crucial in formulating a campaign strategy that resonated with the diverse needs of our constituency.

As I scrutinized the profiles of my opponents, a realization settled in – Roberto Gonzalez posed a more serious threat than Kevin. With backing from the local community, particularly the influential farming sector, and a track record of active contributions to the welfare of farmers, Gonzalez's candidacy held significant sway over a crucial segment of voters. To secure victory, I had to carve out enough votes, strategically peeling them away from both Gonzalez and Kevin, while also appealing to independent voters. The challenge was clear – the delicate art of convincing voters to shift allegiance. It was at this juncture that my insecurities resurfaced, questioning whether I was in the wrong place at the wrong time. I resolved to add this concern to the agenda of our upcoming core committee meeting.

My next task demanded a deep dive into the labyrinth of legislation passed in the last three years, which proved to be the most challenging item in this campaign. With an engineering background, these political and legal intricacies felt like a foreign language, a terrain where unfamiliar terms abounded.

Frequently consulting a legal dictionary became an unavoidable necessity to unravel the nuances and implications of each word and complex term. It felt akin to returning to school, a humbling experience that reminded me of my days as an average student. Yet, this time, the stakes were higher, and the subject matter more intricate.

As an average student, albeit street-smart, I felt like going back to school grappling with an academic challenge that seemed incompatible with my educational background. The weight of political and legal terminology pressed upon me, requiring a level of understanding that surpassed my past expertise.

Amid this sea of complex terms, I realized that my street-smartness, the practical wisdom gained from navigating various facets of life, could be my greatest asset. It was time to leverage this innate resource, to translate my real-world insights into a language that resonated with voters. While my opponents might wield experience in the traditional realm of politics, my ability to connect with people on a relatable level could set me apart.

To enhance my understanding of how the U.S. Congress functioned, James recommended a selection of half a dozen books, which I enthusiastically borrowed from the local library. I was always curious and ready to learn new knowledge and skills. This attitude became an asset. As I delved into these resources, it became clear that the legislative process was intricately designed to foster negotiations and compromises between the two major parties at every stage.

From the assignment of committees to the drafting of legislation, scheduling debates to forming compromises before bills were put to a vote, the entire process seemed to hinge on the ability of lawmakers to find common ground. This realization sparked a sense of skepticism about whether an independent congressman, free from party affiliations, could navigate this landscape and effectively push for a legislative agenda. The system appeared to favor negotiations within the confines of party lines, raising concerns about the extent to which an independent voice could influence the direction of legislation.

Determined to address these concerns, I decided it was worth discussing as we prepared ourselves for the task ahead. James had been a source of wisdom and insight. I was sure that our discussions would provide valuable perspectives on a path to navigate the complexities of the legislative process as an independent.

Without consciously realizing it, I was transforming into a politician.

Eighteen

Lingering doubts

⚜

March 13th, 2066

We gathered for our weekly meeting at 3:00 pm at my home.

"Lady and gentlemen, I present to you our candidate, Mr. Sher Shah," James announced at the start of the meeting, putting me on the spot as he often did. It seems he enjoyed doing that.

I had prepared for this moment by practicing my public speaking skills all week. I stood up and delivered a ten-minute speech. When I finished, everyone clapped to appreciate the new me, except James, who provided his guidance like the good coach that he was.

"I see the improvement, but you're not quite there yet. Work on your body language, eye contact, and auditory aesthetics," he coached.

While I appreciated the feedback, I needed suggestions

about how, "What tools can I use James? I have tried everything that I could think of."

"Practice more following the old axiom, practice makes a man perfect. As you make these speeches there will be improvement. Make sure every event is 3-D recorded so that you can review it later."

Technology has made it possible to make a 3-D recording of an event. There were apps available that synchronized video recording of three mobile device cameras to produce a 3-D video. It could be watched using artificial reality headphones.

"Gina, Alex, and one volunteer should be designated video recorders for each event." James assigned the task. "Alex please find a young volunteer that has multimedia expertise."

As I sat down, I raised a fundamental question that was bothering me all week, "I have no voting record, no political experience, and no affiliation with a national party. Why would voters choose to vote for me?"

"They won't," Gina replied as if waiting for me to ask the question. "That's what my polling data shows." No one was not surprised by this polling data.

"No one knows us," Gina continued sharing her survey results and distributing copies of the findings to all of us. The pollster interviewed one thousand voters and compiled the results. Her team had asked voters whether they had heard about me and whether they would vote for a person with no political experience or voting history. "Voters are hesitant to support an inexperienced independent candidate."

"Devil they know is better than a human they don't know," I interjected my cynicism.

"It's a valid concern, Sher. But remember, 2% of voters have already endorsed your campaign. That requirement is in place to weed out non-serious candidates who lack support," James reassured us. "Let's not worry about losing at the start. We'll tackle these challenges. To boost your confidence, the incumbent Kevin Johnson was also inexperienced and had no political background when he won."

"He had money," Gina persisted.

"And we will have people," I replied, not wanting to dampen the team's motivation. It was my responsibility as a candidate to be motivator-in-chief.

Gina also surveyed voters about their key concerns when evaluating candidates.

"What are the issues that matter most to voters?" James asked her to proceed with the meeting agenda.

Gina then informed us about these concerns, including air and noise pollution from air taxis, the high cost of 3-D printed organs, over reliance on AI in medicine for diagnosis, declining face-to-face doctor visits, declining math and science skills in children, housing pressure on agricultural land, and volatility in American Coin (aÇ) digital currency.

"That's a good list, Gina. Thank you," James endorsed the list to form our political platform.

I couldn't help but ask, "Isn't it true that Democratic incumbent Kevin Johnson made millions in air taxi service?"

"Yes, that's him," Gina replied with a hint of disdain. "I even worked for his election campaign as a volunteer."

"Prioritize the enhancement of air and noise pollution measures at the forefront of our election campaign," I asserted. "I firmly believe this approach could sway Kevin's voters to reconsider their allegiance and choose us. The widespread impact of environmental concerns on people's lives made this a compelling issue, and supporting our cause did not equate to disloyalty to their party. Voting for a Republican was deemed unthinkable by many, further strengthening our position." James nodded in agreement, endorsing the suggestion as a strategic move for our campaign.

James next addressed Jimmy and Alex, seeking information about the progress of volunteer sign-ups. The count fell short of the targeted number of volunteers, prompting a discussion on the challenges encountered during the recruitment process. Jimmy and Alex shared insights into the hurdles they faced while attempting to secure commitments from potential volunteers.

"Jimmy, churchgoers are usually good volunteers. Can you arrange for some of your congregants to meet the candidate?" James suggested.

"Yes, that's possible," Jimmy promised to organize a meeting in the coming weeks.

"Alex, once our advertising campaign is underway, I'm sure we'll get more sign-ups," James encouraged.

Ranbir and Ashraf discussed their upcoming meetings with donors, and the mood of those gathered shifted to excitement. They had scheduled two meetings for next Friday and Sunday afternoons.

"I'll reach out to my acquaintances and arrange a meeting as well," James said, determined to deliver on his promises.

"Sher, you have to prepare your family. As the campaign heats up, there will be moments when they wish you weren't a candidate," James advised, drawing from his experience. This turned out to be prophetic advice in the coming weeks.

Gina's delivery of the dismal polling data cast a long shadow over the team's enthusiasm. The initial excitement of qualifying as a candidate was fading, replaced by a cloud of uncertainty and insecurity. Despite James maintaining his eternal optimism, the team appeared doubtful about our chances of victory. Their expressions and demeanor betrayed a sense of skepticism. Recognizing the need to uplift their spirits, I was determined to find a solution to instill a belief within the team, convincing them that, against all odds, we could defy expectations and achieve the seemingly impossible goal of winning.

Nineteen

Five dollar bill

It has been a month since Sher Shah commenced his writings. The act of revisiting those memories occupied his mind so entirely that he scarcely registered the intensifying pain in his body and the deteriorating state of his organs. The surge in adrenaline, prompted by the thrill of recalling old times, coupled with an increased dosage of painkillers prescribed by his doctor, undoubtedly contributed to a sense of improved well-being, masking the actual condition of his body. The combination of these factors created a semblance of relief that belied the harsh reality of his physical health.

Sher Shah, with difficulty, lowered himself into a seated position, preparing for his daily ritual of filling the notebook. He reached for the front drawer of his writing table. From within, he retrieved a framed five-dollar bill adorned with the handwritten words 'good luck.' This bill held significant sentimental value, serving as his enduring source of motivation and perseverance throughout the myriad highs and lows of his life.

What made this five-dollar bill more remarkable was that its existence was unexpected. Preparing for the donor meeting, Sher Shah did not anticipate receiving a relic from the past that held emotional significance. Adding to the surprise was the fact that, by 2066, paper currency had become obsolete, making the framed bill a relic from a bygone era. Its continued significance in Sher Shah's life underscored its role as a cherished and unconventional lucky charm.

Sher Shah picked up his pen to share the details of the first donor meetings arranged by Ashraf and Ranbir. It would be another milestone in his transformation into a career politician.

* * *

March 13th, 2066

The county office had issued us a unique internet link for collecting campaign funds from donors. The unique link was for keeping track of campaign funding of candidates by government regulators. All contributors had to utilize only the designated link to donate American Coin (aÇ) to an election campaign. Each donor was limited to contribute a maximum of 2500 aÇs, but this limit did not apply to political action committees. The links were programmed to be deactivated as soon as a candidate reached the mandated upper limit, restricting further contributions by unaware donors. Candidates' campaign expenses were capped at one and a half million currency units. All campaign payments for goods or services procured were made through the same account.

I was a little nervous about facing the donors. I had never borrowed money from my friends or relatives in my life. The only borrowing I had ever done was from banks for my education, home appliances, car, and home. These were institutional borrowings with no emotional strings attached. Asking for money from people for a political campaign was something I had never done. I was still not sure why people would fund a political novice. All I had to offer was emotions and no rational basis to get donations. I was also curious to know if educated and rational people would respond to an emotional appeal, as James had suggested. I practiced my speech and prepared answers to possible questions. James and Jimmy helped me with it.

The Friday afternoon funding event, hosted by Dr. Ashraf Ul Islam, was a routine affair. I delivered a speech that focused on my roots in the city, the humble background of my father, and my political position on local issues. It was followed by a question-and-answer session. Interestingly, the doctors appeared to be more interested in taking pictures with me than in engaging in what they might have found to be a dull political conversation. Finally, Ashraf stood up to ask for contributions, to raise 25,000 aÇ. I believed this was a reasonable target for our first meeting, but unfortunately, we fell significantly short and could only generate 10,000 aÇ. Although we didn't reach the targeted amount, this experience boosted my confidence, proving that it was possible to secure funds for the campaign. The amount collected was more than my expectations.

The event on Sunday, arranged by Ranbir with his farming friends, was a memorable one. I stood up and spoke for about ten minutes, this time focusing more on climate change and water supply issues faced by the farming community. It seemed they had come prepared for the meeting and were more politically savvy.

"What is your political experience?" was the first curve-ball thrown at me.

"I have no political experience, but I have experience voting and managing teams. I've made decisions that have impacted the lives of others," I defended my candidacy.

"Are you familiar with Roberto Gonzalez?" Another question I had expected and prepared for.

"Yes, and he has done some good legislative work in the state congress," I replied. I had no intention of belittling the accomplishments of my opponent for political gain. I figured James might consider it my naivety.

"Why should we vote for you and not Roberto?"

"I want you to consider my entire policy position, not just water-related issues. We have many more issues affecting our city and our nation than just water," I explained, doing the best I could. At the end of the event, I shook hands with all the participants and thanked them for coming for a weekend political event.

"Are you the son of the truck driver Shah Zaman?" A man, probably in his 80s with a flowing white beard, asked as we shook hands.

"Yes."

"I was a friend of your father," he said, smiling as he took out his worn-out leather cowboy-style wallet from his back pocket. "I have something that belongs to you."

He pulled out a five-dollar bill with "good luck" handwritten in gold ink across the face of it. "Your father gave me this bill as a good luck charm when I bought my first 50-acre farm. I think you need a good luck charm for your campaign. Please accept it." He handed me the dollar bill.

I looked at the dollar bill with astonishment and disbelief. It had both emotional and antique value.

"This bill is priceless to me. Besides, it has antique value. Are you sure you want to give it to me?" I handed it back to him with trembling hands. Part of me wanted it because I had never seen my father's handwriting.

"It belongs to you. It has brought me luck, and now I own close to 1000 acres of farmland." He handed it back to me with a broad smile. "I have donated to your campaign today and will provide some more next month. We do need some new blood in politics."

I accepted with gratitude and felt a surge of deep emotions. "I've never seen my father's handwriting. Thank you. It is the best gift and donation I could expect." Emotions overtook me. I gave him a hug satisfying an urge to fill the void of a missing father. I got the bill framed to preserve it. This relic from the past kept me on track when the going got tough.

By the year 2066, dollar bills were no longer in circulation. These bills were now sold at antique shops as collector's items. In the 2050s, the government abolished paper currency and introduced a digital currency known as the American Coin, or aÇ for short. I was fresh out of college and in my first job when the government abolished paper currency. People had one year to hand over the paper bills to receive the equivalent aÇ. This digital coin could be used in increments of one-tenth of its single-unit value.

I remember the uncertainty this had caused among the people during the first few years. These coins experienced fluctuations in purchasing power based on inflation, growth, and population figures released every six months by the central bank. Every child born resulted in the issuance of new digital coins, covering one year of the child's cost of living until they reached adulthood at age 18 or secured their first full-time job, whichever came first. This new currency added to the circulation was an investment in the productive citizen that could generate future revenue for the state.

Apart from fluctuations, people felt insecure about a currency they could not touch and feel. The government had to initiate an elaborate marketing campaign to remove these apprehensions. People were told that the digital currency records were securely stored in three different server locations, nestled beneath the mountains to protect against physical threats. The encryption process was handled by a quantum computer, considered impervious to outside hacking attempts. While hackers had tried, their efforts had thus far been unsuccessful. I remember there had also been attempts to create counterfeit aÇ through server breaches and adding it to circulation, all of which had failed.

Organized crime had a hard time adjusting to this new dynamic. Every transaction had to pass through government servers, making tax collection straightforward. Each transaction involved an accounting transfer from one account holder to another, minus any taxes owed. Corrupted funds became increasingly difficult to maintain, forcing criminals to rely on alternative cryptocurrencies outside of the USA. Corporations were mandated to repatriate their foreign profits to bolster the digital currency's purchasing power compared to other currencies.

Banks no longer held cash deposits due to the absence of

paper currency. Instead, depositors allocated digital currency to banks, which could then lend and generate profits. This simplified the monitoring of the money supply and granted the state absolute fiscal control over its economy.

Although, like everyone else, I was apprehensive about the new virtual currency, the digital currency had its shortcomings but offered two significant benefits. Banks could lend a digital currency unit only once, curbing capitalist greed and averting a mortgage and hedge fund crisis reminiscent of the one recorded fifty years ago in the first decade of the 21st century. It had a significant impact on restricting speculation in stock, bond, and commodities markets.

The state was constrained to spend as much as it generated in revenue because issuing new coins that were not backed by income could impact the purchasing power of a citizen's currency account. Every elected government was afraid of a backlash from citizens. It helped contain the spiraling rise of the national debt. The government had to adhere to a balanced budget because extraordinary borrowing from the public was impossible, as money could be lent only once. The crowding out of digital currency for government funding had previously led to economic recessions and protests. It made the elected governments cautious about spending beyond their tax revenue collection capabilities, prompting Republican and Democratic parties to prioritize budget compromises to avoid public backlash.

While we didn't collect as much in funds as Ranbir had hoped for, the five-dollar bill with my father's handwriting gave me a significant boost in motivation and determination to win. For an illogical and irrational reason, I believed that this good luck charm could solve all my campaign problems.

Twenty

Lone wolf dilemma

~⚜~

May 15th, 2066

We spent two months executing what we had agreed upon. I attended over two dozen donor meetings. With each event, our collections increased, but it was always less than planned. In six weeks, we could hardly reach 100,500 aÇs. Our 'by the people' marketing campaign also produced a low response, with a little over 500 people contributing to our campaign, which was less than 10% of our target. Our total funds stood at around 127,000 aÇs.

My father-in-law, Dr. Rabbani, had never fully accepted me as a son-in-law. He could not forget that I was the son of a truck driver. He grew up in a class-divided culture and this attitude was part of his upbringing. Our interactions were infrequent and limited to family and social events. I was in for a surprise when he arranged a donor meeting and invited his doctor friends and wealthy patients who owed him their lives for taking care of their hearts.

That meeting turned out to be our most successful one, as we raised over 75,000 aÇs, and some of them promised another 50,000 aÇs if we improved our favorability ratings among the voters.

As my father-in-law walked me to the door, he put his hand on my shoulder and said, "You remind me of my youth when I ran for the presidency of the student council in college."

My shift into politics altered his perception of me, over-shadowing the value of my engineering degree, which, in a conventional sense, should have garnered approval and respect. I harbored a steadfast belief that something was awry in a society where celebrity status wielded more influence, garnering greater respect and acceptance than substantial achievements and diligent effort. In this societal framework, it seemed that fifteen minutes of fame held more significance than decades of labor dedicated to contributing to society and cultivating a community.

While our volunteer ranks were expanding, akin to our funds, we still fell short of achieving the ideal team size. It seemed as though we were entrenched in a quagmire, facing a challenge to make substantial progress.

"Why are we failing on every statistic, Gina?" I asked during our weekly core group meeting on May 15th.

"Your name recognition is growing, but at a snail's pace," Gina explained, showing us the graphs on her device.

"How can we improve name recognition?"

"The mainstream media is not mentioning us at all. They only report campaign activities of the two major parties," she informed us with a hint of worry in her tone. "They are not interested in an independent candidate without a national political platform."

"We can get their attention through a thousand cuts," I suggested, distorting an axiom. "Have you heard of that, Gina?"

"No, but please explain."

"Let's ignore the mainstream media and focus on social media influencers and upcoming young reporters. Contact them, and let's set up meetings with them," I proposed, recalling James's advice that underdogs tend to support underdogs.

"Another significant hurdle is that people believe a lone congressman can't work. Sixty percent of voters who have heard of you feel they can't vote for you because of that fear," Gina continued with her presentation.

"People are right. The Senate is split in half between the two parties," James said, wearing a thoughtful expression. "So, a lone wolf can dictate terms. But the U.S. House of Representatives is a different story. One lone wolf or a few votes cannot do much."

"Didn't you say people are not happy with the hold of the two major parties?" I asked him.

"Yes, and it has been growing with each election cycle."

"Then, don't you think there are candidates like us around the country facing the same dilemma?" I quizzed him.

"Yes," James said, sitting up, his old sportsman's killer instinct returning. I was sure James considered politics a sport. It was the excitement of this game that had drawn him into the campaign, fueled by his frustration with the two major parties.

"Let's find out how many independent candidates are running and explore if they are willing to form a national platform."

"When there is a will, there is always a way," James said smiling. He was eager to expand the horizon of our campaign to match his own ambition of forcing the two dominant parties to change their politics.

It marked yet another pivotal juncture in my political evolution. Never in my wildest dreams did I envision embarking on a journey to establish a national political platform. On that particular day, doubts lingered about the feasibility of this venture, but the imperative to try and explore was undeniable. As the adage goes, a person must take the first small step to commence a thousand-mile journey. The uncertainty loomed large—where to start, whom to approach, how to proceed, and what inquiries would come our way were all unknowns. Yet, James' wealth of political experience infused me with confidence that, even if the results were modest, we would achieve something meaningful for our prospects.

In the last two weeks, I noticed expensive billboards were promoting the Republican and Democratic Party candidates. Radio, television, and social media were slowly but gradually starting to host discussions and analyses for the upcoming elections. The two major parties were finally getting into the act as well. These were costly advertisements, and I wondered how they could afford such marketing tactics within the restricted budget of a million and a half American Coins.

We did not have enough coins to afford these expensive avenues for promotion. Instead, we were relying on social media through our volunteers and supporters. We were testing the fundamental premise of democracy, which is that the people choose their representatives based on who can serve them best. The criteria for the "best" should not be determined by who has deeper pockets but by better ideas and innovative solutions. Politicians were brand-marketed like consumer products, relying on the same techniques suited for impulsive buying without deep thinking. Deceptive marketing was aimed at voters to compel them to ignore evaluating the pros and cons of a particular candidate's skills, capabilities, and motivations. It was an ideological contest.

Twenty-One

The conclave

⚜

Sher Shah entered the room. He walked to the shelf with difficulty holding his lower back with his left hand. On display on the top shelf was an object that he retrieved—a striking owl-shaped award caught his eye. Six inches tall, the trophy boasted a wooden base with a metal plate, proudly displaying his name and the year 2068. The bronze statue of the owl, with its penetrating large, round eyes, seemed to gaze into the depths of the soul.

Affectionately holding the owl statue in his right hand, Sher Shah carried the award to the writing desk. Placing the owl statue prominently before him, he was ready to inscribe —a journey poised to create a national platform that would boldly challenge the entrenched supremacy of the two prevailing political parties.

* * *

May 15th to June 30th, 2066

For the next four weeks, James and I worked closely together. We decided to meet every morning. At first, we didn't know where to start or what to look for. Our first task was to prepare a plan and then get into execution mode because we had limited time.

We met the next day after our core committee meeting using a virtual reality headset. The technology was ubiquitous to replace face-to-face meetings with virtual reality. Colleagues were meeting in social events organized to get to know each other, while the business was conducted in cyberspace.

"How do we tackle this, James?" I initiated the discussion. We were sitting in a virtual replica of my study room.

"There have been past attempts in the Presidential elections to develop a third party, but it has never succeeded. The best one I can remember was almost seventy-five years ago when Ross Perot secured 19% of the vote in the 1992 Presidential elections and then formed The Reform Party in 1995." James gave me a quick history lesson to highlight the extent of difficulty ahead of us. "It is a Herculean task to develop a third party. Others have failed to succeed."

"Are you suggesting we give up?"

"Not at all. I am only emphasizing the level of difficulty." James, with his athletic instinct to compete, never said no to any obstacle regardless of its size and complexity. "If we appreciate the difficulty, then we will be better prepared for it. That is all I am trying to point out."

"How do you propose we proceed?"

"Let's not make the mistakes others have made and failed. Our first step should be to research to gather facts about other constituencies and candidates. We don't know how many candidates are in the same situation as us."

"I agree. Let's go on a scavenger hunt to find our potential friends in the field." As I made this comment, I fondly recall my children's favorite pastime, a game where we would hide treasures around the house for them to discover. The joy they derived from the hunt was immeasurable, and it instilled in them a sense of earning the treasures through deliberate efforts, rather than simply receiving them. It resonates with the notion that the human ego is a powerful force, one that thrives on challenges and the need to overcome obstacles to feel a genuine sense of accomplishment.

There were four hundred and forty-two US congressional constituencies. We first identified those where disenchantment with the Democratic and Republican Parties had grown substantially in the last five years. All the data we needed was not in one place, so we had to tap into multiple sources, which was time-consuming.

After burning midnight oil for about a week, we identified two hundred and seventy-five such constituencies. We looked for places where the incumbent had been serving for ten years, as that was long enough for a politician to serve effectively. Any term longer than that resulted in the growing influence of vested interests and complacency in the office holder.

It brought us down to two hundred and twenty-five. Next, we looked at how many constituencies had a third candidate. The list went down to two hundred and ten. Out of these, we removed constituencies where an angry party member was contesting against his own party, as well as billionaires contesting. The list was reduced to 195 constituencies. It was not a perfect method, but at least we were sure to make good use of our limited time.

We divided these 195 constituencies among ourselves to research the profiles of the third candidate and evaluate them to see if we could find common ground. We formed five-point criteria to shortlist our potential partners. It included education background, past work experience, community service track record, past political affiliations, and ethical standards.

It required a lot of reading, and I had to stay up late to finish my task because I was still keeping my job, as well as campaign commitments. At the end of three weeks, we shortlisted 180 constituencies where we could reach out to the third candidate to explore if we could form a national platform.

We agreed on a script to approach them and divided the list. We developed a profile including the purpose of our outreach and communicated it to our targeted list. Initial reactions were not encouraging. The other candidates did not know us well. They were skeptical about the success of a new national platform to breach the ironclad hold of the two parties with deep-pocketed, well-trained, and experienced organizational apparatus. They also felt this exercise could drain their resources and dilute their focus on their election activities. Despite this coldness, most of them faced the same question from their voters about the effectiveness of a lone-wolf congressman. They appreciated that independent candidates needed a national platform to improve their chances of winning. After multiple calls and cajoling, we convinced most of them to participate in a meeting to explore the idea.

We organized a virtual reality meeting and invited all one hundred and eighty candidates out of these hundred and fifty showed up for the meeting.

The first few meetings were chaotic, and everyone wanted to speak. The discussions continued for over ten days, but slowly and gradually order emerged. Finally, during our last meeting on June 30th, the consensus was reached that it is worthwhile to form a national platform even if it meant to improve the chances of the candidates and nothing else.

The majority agreed to adopt the name "The Third Way." A single tagline would be used by all: "Nation first. Local second. No to special interests." They agreed to adopt purple as the party color, as we did for our campaign because it was made by mixing the party colors of the two parties, Democratic blue and Republican red. An owl was adopted as the party mascot, as was the tradition to compete with the donkey and elephant of the other two parties. The owl was a curious choice as it was a symbolic suggestion that it stayed awake when everyone else slept.

All party candidates had the option to formulate a political agenda that resonated with their constituency voters.

A thirty-member committee was constituted to formulate a national agenda for the party. I was made a member of it. It was decided that the party constitution and other organizational matters would be tackled based on the party's performance in elections. No one had any foresight about the possible outcome as nothing of the sort was attempted in the three hundred years of political history of the USA. The committee would meet once a month to discuss progress and issue directives. James would become the official spokesperson of the party. After the conclave, he issued a press release to the media announcing the formation of the party and its political agenda.

The next day, early morning, I received a message from

Gina on my device: "For the first time, mainstream media have mentioned you in greater detail as a candidate for the 23rd US Congressional District."

"What did they write?"

"An inexperienced congressional candidate has spearheaded the efforts to form a national front. And then they wrote a brief profile of you."

"Are you happy now that we have a name recognition?"

"Not yet. I am conducting another pollster survey to find the impact." Gina was a hardcore political analyst who only believed the data.

I took a whole week off from the election campaign. For that one week, I went to the mountain every day. On the first day, I shouted at the top of my lungs to get the pent-up pressure off my chest.

Twenty-Two

Anderson Allen

❧⟨ೈ⦿ೈ⟩❧

A s illness continued to sap Sher Shah's vitality, he noticed his once-sharp mind growing increasingly dulled. Simple tasks, like reading messages from the past, became both thrilling and exhausting. His journey, as chronicled in these archived messages, unfolded like a narrative of determination, setbacks, and ultimate triumph. The text vividly described the challenges they faced in securing a spot in the debates, highlighting the tenacity and resilience of the campaign team. It was a testament to their shared commitment to participating in the democratic process, striving to be heard on a significant platform.

As Sher Shah delved into the past messages, each one became a portal to a different moment in their political campaign. The exchanges with fellow campaigners reflected the camaraderie, strategic planning, and sheer hard work that went into their efforts. Despite the passage of nearly two decades, the memories encapsulated in those messages remained potent, offering a window into a pivotal chapter of Sher Shah's political journey.

In the face of his declining health, revisiting these memories not only served as a trip down memory lane but also inspired him. The recollection of their past triumphs fueled a sense of pride and accomplishment, reminding Sher Shah of the meaningful impact they had made during a crucial juncture in their political endeavors.

The notebook, a repository of memories and reflections, opened once again as Sher Shah prepared to document the challenges encountered to gain entry to the debate platform organized by national news channels during this yet another critical juncture of the campaign. Every turn offered a new challenge and opportunity. Little did the campaign team realize that the barriers they faced would set in motion a chain of unintended consequences, reshaping their trajectory in unforeseen ways.

* * *

July 12th, 2066

I thought organizing a national platform would open all closed doors for us and provide access to mainstream media. But it was an unfounded optimism far from the harsh reality of life. I had to struggle to fight for screen time for our election campaign.

In the morning, a few days before July 12th, I received a message from James: "MSBC in collaboration with CNNBC announced there will be three debates on August 16th, September 13th, and October 18th between Democratic and Republican candidates."

I called him right away and asked, "What? We are not invited to participate?" I felt angry for not being accorded due respect by the media that claimed to be the representative of the voice of the people, and protector of their interests by holding people of power accountable.

"No," James responded lacking his customary enthusiasm.

"What are we going to do about it?" I asked, thinking of my chances and possible options to cross this new hurdle.

"I am going to set up an appointment with debate moderator Anderson Allen."

Later that day, I got a message from James, "We have an appointment with Anderson scheduled for Wednesday, July 12th, at 2:00 pm."

"Where?"

"At their offices. I got the address from Anderson."

I met with James before we got to the appointment to discuss our strategy.

"Anderson wants higher ratings and maximum viewership because his job depends on it," James laid the card on the table.

His advice was that viewership and ratings were the top priority for any anchor. We should play on that weakness and emphasize the freshness of our ideas to have the potential for higher ratings. It was a do-or-die situation for us, and we agreed to go to any length to gain access to these debates.

MSBC offices and studios were situated on a campus in the suburbs. Management, administration, marketing, and content creation departments were all nearby on the same campus in separate buildings. I wondered how this could create the separation between sales and editorials that the legislation demanded when they were so close in proximity. I decided to raise this point in our meeting with the anchor. It could be a trump card we needed to break through and gain access.

Anderson received us in his office adorned with various awards won by his hourly prime-time news program. His appearance was more like an actor than a journalist, an air of arrogance and showmanship rather than that of an expert in a craft that makes a person humble and down-to-earth. It was evident from the spacious room and decor that he was a top earner for the network. Yet another card to play in our negotiations.

He got up from his plush ergonomically designed chair to greet us with an air of condescension. I knew because I was sort of an expert on work chairs because of my chronic lower back pain.

"What can I do for you, gentlemen?" He said, sitting down behind his work desk made from expensive wood and squeezing a stress-releasing softball. A gold bracelet adorned one of his wrists and a smartwatch kept him updated on the other. He was wearing a formal white shirt; it was unbuttoned with an open collar. There was a small wardrobe in the room with half a dozen suits, shirts in many different colors, and ties.

"Include us in the debate," I decided to be upfront and not intimidated by his arrogance and opulence.

"Politics is serious business," Anderson maintained his condescending manners. "We want to give candidates maximum time to explain their political position for people to make an informed choice on Election Day."

"The county clerk has placed me on the ballot paper. Or do you have your criteria to qualify a candidate?" I made no effort to hide my annoyance at this arbitrary selection.

"Maybe we need to review this legislation," he brushed aside my single most significant success up to that point.

"Yes, maybe. But until then, I am a candidate, and on the ballot paper," I became a little more aggressive.

"What does your poll data show as of today?" Anderson wanted to move past that point.

"Around 10% of people support us," I decided facts should speak for themselves.

"This is not enough support for us to consider you a serious candidate."

"Your opinion is not above the law. And the law states that every candidate should get a fair chance to reach voters. That includes being at the debate stage," James jumped in to provide support and not be left out in this jostling. We had already discussed our one-two-punch strategy. He would be an expert strategist and I would be an emotional candidate. He would use law and I would use my self-interest.

"Anderson, you can't expect to get maximum ratings for your debates by presenting the tired faces of the two parties," I felt it was the right time to play that card to invoke his self-interest to excite him about us. "You need a fresh perspective."

"I will check with my legal department on this and get back to you," Anderson rose from his seat, signaling the conclusion of our meeting.

"OK, sure, and when you do that, also ask them if maintaining marketing and content in the same proximity is breaching the law or not," I decided to use that trump card to show our seriousness to go to any length if required.

"We are aware of the legislation that demands maintaining offices in separate buildings."

"That shares the same parking lot where people from the two departments interact and exchange communication without being noticed by the prying eyes of the law," I refused to relent. It had an impact as Anderson gave me a look.

On our way to the car, I asked James, "What is our plan B to get access to the debate platform?"

"I am going to file a petition with the court about the infringement of our fundamental rights," James responded without hesitation. "There will be no debate without us."

"Let's talk to other candidates of the Third Way and learn from their experience," I did not want to rush to the courts. "It is our last resort and should be used after we exhaust all other options. In the meantime, I am going to instruct Gina to ask all our supporters to send emails and initiate a social media campaign to pressure MSBC and CNNBC to include the voice of the people."

While driving home, I sent a message to Gina explaining what had happened in the meeting with Anderson and our strategy to counter it. She liked the strategy and got on it right away.

Next, I sent a message to Alex and Jimmy to prepare our volunteers to be ready for a protest outside MSBC's office if needed.

I was idealistic and naive, believing that the media, traditionally regarded as the fourth pillar of the state along with the legislature, executive, and judiciary, would serve as the bearer of the voice of the people and hold the ruling elite accountable. In theory, that's how it should work, but reality was starkly different. The media was predominantly owned by for-profit corporations driven by greed for more and more profit motives. Without the backing of advertisers, they couldn't sustain their profitability. Consequently, big business became a significant stakeholder, influencing the media's content. These were the same corporate giants that funded the two political parties that controlled the levers of state and government to benefit them. This alliance of political, media, and business elites functioned as kings while the ordinary people were relegated to the status of pawns. The supposed division between the editorial and the business side of media was merely a false facade.

I had read unconfirmed reports on social media that despite the law separating marketing from editorial, big business still exerted its influence on content. Social media was ripe with rumors and some facts that parking lot meetings and off-site discussions worked out to avoid breaching the law requiring no contact. Big business was in control of ensuring the 'by the people' part of the democratic equation only chose from the candidates they preferred.

People were increasingly disillusioned as they observed the media, which should have represented their voice, aligning itself with the interests of exploiters. In response, there was growing support for social media counterculture, a movement aimed at exerting pressure on the ruling elite. A new breed of social media influencers emerged as the guardian of the people. However, these influencers lacked editorial oversight and operated without the constraints of a professional code of ethics.

I distinctly remember that when mainstream media rejected our campaign when we started, we had to rely on social media influencers to gain traction. Our strategy of leveraging social media influencers proved effective in gaining name recognition, primarily because people placed more trust in these social media reporters than qualified, trained, and editorially controlled counterparts.

In the 2020s, the proliferation of fake news, misinformation, disinformation, and the manipulation of emotions polarized society. The presentation of fake news had become so sophisticated that distinguishing it from genuine reports was a formidable task, especially with the advent of artificial intelligence. The consequences of this trend became evident when it bolstered the anarchists in the riots of 2024. In response, the state enacted legislation that mandated the assignment and provision of communication IDs by the government, deeming it a necessary utility. All social media activity underwent non-intrusive monitoring, with the state only intervening when it sensed the emergence of an organized anarchist movement.

During my preparations to understand the legislative process for the election campaign, I came across one of these pieces of legislation. It imposed stringent conditions on media ownership by private commercial corporations, mandating a clear separation between marketing and editorial functions. Any form of direct contact between the business managers and the creators and editors of content was strictly prohibited. This regulation provided us with leverage during our meeting with Anderson.

The law also stipulated that no corporation could own multiple forms of media, including television, radio, social media technology, entertainment, book publishing, and written news. Social media platforms were required to eliminate anonymous accounts and permit only a single account per person, linked to their officially issued state communication ID. While the state issued the communication ID, individuals had the option to use private service providers.

All messages were routed through government servers, and a permanent copy was stored, although state access required court authorization.

Despite the temporary chaos, the social order was eventually restored through these controls by the time I started my election campaign. Nonetheless, the memories of the anarchy experienced in the 2020s remained fresh in the minds of the people and state authorities alike. Frustration had been my companion when the media refused to acknowledge me as a candidate due to my humble origins and the absence of support from big business. I believe this prompted them to deny me access to the three debates.

The irony lay in the fact that the legislature had passed laws to establish a level playing field for all and to ensure the state acted as a neutral arbiter. However, the practical application of these laws did not align with their intended spirit. It was the norm, and I was not an exception. The weak were in a constant fight with the powerful. These elites consistently found ways to circumvent the laws, pursuing their self-interest at the expense of society. The law explicitly demanded media independence, free from the influence of vested interests. Instead, a *de facto* cartel-like alliance was formed between big business, media, and the two dominant political parties.

When we are corned our instinct is to fight back for survival. I resolved not to allow my rights to be denied without a fight.

Twenty-Three

Change of heart

❦

July 15th, 2066

As per our plan, James took the initiative to convene a meeting of the central committee, consisting of 30 members of the Third Way party. During the discussions, it became evident that other candidates were grappling with the same frustrating situation. They shared the collective sentiment that media companies were operating as powerful cartels, wielding control over the political landscape and depriving citizens of their fundamental constitutional right to choose. These media networks were poised to reap substantial profits from the enormous advertising budgets funneled to them by the two major parties, which were influenced and controlled by big business.

In response, our group decided to mobilize public support for our inclusion in the debates and, if necessary, take the matter to the courts. We arrived at a consensus that James would issue a press release addressing this collusion between the trio and expressing our party's intent to file petitions with the courts, seeking to safeguard candidates' freedom of expression, people's right to choose, and ensure a level playing field, as mandated by the law. Third-party candidates were instructed to prepare their petitions for local courts but withhold them until we could gauge the public sentiment. Additionally, we encouraged our supporters to voice their opinions on social media and news platforms, emphasizing the importance of preserving democracy and ensuring that it remains "by the people" not just in letter but also in spirit, as intended by the founding fathers.

Our research showed that big businesses, ever wary of public opinion turning against them, recognized the potential threat posed by consumer boycotts and damage to their corporate image. The fear of these consequences could be a powerful motivator for them to relent and allow space for us. We wanted to test this theory and make it the nucleus of our plans.

The following day, prominent newspapers featured headlines proclaiming, *"The Third Way Takes Election Dispute to the Courts."* It was farther from the truth, but we hoped it would have the desired effect. The online comments on these reports were a testament to the public's discontent. As we anticipated, people expressed outrage at the media, big business, and the two major political parties. There were also calls for nominated candidates of these parties to boycott debates that excluded other candidates listed on the ballot paper, deeming it an undemocratic decision that went against the principles of social justice and fairness of the process.

The momentum was undeniably in our favor. Our dual-pronged strategy, utilizing the power of public opinion and the looming threat of legal action, had yielded results. I received a message from James regarding a meeting with Anderson.

"Anderson wants to meet but not at his office," he informed me.

"When and where?" I inquired.

"Tomorrow afternoon at a game of golf at Royal Club," James confirmed.

"I've never played golf," I admitted. I had always considered it a pastime favored by affluent individuals for socializing. The sport seemed to involve minimal physical exertion, with many players relying on golf carts to travel from one hole to another. The golf terms iron, birdie, and under par were also alien to me.

"I play, you talk," he responded, accompanied by an emoji that displayed hearts as eyes. Emojis have a unique way of conveying emotions.

"Great. Let's meet before the game to discuss our strategy."

I was uncertain about what had prompted Anderson's willingness to meet. Was it the public's reaction, the threat of a lawsuit, or perhaps his desire for higher ratings? To be proactive, I instructed Gina to arrange a vlog interview with a prominent social media influencer, and it had to take place on the same day. I also sent a message to Alex and Jimmy to announce on social media that we were planning to hold a public rally in front of the offices of MSBC and CNNBC in the next few days.

I couldn't afford to assume that Anderson had experienced a genuine change of heart, and I intended to keep the pressure up until we were allowed to participate in the debate.

Twenty-Four

Off the record

⌒☙❧⌒

July 16th, 2066

James picked me up at 1:00 pm to drive together to the Royal Golf Club and discuss our strategy on our way to the appointment. His car was a wonder of human creativity. It was a fully automated self-driving car that could handle all kinds of weather and emergency conditions on the road. It had a digital steering hidden in one of the corners and could be retrieved if needed. The roof was an energy generator equipped with high-efficiency solar cells that converted almost 40% of sunlight into electric current, charging batteries that could also be done through a wall charger. It could drive five hundred miles on a single charge. The car door windows could be used as a display to watch news or entertainment or kept as clear glass to see the view outside. It had air filters to supply fresh air free of almost all allergens and pollution. It also had a small fridge containing drinks and water. Sounds emanated from pores in the doors, enveloping the entire interior with soft, crisp music.

Two seats were facing each other, making the inside look more like a small living room than a car. I spent a few minutes learning about all these features before we could discuss our plan for meeting Anderson.

"Why does he want to meet?" I asked James as soon as he finished talking about his car.

"I am not sure."

"Why outside his office?" I was talking to myself rather than James.

"We are going to find out in an hour."

"What should be our strategy?" I wanted to be prepared for all eventualities, as this meeting was a make-or-break for our campaign.

"We should be aggressive." James was in his usual element.

"I agree. Either he accepts us at the debate, or we will knock the doors down to gain entrance." I said it more to release my internal suffocating pressure than to present a workable strategy. James nodded in agreement, and we remained silent the rest of the drive. Inside the car, it was pleasant thanks to climate control technology, but outside in Fresno, it was sizzling with the mercury touching 110. The dryness of the air made it hard to breathe at times. Humans have contributed significantly to this deteriorating climate.

I wondered why Anderson would play golf in such hot weather although the club had trees all around to provide shade. It was also true that the hottest time in Fresno was not 2:00 pm but 5:00 pm when a person expected it to be cooler rather than hotter.

Anderson met us at the clubhouse, and we immediately

proceeded to the golf course in the self-driving golf cart. We sat facing each other, with James to my right. James and Anderson started talking about their golf handicaps and the brand they preferred for their golf clubs. I listened to their small talk, as I had no knowledge or interest in the game of golf. I was enjoying the soothing views of manicured grass and the abundance of trees on the golf course. Their use of terms like birdie and iron was alien to me. I was familiar with the lingo but never understood how they were applied. Golf seemed like a rich man's game, a way to form business deals away from the prying eyes of the state and its law enforcement.

My preferred games were team sports: cricket, soccer, baseball, basketball, and American football. Sports were, for me, a contest between teams for the glory of the collective rather than a gladiator contest to satisfy an individual ego. I always enjoyed how a team worked together to score a goal in soccer or a touchdown in American football. Every person in the chain had to be perfect for the team to achieve an objective. It was another reason that the individualistic aspect of politics bothered me. My chain of thoughts was interrupted by Anderson.

"I read your profile, Mr. Sher Shah," Anderson spoke to me for the first time after they hit balls at hole number one.

"Did you find it interesting?"

"You have to understand, I started as a reporter for the city council and remained languishing at the third tier of the content ladder for a long time." Apparently, he was more interested in talking about himself and completely ignored my question. I saw an expression of pain pass through his eyes, and for the briefest of moments, there was no arrogance in his attitude. He was a different person than the one we met at his office. The friendly and informal demeanor of Anderson gave me hope that we were meeting to form a compromise.

"It took me over a decade to rise through the ranks and reach where I am today," he continued. "I work for a corporation that wants eyeballs and hefty profits. People come third in priority in this list." He blamed the corporation for rating hunger rather than implicating himself in it. It seemed to me he understood that he had become the slave of this entrenched system.

"I understand," I expressed as much empathy as I could.

"Between us, off the record, I don't even like the two parties," he said in almost a whisper, using his reporter disclaimer.

"That is good to know," I said, throwing a curious glance at James.

"You have adopted the right approach by threatening to go to the courts and using public opinion in your favor," Anderson gave his expert approval to our strategy. I could see a faint smile appear on James's face.

"I want to help you," Anderson surprised me by saying that.

"I can use every help that I can get." I was now sure we would form a deal today to gain access to debates.

"I will ask the producers to include you in the debate," he removed a heavy burden from me, as I did not want to be aggressive.

"But you need some expert help to prepare for the debate," Anderson transformed into a media advisor from an adversary. We had converted a hurdle into an opportunity.

"I appreciate it. Who do you recommend for it?"

He asked me to save the contact details of Aaron McDonald.

"I spoke to him yesterday during the game of golf and asked him to help you prepare for the debate. You don't have to

pay him. I checked your finances, and you can't afford him."
Anderson had become an ally. I still did not know how this
transformation had happened, it made me remain skeptical
of his intentions.

"Why are you going out of your way to help us?" I was now
relieved but still curious.

"For ratings, and I was an underdog once. I have to repay
an old debt."

James was right – the media needs ratings, and underdogs
help underdogs. To repay his change of heart to support us,
James let him win the game of golf. At least that's what he told
me on our way home. I smiled hearing that because it must
have been hard for him to defy his nature to lose. I considered
him a person who wants to win and is a source loser.

The next day, the breaking news in the local media was that
I was invited to the debates organized by MSBC and CNNBC.

This new development broke the stalemate in our campaign.
Our volunteers doubled overnight, reaching the numbers we
needed. We received more donations from the donors that
had already contributed. But the number that mattered most
to me was that our small donors breached the target of 5,000.
We received 50 aÇs donations from over 6,100 people.

The power of the media was on full display, but it was the
fear of people that made it happen.

Twenty-Five

Aaron McDonald

S her Shah looked at the wall photo display. It was showing his wedding photo. They were sitting on a sofa holding hands, their heads tilted towards each other as if whispering. He looked at the picture without blinking because the person in the picture transformed into a different person at each stage of his life. His story was not of one but many personas from a shy introvert to a politician and then to a statesman.

Sher Shah recalled his feelings of inadequacy when he first met Aaron McDonald. It was an interesting, life-changing experience. He opened his notebook to write about it.

* * *

July 17th to August 10th, 2066

Until I decided to pursue politics, I was a shy, introvert who avoided the limelight. I wasn't even aware that a significant untapped part of my personality was lurking in the dark corners of my consciousness. The boiler accident exposed that hidden part and changed me into a different person. The accident of birth brings us into the world, but the accidents in living a life bring out our hidden selves. Failures and successes both leave an imprint on us that becomes part of our history and personality.

Even at social events, I would avoid cameras and was a backbencher in the class during my school days. My family had to drag me to be part of the family photos. My daughters and son, members of Gen Alpha, were addicted to selfies and posting pictures of mundane daily chores like breakfast or their preference for clothes or shoes. I never understood the value of sharing pictures of a meal with social media friends and followers. My kids considered me a dinosaur because of this attitude. I could not have imagined, in my wildest dreams growing up, that one day I would be standing on a TV stage participating in a debate watched by hundreds of thousands of people if not millions.

The next four weeks were bustling with regular campaign activities, including knocking on doors, meeting donors, attending weekly meetings with volunteers, responding to questions through my communication ID (selected by Gina for responses), participating in our weekly core committee meetings, and preparing for the upcoming debate. Modern democracy was dependent on the media to reach the numbers that were impossible to achieve by sheer hard work. Tools were available to gauge voters' moods and preferences as debates progressed using smart devices and artificial- intelligence helped pollsters gather live data.

Political debates had transformed into reality TV spectacles, filled with drama, suspense, and anticipation. Candidates competed for camera attention, and moderators sought punchlines that would boost their ratings. Rating agencies used these debates to gauge public interest in politics, which, in turn, influenced voter turnout on Election Day. The Democratic and Republican Parties had crafted a contract that candidates and the media had to sign to secure more airtime for their candidates.

Many political pundits believed people voted based on emotions rather than facts and rational thinking. The candidates appeared to adhere to this theory, often behaving more like actors than politicians on the debate stage. They aimed to become shock jocks, high on entertainment value but often lacking substance. I pondered whether I could play this role effectively, given my deep-seated shyness and no experience with live TV. Stage fright was a real concern for me.

One week after our encounter with Anderson at the golf club, James and I landed in the downtown studio of Aaron McDonald. Clad in a green T-shirt, khaki pants, and leather boots, Aaron's attire signaled a technician immersed in his work without respite. Despite his rather short stature, he exuded a high-energy persona that defied expectations. His piercing blue eyes seemed in constant motion, absorbing every detail around him.

Aaron, a middle-aged man with a background in film production, now specialized in coaching actors, including politicians preparing for debates. His expertise drew us to his office and studio, strategically situated in a downtown Fresno office building. The visit to Aaron's studio promised an insightful experience, given his reputation for honing the skills of individuals navigating the challenging landscape of public discourse.

After the initial introductions and pleasantries, Aaron handed me a series of forms to fill out. These forms delved into my experience in public speaking, my comfort level with cameras, and any prior experience performing in front of live audiences. It was not hard to fill out these forms, I had none of it. My only experience speaking to a group of people was during the election campaign, and I did not particularly relish it. The holographic video was my lone experience of speaking to a camera and that took more than two dozen takes. I preferred face-to-face meetings over these stump speeches.

As I diligently filled out the forms, I couldn't help but feel a growing sense of insecurity and anxiety. These insecurities were recurring too frequently because I was faced with new challenges on an almost daily basis. Challenges I was neither equipped nor experienced to handle. Before entering politics, I believed that I had no desire or inclination to be in the limelight and enjoy it. Little did I know that events in the coming days would challenge this self-analysis. It turned out that sometimes we don't truly understand ourselves, and circumstances reveal hitherto hidden aspects of our character. We transform many times in a lifetime. Shakespeare called it the seven ages of men.

Aaron looked at the forms with a thoughtful expression, his brows furrowed in concentration. I was not sure if he could help a person like me who had zero experience or capability. I sought some reassurance from the expert, asking if I could adequately prepare.

"That depends on you," Aaron remained non-committal.

I pressed for a more concrete answer, given his expertise.

"You are an expert, and these forms should give you an idea," I pointed out.

"Past cannot be changed, but the future can be different and defy the past," Aaron responded, ready to embrace the challenge. I admired his resolve to accept a challenge. I liked his straightforward and methodical ways.

He went on to share his experience of coaching incredibly introverted actors, yet they transformed into different individuals when facing a camera. This revelation lifted my spirits, and I felt more hopeful about the process.

Aaron explained that, during the debate, I would hardly see anyone in the audience due to the stage setup. To help me acclimate to this unfamiliar environment, he invited us to the studio, where he had recreated a replica of the debate setting. He encouraged me to step onto the stage and stand behind one of the three podiums. However, just as I was getting accustomed to this strange experience, Aaron switched on all the spotlights, blinding me with their intense brightness.

"How does it feel?" I could only hear him ask as the lights had blinded me to what was beyond it.

"Overwhelming," was the first word that came to my mind. It accurately captured my initial response to the blinding lights.

Aaron turned off the lights and joined me on the stage with James. He emphasized the need to overcome the overwhelming feeling and become familiar with the environment. He believed that developing a debate argument would be the easier part of the process.

I asked, "When do we start?" as I realized I needed his coaching urgently. The first debate was only three weeks away.

"We begin tomorrow and meet every other day for two hours. When you come next time, bring two more people with you," Aaron instructed.

Concerned about the costs involved, I inquired, "How much would it cost us?" to ensure clarity about the terms of his services.

Aaron reassured me, saying, "It will be my campaign contribution." This statement aimed to put me at ease, though I couldn't help but wonder why he would contribute to my campaign when he hardly knew me.

James appeared to have read my mind and asked him, "Alright, but we will also need a disclaimer stating that no one else has paid you for this coaching."

"I will sign it," Aaron had no objections to this request, demonstrating his experience in dealing with politicians and campaign managers. As our first meeting concluded, he extended his hand, "See you all tomorrow at 3:30 pm."

It marked the beginning of my journey to transform from a political novice into a stage actor who masqueraded as a politician. Aaron's initial focus was on my posture, hand gestures, eye contact with the camera, and other body expressions. In the next phase, he assigned roles to Gina and James as my opponent candidates and himself as the moderator. Alex was designated as the observer who would determine the winner of these mock debates.

As we continued to practice for two weeks, Gina monitored our progress through weekly voter surveys. Our favorable ratings were gradually improving, and I moved to become the second option for most voters, although I was still not the first choice of the majority. I trailed behind Democrat Kevin and Republican Roberto as a first choice. The gap had narrowed but remained an eyesore for us. It concerned all of us, and we knew we had to overcome this hurdle soon.

The Third Way party emerged as a formidable contender as an alternate third choice seeking to erode the domination of the two-party system. National surveys indicated that we were poised to win enough seats to influence the legislative process, which boded well for my election campaign.

However, political action committees (PACs), originally intended as pressure groups to influence policy, had transformed into secret weapons in the hands of the two major parties to target Third Way candidates. I was one of the candidates in their cross-hairs.

These experiences taught me that the ideal of democracy "for the people" was often an illusion, and "by the people" was a farce. It needed liberation from the clutches of special interests. The election could be a significant milestone in this ongoing journey to introduce democratic reforms, but it was not the end.

Twenty-Six

The adversaries

August 13th, 2066

I received a message a day earlier from James informing me that Anderson had arranged a meeting for all the candidates to discuss the debate format, ethics, and rules. The meeting was scheduled for 3:00 pm on August 13th, at the MSBC conference room located in the same building as Anderson's office. Each candidate could bring one person from their staff to accompany them to the meeting, and I decided to have James accompany me. Other candidates had more elaborate organizations comprising of campaign manager, media advisor, and financial controller. They could afford it. For our campaign, James wore all these hats.

At 2:30 pm, James picked me up from home. As we drove to the meeting, I asked him if he had any experience with these negotiations, as I wasn't sure if he had been in such situations before.

"No, I don't," he replied. "But I reached out to a friend who has attended these meetings in past elections."

"What did your friend advise?" I inquired.

James shared with me the purpose of these meetings. Essentially, they were meant to arrive at an agreement on the debate format and set expectations for candidates. Cable news networks needed to ensure that their debates were compliant with election laws to protect themselves from potential retaliation or lawsuits from the supporters of the major parties. We were invited more for the sake of maintaining compliance with election laws and had little influence over the eventual arrangement.

"At least it gives us a chance to meet the other candidates and get a sense of their personalities," I remarked as James finished his explanation.

The atmosphere in the MSBC office building exuded professionalism and prestige as we were warmly received at the main entrance. The escort provided by the MSBC staff added a touch of formality, guiding us to the conference room where the upcoming meeting would take place.

Upon entering the conference room, I noticed the tasteful and elegant decor that characterized the space. The dark gray walls and Brazilian cherry wood floor contributed to a sophisticated ambiance. The room was not just a functional space but a showcase of the network's success and influence.

My eyes were drawn to the pictures on the walls featuring celebrities who had visited the network's offices for interviews, indicating the network's prominence in the media industry. Additionally, a shelf proudly displayed the awards the network had won, showcasing its excellence in covering a range of events, from wars to natural calamities. This visual representation of achievements added a layer of credibility to the network's reputation.

The centerpiece of the conference room was the long, expensive-looking wooden table, suggesting a commitment to quality and professionalism. The table was complemented by chairs upholstered in black and dark green leather, not only adding to the aesthetic appeal but also ensuring comfort during extended meetings. The seating arrangement for two dozen people indicated large meetings were held in the room.

As we waited for the other candidates to arrive, the surroundings of the conference room subtly conveyed the network's history, achievements, and commitment to excellence, creating an impressive backdrop for the discussions that would soon unfold.

As the clock struck 2:00 pm, the door swung open, and Anderson entered the conference room with his customary expression of arrogance. Following closely behind him were the Democrat candidate, Kevin Johnson, and the Republican candidate, Roberto Gonzalez. Both candidates were accompanied by their respective staff members, creating an air of formality and significance to the gathering.

I couldn't help but steal a glance at James, my curiosity piqued by the possibility of a separate meeting that we might not have been informed about. However, James' expression remained composed, not indicating any exclusivity in the encounter.

As a sign of courtesy and professionalism, we rose from our seats to greet one another. Handshakes were exchanged, signaling the beginning of what promised to be a pivotal meeting.

Kevin Johnson was a tall, lean man, roughly the same height

as me, standing at six feet. He had gray-blond hair, piercing blue eyes, and tanned white skin that had grown somewhat leathery with age. He looked like a retired soldier who stayed in shape to defy aging. His handshake was firm, and he offered a mechanical smile that appeared more out of habit than genuine warmth.

Roberto Gonzalez was shorter, around five feet ten, and a couple of years younger than me. He had straight black hair with a touch of gray at the temples, parted down the middle, giving him a boyish appearance. His brown skin, black eyes, and ready smile made him appear younger than his actual age. His appearance defied his age, he looked more to be in his early forties rather than in his early fifties as his year of birth suggested. His smile was warm and his handshake firm as we exchanged greetings.

The atmosphere in the room shifted in anticipation of a serious discussion, and the candidates took their respective seats around the impressive wooden table. The stage was set for a meeting that would likely shape future events, and the air was charged with expectations.

"Gentlemen, I wanted to review the rules, procedures, and structure of the debate to avoid any surprises," Anderson began. He proceeded to explain the laws, ethics, and structure of the debate. Each candidate would have two minutes for an introduction, one minute to answer a question, thirty seconds for a counterargument to an opponent's claim, and two minutes for a closing statement. The debate would last ninety minutes with a fifteen-minute break after the first forty-five minutes. Use of curse words or hate speech, as defined in a list provided to each candidate, would be prohibited. Anderson showed pictures of the debate studio and the positions of each candidate on the stage. I would stand on the left, Kevin in the center as the incumbent, and Roberto to the right of him.

As Anderson finished his presentation, Kevin Johnson and Roberto seemed somewhat disinterested, having heard this information before. We were all given a contract to sign and return a day before the debate. Anderson then opened the floor for questions.

James began the discussion on our side, "How did you decide to position us on the stage?"

"Traditionally, the incumbent is placed in the center, with the other candidates on either side," Anderson explained.

"We object to that. The election is between candidates for a fresh mandate, and being an incumbent should not matter," James argued.

"I understand your point. We're open to new ideas," Anderson responded.

"We propose that candidates be placed in alphabetical order of their first names," I suggested. It was a clever suggestion as our research had shown that candidates on the far left were not as well-focused by the camera, affecting their visibility to viewers. Even if the alphabetic order followed the last name convention, it would not have a significant impact on us, as we would still be on the right side of the stage. This strategic move aimed to provide us with better visibility during the debate. As well as to send a message that we should not be taken lightly by our opponents.

"Gentlemen, any objections?" Anderson looked to the other two candidates.

"I have no objection, but I do worry that ninety minutes might not be enough to fully inform voters about our election manifesto," Kevin expressed his concern.

"I agree with Kevin. How can we ensure that the top four or five issues are discussed in depth to inform voters?" Roberto supported Jim's view.

"Our political consultants have conducted surveys to identify the top five issues that are important to voters," Anderson explained. "We've had ninety-minute debates in the past, and time has never been an issue."

"We also have another concern to address. How are the questions developed, and who formulates them?" I inquired.

"Questions are developed by our political consultants, and no candidate has access to them," Anderson responded with irritation for questioning their integrity. "I want to assure all of you that our channel is unbiased and neutral in this contest. We will provide a level playing field." He defended his employer.

"We suggest that each candidate should have one minute to respond to each question, with rebuttals to follow after they've all had their turn," I suggested. I wanted to make it clear that we wouldn't allow other candidates to have a free ride just because we were less experienced.

After a lengthy discussion of the debate format, we all agreed to the proposed changes. The meeting allowed me to have a better understanding of the personalities of my two opponents, which would help prepare my counterarguments. Kevin appeared for his re-election and Roberto was enthusiastic to elevate to US Congress from state parliament. I was sure Roberto would focus on Kevin in the debate and leave me alone. The events would prove me wrong yet again. I was going through the school of realpolitik in real-time. I hoped I would graduate with flying colors on Election Day.

On our way home, I asked James, "How do you feel about our meeting today?"

"Pushing Kevin to the far left was a win for me," he replied with a mischievous smile.

"Did you have any past scores to settle with him?" I inquired curiously.

"Yes, he defeated one of the bills I prepared for the Congressman as a staff member. We proposed to cut subsidies for tech companies and redirect that money toward fighting climate change," James explained with a tone of satisfaction.

"Well, I'm glad you found some closure today," I said with a smile.

Twenty-Seven

Gladiator contest

S her Shah looked at the notebook he was using, realizing he was already halfway through the second of the three notebooks he had purchased. Recognizing that he had a substantial more to document, he foresaw the need for additional notebooks soon.

Concern creased his brow as he pondered the scarcity of these antique items. Knowing they weren't readily available, he worried that they might be sold out when he eventually required them. Understanding the importance of maintaining a continuous record, he decided to make a mental note to ask Nour to get it for him.

Given his physical weakness, which limited his mobility, Sher Shah increasingly relied on Nour to help with various tasks. In this case, he planned to delegate the responsibility of obtaining at least two more antique notebooks from the store to ensure he could continue his meticulous documentation without interruption. This small yet crucial task underscored his dependence on Nour for support in both his personal pursuits.

Sher Shah took hold of the pen, preparing to recount his experience of the first election debate. This event had thrust his name into the national spotlight, albeit for reasons he would have preferred to avoid.

* * *

August 16th, 2066

Aaron had prepared me thoroughly for the upcoming debate, yet I couldn't shake off the persistent nervousness that gripped me all morning on the day of the debate. Seeking solace and a way to alleviate my stress, I decided to escape to the mountains, seeking solitude and time to gather my thoughts and composure. The summer heat was relentless, even in the morning hours. While the mountain temperature was some twenty degrees cooler, it still reached the mid-80s, feeling much warmer than the weather forecast had suggested. I found a boulder beneath the shade of a tree and settled down, gazing out at the valley.

There's always been something profoundly soothing about the tranquility and quiet of the mountains. The giant sequoia trees loomed tall and motionless, seemingly untouched by the concerns of the world. These ancient sentinels, standing there for over a century, had witnessed countless election cycles, presidents, and changes. They witnessed the American Civil War and the two world wars. None of these devastating events moved them. Their serenity served as a potion for my frazzled nerves and anxiety.

My mind was plagued by a barrage of questions and worries. What if I stumbled or stammered, something that occasionally happened under stress? What if my voice didn't project strongly enough? What if I lost my train of thought, or worse, faced questions about legislation I wasn't well-versed in? These thoughts swirled in my mind like a tumultuous whirlwind.

In search of peace, I closed my eyes and tried to retreat to that mental place where I could find calm. I recalled my father's advice: "Son, you were born during the height of spring when no one thought you'd survive. Always remember that and shine like the warm spring sun." It boosted my confidence, and my normally critical mind became an ally today, reassuring me to focus on the positive aspects. I was participating in a debate that had been an unimaginable goal until recently. I helped establish a national platform for the Third Way. I had to relax and savor the moment.

After an hour of meditation, I returned home, took a refreshing shower, and decided to unwind with an hour of music. During lunch with my mother, Nour, and kids. Nour expressed her nervousness about my performance, while our children and my mother were excited that I would be on television.

Nour agreed to accompany me to the debate, my mother stayed home looking after the children. She wore a saree, a choice I particularly liked, and selected a purple one, matching the color of our party. A pearl choker, earrings, and bracelet added elegance to her outfit. Her Asian features and fuller figure complemented the saree beautifully. She didn't go for heavy makeup; just a shade of dark purple lipstick to match her dress. I often teased Nour that men dressed more quickly than women because we had limited options to choose from, saving us time.

For my part, I had chosen to wear my black pinstriped suit, a pastel purple mandarin-collar shirt, pearl cuff-links to complement Nour, black patterned socks, and black oxford shoes. My receding hairline and short-cropped hair spared me the concern of a complex hairdo. I had trimmed my full beard to look more professional than I usually did.

James arrived to pick us up at 4:00 pm, aiming to spend some final moments with me for a discussion before we reached the debate venue around 6:00 pm. The debate was scheduled to commence at 6:30 pm.

During our drive, we made a pit stop at a coffee shop. "How are you feeling, Sher?" James asked, sounding like a seasoned coach motivating his team before a pivotal match.

"I feel good," I replied, offering a smile while concealing the inner turmoil one typically experiences before a significant event. Technology may have progressed, reshaping our lifestyles, but the hunter-gatherer instincts of humans remain unchanged. Despite our advancements, at our core, we're still the same people who lived during the times of Noah, Abraham, Moses, Jesus, and Muhammad.

"Is there anything you'd like to discuss before the debate?"

"No," I answered. I was ready to enjoy the evening and not take myself too seriously. Taking oneself too seriously often leads to unnecessary stress. I had decided if I did not know an answer to a legislative question, I would say it and give my opinion on the issue it addressed rather than the content of the legislation.

The MSBC studio staff warmly welcomed us at the door and guided us to the conference room where all the candidates were gathering. Anderson, accompanied by his production team, was already in the room. We all arrived within minutes of each other. Kevin was dressed in a black suit, white shirt, and a blue tie, while Roberto was wearing a dark gray suit, a white shirt, and a red tie. It almost seemed as though they were following an unwritten code, sticking to the conventional attire of their respective political parties for such events. Both candidates were accompanied by their spouses and campaign staff. From our side all members of the core committee, Gina, Alex, Jimmy, Ashraf, and Ranbir were present. Roberto and Kevin both had over a dozen staff members each. They all mingled to get to know each other. Despite the upcoming clash on the debate stage, we all exchanged pleasantries, acknowledging that tonight we were modern-day gladiators, to be judged and possibly voted up or down on Election Day based on tonight's performance.

The makeup artist carefully worked on each person, skill-fully applying a light dusting of powder on their foreheads and cheeks. This meticulous touch was not just for aesthetics but served a practical purpose, aiming to eliminate any shine that could result from perspiration under the intense stage lights.

The rationale behind this makeup technique became clear as it was explained that the camera didn't favor the natural sheen that could appear on the skin under such conditions. Under the scrutiny of high-intensity stage lights, even the tiniest beads of liquid could be accentuated, potentially giving the impression of nervousness or sweating.

By skillfully addressing this potential issue with the application of powder, the makeup artist ensured that the individuals would present themselves in the best possible light on camera. This attention to detail highlighted the importance of not just enhancing appearance but also managing the practical challenges posed by the technical aspects of the production, contributing to a polished and professional on-screen presentation. After all, it was the best reality show in town.

Anderson reiterated the sequence of events that we had already agreed upon a few days earlier. We would be called to the stage in alphabetical order. Kevin would lead, followed by Roberto, and finally me.

In the debate studio, there was a select group of people, including campaign staff, party members, and constituents from the district. They were given strict instructions not to applaud any candidate and to maintain complete silence throughout the debate.

Precisely at 6:30 pm, the debate began. Stepping onto the stage, I was struck by the piercing brightness of the spotlight. It felt as though it was penetrating my very soul, and I had an unnerving sensation of standing there exposed and vulnerable, like being naked. A wave of shyness and a blush washed over me as the blinding lights played tricks on my eyes. Unable to see any faces in the room, I silently thanked Aaron for his coaching, knowing it would have been a sure disaster without his expert guidance to manage stage fright.

On stage, we greeted each other with a handshake for the camera and returned to our assigned podiums. According to the agreed arrangement, I was placed on the right, with Roberto in the center and Kevin on the left. I couldn't help but notice that their podiums seemed slightly closer to each other, and I couldn't shake the suspicion that I'd been pushed to the side. I resolved to ask James to investigate whether this was a deliberate tactic or merely a figment of my imagination.

Anderson commenced the debate, and I began my introductory statement, a speech I had delivered well over a hundred times by now. It was the start of a challenging but essential evening.

The questions began to flow, and our responses followed. Things took an interesting turn when Roberto questioned the qualifications required for congressional candidates, and it felt like a thinly veiled attack on my lack of political experience. It was a surprising early onslaught.

Anderson turned to me and offered the opportunity for a rebuttal. I seized the moment, responding with a tactful counterattack. I accused Roberto of not addressing real issues important to people, such as air and noise pollution from air taxi services, subtly highlighting Kevin's financial ties to these companies. I reminded the audience that Kevin was a political freshman when he was elected for the first time. A fact that Roberto conveniently overlooked in his attack on me. This countermove was designed to suggest Roberto and Kevin were two sides of the same coin and aligned with each other. It pushed him into the spotlight. I could imagine James smiling at my transformation into an astute politician.

I decided to shift the debate into uncharted territory, seeking support for an idea that had long bothered me.

"We are often concerned about a candidate's inexperience, yet most management and leadership studies suggest that the effectiveness of a public office erodes after a decade," I paused, turning to Kevin on my left. "Kevin has been re-elected for two decades, serving the interests of high-tech companies. It's time voters tell him to retire because he is not serving their interests."

The unexpected statement caught everyone off guard, given my status as a newcomer without a debating track record.

"Mr. Shah seems to question the collective wisdom of our voters and even point fingers at our constitution," Kevin retorted, visibly agitated. "He seems unaware that the US Congress is the longest-serving constitutional body directly elected by people since 1789."

Anderson enjoyed the back-and-forth and turned to Roberto to contribute.

"I believe the constitution has served this nation well," Roberto said cautiously. "I'm not sure why an inexperienced candidate would question its foundation."

Roberto chose to focus on me instead of his main opponent, who was potentially denying him entry onto the national stage.

"Do you have anything to add, Mr. Shah?" Anderson asked, unsure of my intentions.

"I did not make any suggestion that could be undermining the constitution. The Constitution is a living document that has changed over time. It has to adjust to changing times and social evolution to continue serving the people. We have had 27 amendments so far," I turned to Kevin to conclude my argument. "I propose that the term of the US Congress should be three years with a maximum limit of three terms. We need periodic turnover for the induction of fresh ideas and the development of younger leaders."

I felt I was able to shift the debate from my inexperience to the stalemate that resulted from the overstretched reelection of a congressman.

As time progressed, I grew more comfortable and confident in my responses, letting go of the initial nervousness that had gripped me. I was beginning to feel in my element, ready to tackle the challenges ahead.

Anderson then shifted his attention to Kevin, posing a question about the United States lagging in scientific research, in light of recent developments in robotics and medicine in other countries. The debate was in full swing, and it was anyone's game.

"The Democratic Party has always supported innovation and recently announced a budget of $75 billion for scientific research in medicine, robotics, and space mining," Kevin delivered his typical party response. "We are not as far behind as you might think. We have already been using robots for knee and other non-life-threatening surgeries."

"Democrats by raising taxes and increasing compliance costs for new research, have actually hampered innovation," Roberto countered, highlighting his policy stance that was the mantra of his party. Such minor differences between the two major parties had made them less appealing to the public, creating a space for the emergence of the Third Way.

Anderson promptly turned to me after Roberto finished, asking for my perspective.

"Healing involves the human touch. Scientific research has confirmed this fact. Premature babies recover more rapidly when held by nurses and mothers rather than being placed in incubators. While machines can be trusted to fix what can be considered machines, humans are far from being mere machines. We possess emotions and feelings," I articulated, strengthening my argument. "This demands tender care and touch. Routine surgeries like knee replacements and other non-life-threatening procedures, we have been employing robots for many decades."

I took a brief pause to catch my breath before continuing.

"However, for life-threatening surgeries such as heart, liver, brain, and kidney transplants, I believe human supervision is paramount. My personal experience with a self-driving car led to the loss of my father when it misread data and took a sharp turn on a busy highway during severe weather conditions. We've witnessed airplane crashes resulting from sensor misinterpretations, where autopilots failed to make the right decisions. While these critical procedures can involve robotic assistance, human surgeons should always be present for supervision. Voters are already expressing their concerns about the need for more face-to-face doctor visits rather than relying on artificial intelligence-powered medical assistants for diagnoses." I remember Gina listed it as one of the five issues we would focus on.

I took a deep breath, maintaining direct eye contact with the camera as I concluded, "We are falling behind in innovation and research because we are becoming a closed society. Creativity cannot be reduced to a matter of money alone. America has always attracted top talent because our universities were renowned, our infrastructure top-notch, our barriers to entry minimal, and we rewarded success regardless of an individual's skin color, faith, or social status. The American dream needs revival, and this cannot be achieved through budget allocation and fiscal incentives alone. The two major parties serve as obstacles to this revival, rather than facilitators; they have contributed to the weakening of the American dream."

We continued the debate for 45 minutes, addressing a wide array of topics that concerned voters. A 15-minute break was announced by Anderson, during which James and Gina approached me. Gina shared the encouraging news that voters were responding favorably to my responses. I was relieved to hear this, as my focus during the debate had been solely on presenting what I believed to be in the best interest of society. Little did we all know that a significant turning point awaited us in the second half of the debate.

* * *

A sharp pain in his fingers abruptly interrupted Sher Shah's focus, causing the pen to slip from his grasp. Becoming aware of the mounting discomfort in his lower back and shoulders, he took a moment to rub his fingers in an attempt to find relief.

Glancing at his watch, he was surprised to realize that nearly two and a half hours had passed since he began his writing endeavor. The intensity of his concentration had made him oblivious to the physical strain.

Contemplating whether to postpone the narration of the first debate until the next day, Sher Shah weighed his options. Despite the discomfort, he decided to push through and complete the task on the same day. Recognizing the need for a brief break, he made his way to the couch with the intention of lying down to alleviate the strain on his back and shoulders. He set up an alarm on his device to remind him to restart after 30 minutes.

Twenty-Eight

A misstep

───✦───

A s the debate resumed after the break, I felt a sense of confidence and control. However, a lingering concern persisted that my responses might not have the necessary impact to sway voters in my favor. Gina had confirmed my suspicions, reminding me that we needed a significant boost in approval ratings from the first debate. Her live data monitoring showed marginal numbers of supporters choosing me as a first or second choice after the first half. Seeking guidance, I turned to James for suggestions.

"Women make up over 52% of registered voters. Their primary concerns revolve around family and their well-being. Find a way to incorporate that into your responses," James offered some invaluable advice. Recognizing the strategic importance of addressing these concerns, I prepared to integrate these insights into my subsequent debate responses, aiming to resonate with a crucial demographic and potentially enhance my appeal among voters.

Anderson restarted the debate by directing a question to Kevin, inquiring about the growing number of illegal immigrants seeking asylum. The demographics of Europe have changed significantly over the last five decades, with native populations aging and having fewer children while immigrants from Africa and Asia contributed to exponential population growth. In response to this shift, Europe adjusted its citizenship and permanent residency laws. Meanwhile, America had grappled with an increasing number of illegal immigrants exploiting asylum and UN refugee laws.

Kevin presented the Democratic Party's position, explaining their efforts to cooperate with governments in South America and Southern Africa to curtail human smuggling networks and process asylum applications there. They had also worked with the Republican Party to pass legislation discouraging on-land processing of asylum applications.

Roberto, seizing an opportunity to score political points, criticized the Democratic Party's track record on immigration.

When Anderson turned to me for my perspective on the immigration issue, I took a moment to collect my thoughts. I was well aware of the positions held by the two major parties, but I believed they didn't grasp the root causes of the immigration issue. Additionally, my family's history was intertwined with immigration, particularly my father's experience as an asylum seeker, which made the topic particularly personal.

"I believe the two parties aren't fully addressing the immigration issue with sincerity," I began, once again framing them as allies rather than adversaries. "We need to understand why people choose to immigrate. Leaving behind family and friends to live in a foreign country isn't an easy decision. Data shows that when home countries are doing well economically, politically, and socially, a person is less inclined to emigrate. We're seeing reverse migration among Indian and Chinese communities as their home countries offer greater opportunities. However, we haven't done enough to help South American and African nations improve their governance."

Anderson probed further, asking for my proposed solutions to the problem. I seized the opportunity to share my research that barriers to freedom of movement have disrupted global population balance over the past two centuries. Throughout history, people migrated in search of better opportunities, often moving toward regions with more avenues for prosperity. However, in the last two centuries, barriers to freedom of movement have led to a population imbalance among various world regions resulting in an ecological disaster. Some countries faced overpopulation, while others grappled with aging and declining populations, resulting in strained pension systems.

I went on to advocate for a radical redesign of global visa and residency programs. As a global superpower with economic, political, and military influence, the United States was uniquely positioned to lead such an effort. It was also distinct in its status as a melting pot that welcomed diversity, in contrast to other leading nations that predominantly represented the ethnic identity of their majority populations.

America had the potential to pioneer an approach that celebrated diversity and addressed the root causes of global immigration issues. This stance could set the nation apart from countries like India, Japan, Germany, Russia, Turkey, or China, where ethnic homogeneity held a central place in national identity. While these nations were hesitant to adopt diversity, America thrived on it.

Kevin and Roberto viewed my perspective as impractical and a testament to my political and legislative inexperience.

"My Republican and Democratic friends often label me as inexperienced and idealistic," I countered in response to their critique, "but the reality is that their border walls and restrictive legislation have proven to be failures to contain the tide of illegal entrants. In the last five years, we've seen more illegal immigrants than ever before, as even their own congressional reports indicate. Their experience has failed to produce results, and it's time to consider alternative ideas and options." At that point, Anderson decided to shift to the next topic.

"Mr. Roberto, if the Republican Party defines marriage as a union between a man and a woman, do you oppose or support a tax incentive proposed by the Democratic Party?" Anderson directed a question to the Republican candidate, focusing on a recent hot topic that had been making headlines. It surprised me, I felt that a relatively minor issue was being exploited for ratings rather than addressing matters of significant public interest. Gina's research also confirmed that voters were least concerned about such personal lifestyle preference choices.

Roberto responded with the shrewdness of an experienced politician, emphasizing the need to separate the union of people and the tax policy. In his view, tax incentives should not be tied to the specific form of the union between citizens.

Kevin countered Roberto, advocating for tax incentives that would address the additional challenges faced by the LGBT community due to their marginal status. He argued that, given the ongoing societal discrimination, it was essential to offer support, as we had historically supported communities facing workplace discrimination.

The two candidates continued their back-and-forth, largely reflecting their party lines. All the while, Anderson conveniently overlooked my raised hand. Frustrated by this disregard, I impulsively interjected into the microphone, "LGBT relations are an anomaly and should not be considered the norm."

A murmur swept through the hall, and the other candidates on the stage momentarily fell silent. Anderson responded, "Are you against LGBT couples?" He finally paid attention to me and acknowledged my participation in the debate.

"No, that's not what I'm saying. People are free to live their lives and adopt any lifestyle they choose within the confines of their homes. However, society shouldn't embrace such relationships as the norm," I clarified.

Roberto and Kevin both responded in unison, labeling my statement as anti-LGBT. I was sure to the audience they would appear as members of one rather than two separate parties. It was the reality; on most issues they had minor differences.

Refusing to change my position, I argued, "We are challenging the natural order by accepting these relationships as the norm. Look at other animal species that have existed for millions of years longer than us. They exhibit a union of two sexes with distinct roles. We are the youngest species relative to them. All these other species rely on the union of two sexes to procreate and nurture offspring. Are we wiser than Mother Nature?"

Anderson probed further, inquiring whether I wanted the state to control whom individuals could love and marry. He seemed to revel in the rising ratings due to the controversy.

"No, that's not what I'm suggesting either. The state intervenes in matters like smoking and drinking to protect public health. If the state can impose restrictions on such behaviors, it should also protect society from potential adverse consequences, without infringing on individuals' privacy within their homes," I responded.

Kevin interjected, highlighting the importance of not dictating people's sexual orientation, Roberto supported this view, emphasizing the medical evidence indicating that an individual's physical attributes may differ from their sexual orientation.

I continued my argument by posing a hypothetical situation, "How would we feel if someday people decided they no longer wanted to wear clothes because being naked is a natural state?"

Kevin responded with sarcasm, claiming that I was confusing the issue and that my statements were discriminatory bordering on hate speech, insisting that Americans didn't support any form of discrimination.

I countered by pointing out that humans were the only species to cover themselves with clothes, acknowledging that some people might have different physical conditions and emphasizing that they could express themselves within the privacy of their homes. However, society shouldn't accept these behaviors as norms that defy the nature of existence. I believe that exceptions should be accommodated for social justice, but not to an extent that has long-term adverse effects on society. I argued that a child needed both a man and a woman to develop a stable personality and reach their full potential since men and women brought diverse physical and emotional qualities needed to create a balanced home and society.

I continued, "Humans are failing to learn from past mistakes. We've already damaged the climate by polluting the air, water, and soil, leading to man-made disasters such as the disappearance of glaciers due to rising temperatures and rising water levels that have submerged vast areas. Now, we're disrupting the balance of society by accepting an exception as the norm."

Kevin wanted to emphasize that same-sex relationships had existed throughout human history, seeking to clarify his political stance and make it appear credible.

I responded, "Yes, but it was never accepted as the societal norm. That's all I'm saying. I won't support any legislation that allows discrimination against citizens based on their lifestyle preferences when renting an apartment or seeking employment, for instance. However, we must draw a line somewhere to protect society from decay. Marriage should be recognized as a union between a man and a woman."

Recognizing that we had spent enough time on this topic, Anderson shifted the discussion to other subjects. Little did I know, at the time, that my comments would unleash a storm that threatened to engulf us all.

After the debate, when I met James and Gina, they were deeply concerned about my comments on LGBT issues and believed it would be a severe blow to our election prospects.

"Why did you do that? You were doing so well," James asked in apparent frustration, akin to a coach whose team had just lost a match.

"It was the right thing to say. I stated what I believe is good for society."

"But it was the wrong moment," Gina added.

I remained steadfast about my debate position. "Should

I follow the people, or should I lead people to convince them about something I believe in? LGBT individuals make up around 7.5% of the population. Isn't democracy about accepting the values of the majority?"

Gina then revealed a personal connection, "Did you know my sister is a member of the LGBT community?"

"The one that came to our election qualification party."

"Yes."

"I had no idea," I responded. It reflects the nature of American society, where individuals often exist within their own bubbles. People frequently remain unaware of the personal lives of those outside their immediate circles. Most of us have limited knowledge of our neighbors' or colleagues' families and loved ones. We engage with them as necessary to accomplish tasks and then retreat to our own bubbles during our leisure time. While occasionally, we may forge closer relationships with a colleague or neighbor, these instances are infrequent. The prevalence of social media has exacerbated this situation, making it even more challenging to connect with others on a meaningfully deeper level.

"She has been sending me messages, saying I'm working for the wrong person. I don't know what to tell her," Gina said, her concern evident.

"Have I lost you as a team member and your vote as well?" My gaze locked onto her eyes, attempting to glean the genuine emotions hidden within. Eyes are often described as the window to the soul, revealing what a person feels even when their facial expressions may suggest otherwise.

"I'm not sure. This all happened so unexpectedly. My sister wants me to leave this campaign."

I tried to calm everyone down, suggesting, "Let's discuss this and avoid making hasty decisions." My entire core committee was present, listening to our conversation.

James declared, "We've lost the election tonight." It was rather unusual for him to be so pessimistic. It was the first sign of the gravity of the situation and what lay in store for me the very next day.

"We should not jump to extreme conclusions. It is an important social issue. I am glad Sher decided to speak his mind." Jimmy came to my rescue. Ashraf and Ranbir agreed with him.

I reminded James of our deal, "James, you seem to have forgotten our agreement. An election is not an end but a means to an end. We must not get lost in pursuing a victory and lose sight of our ultimate goals. To improve and better the society"

James replied, "There were two parts to the deal. You were going to do exactly what I asked you to do."

"I am doing precisely what you wanted: to speak my beliefs and expose the hypocrisy of the two parties."

Gina then delivered surprising news, "I just received another message from my sister. She's part of an LGBT activist organization, and they're calling a meeting tomorrow morning."

I had no idea that the next day, I would become the focal point of a debate not only in our city but across the entire country. Nonetheless, I slept soundly that night oblivious of the storm gathering at my doorstep.

Twenty-Nine

A storm in a teacup

August 17th, 2066

I awoke to a storm, at home and in the world beyond my home front yard. In all fairness, I had expected some backlash from LGBT groups and had mentally braced myself for it. However, the actual events that unfolded were beyond my wildest expectations.

Nour, my wife, received messages from her colleagues and former students, accusing her of living with a discriminatory hate monger and anti-LGBT individual. She had woken up earlier than me to prepare for her day and checked her messages as a habit. She woke me up.

"It is a steep price to pay for your politics," Nour lashed out angrily at the breakfast table. "Kids are scared to go to school today."

"It will pass," was all I could offer. I was expecting it to subside soon. I was still operating under the assumption that these were usual reactions from some people. The attention span of people has gone down since the ubiquitous use of social media. Reactions would boil over if people did not agree with a comment or opinion and would subside as quickly as they had risen.

"You had warned us about political opponents attacking you," Nour continued to vent her frustrations. "But you never prepared us for this. Now, we're in the eye of the storm, through no fault of our own."

She was right about her concerns. Later that day, my children were bullied at their school and on social media. I told her to take the kids to her parent's home after school and spend a few days there to be away from any potential protest in front of our house.

My communication inbox and social media were flooded with messages branding me as an enemy of the people, as someone full of hate against those different from us, and as someone who had no right to be a candidate.

The reactions of people were quite possibly triggered by the media's coverage of my comments. Newspaper headlines screamed something like, *"The Third Way party is anti-LGBT,"* or *"The Third Way Party wants to deny rights to LGBT and turn us into an intolerant society."* The reports cherry-picked segments of my comments from the previous night's debate, creating a narrative that suited their agenda. Media thrived on concocting a controversy and it was another reason people did not trust them.

Morning shows on almost all channels were exploiting the controversy. They had found an event that served as a catalyst to whip up a frenzy out of thin air, stoking emotions. It was what they called a "storm in a teacup." They raised concerns about rising intolerance in society, playing a ten-second snippet of my statement, where I referred to LGBT relations as an anomaly, but conveniently ignored the rest of my speech explaining what I meant. Pundits from both the right and left concurred that hate and intolerance were on the rise, and something needed to be done post haste about it.

I noticed missed calls on my device from the media. I sent a message to James: "Issue a statement stating that we have nothing more to say on the subject. Remind them that they should show all my comments, rather than just a small piece of it."

"I told you last night we are in deep waters. But we will do whatever it takes to regain lost ground." James's response made me happy. I did not want to lose him over this controversy. That would be the death blow to my campaign.

There were messages from other candidates of the Third Way platform expressing concern about the impact of my comments on their campaigns and demanding an urgent meeting of the party central committee. James promptly scheduled an emergency meeting for the next day.

Gina provided an update early in the morning, revealing that our support had plummeted by almost 40% overnight. I tried to lighten the mood with some dry humor, "At least my name recognition issue is resolved. The whole nation knows about us." Gina responded with a worried face emoji, and I couldn't help but smile. In every crisis, a bit of comic relief can make it more bearable.

Alex and Jimmy reported that half of our volunteers had withdrawn their commitment to work for our campaign. Ranbir and Ashraf informed us that donors had backed out from their pledges and refused to provide further support. We were losing ground on all fronts, and what we thought would help us—the debates—was now causing considerable damage.

As I was getting my head around this multitude of crises, an unexpected message from James delivered a blow to my efforts. I learned that MSBC and CNNBC decided to deny us the platform for the remaining two debates. It was a significant setback. Seeking clarity, I questioned James about the reasons behind this decision.

"Why?" I asked, trying to make sense of the situation.

James responded, "They cited impingement of civil rights and hate speech as their reasons to deny us the platform."

"Did you try to contact Anderson?" I was still under the impression that Anderson supported us.

"I sent him a couple of messages but no response. I will wait until tomorrow to send another message." James did not sound very hopeful.

This development left me perplexed, especially considering the high ratings our campaign had delivered for the Congressional election debate. Generally, these debates were watched and broadcast for local audiences and not meant for national consumption. I had been allowed to participate in these debates with reluctance. The media's decision to withdraw their support at the first sign of trouble seemed abrupt but not unexpected.

It became apparent that the media outlets were using the pretext of civil rights concerns and hate speech as a cover for their true motive. The real reason behind denying us the platform could be an attempt to preserve the status quo dominance of the two major parties.

Faced with this unexpected turn of events, we had to develop a strategy to regain it. I told James to prepare a list of options we could consider, and we agreed to discuss it as soon as possible.

Sitting alone at this very writing table, I contemplated the rapidly unfolding events. I ran my finger over the five-dollar bill with the handwritten "good luck" words, but it felt like my good luck had run out. I pondered how a small segment of society could have such extraordinary power, even to the extent of magnifying a simple disagreement was blown out of rational proportion. This issue highlighted a flaw in modern democracy, where a vocal minority could often dominate the silent majority, just as the elite and warlords did in ancient times. In today's world, special interest groups and passionate organizations play a similar role.

I debated whether I should retract my words and issue an apology. But an apology for what? To express my views? For disagreeing with the opinion of one group? If they had the support of the majority, they could express it on Election Day, rather than resorting to aggressive tactics that bordered on bullying and infringed on the rights of others. I had not made a hateful statement; I had simply expressed my opinion about the social situation. I decided to stand by my earlier statement and not yield to public pressure.

Around 1:00 pm, I received an urgent message from Gina, informing me that about a hundred people had gathered outside our campaign office with placards, demanding my withdrawal as a candidate and an unconditional apology. Every politician faces a choice between standing firm on his ideological belief or succumbing to public pressure for the sake of votes. I could change my views if convincing arguments were presented. But no one was suggesting a debate on the merits of the issue. They were demanding my submission to their will.

I replied, "Call 911 to request police protection. Do you recognize anyone in the crowd?" Remembering that Gina's sister had called a meeting of her LGBT organization this morning.

"Yes. I see my sister among the crowd." Gina confirmed my suspicion.

"Order food, snacks, and drinks for the protesters. I am on my way to the office." I was relieved that the leader of the protest was known to us, and it could be something that we could work with.

After a quick shower and change of clothes, I headed to the campaign office. I made sure to wear casual clothes to convey my middle-class roots and my empathy with the protesters despite our disagreements. Upon arrival, I found the crowd had grown to over 200 people. They were peaceful but resolute in their demands. Music played, some danced to the tune, and LGBT couples waved rainbow flags. I decided to address them from across the road, with the police behind me preventing anyone from reaching our office.

In a brief speech, I told them, "I respect your right to peaceful protest. I respect your opinion about adopting and supporting a particular way of life. I respect your right to disagree with me. But you must grant me the same rights as a fellow citizen. Fortunately, we live in a democracy where diverse views are heard, considered, and protected. The police behind me are here to safeguard the rights of every citizen. I respect your demands, but they are undemocratic. If you disagree with me, rather than protesting, go out and vote for the candidate you support. I will accept the people's verdict on November 2nd, and I hope you will do the same."

Whether it was the free food, my speech encouraging them to express disagreement through voting, or simply exhaustion, the protesters dispersed by 5:00 pm.

The day ended with some positive news for our campaign. The interfaith alliance issued a press statement, stating that they did not consider my comments on LGBT couples as hate speech, although they did not endorse my campaign. I still appreciated the gesture.

I sent a message to Jimmy, "Thank you for at least some good news on a hellish day." He was one of the founding members of the interfaith alliance in the city.

"I admire your courage to say things that require a lot of character. It is not every day we see such courage in today's politicians. I am glad I am part of the team," Jimmy responded to give me strength and courage.

"We're ending the day on a positive note, so I remain hopeful," James remarked, his sportsman's instincts were back in play.

The five-dollar bill with the handwritten "good luck" remained my lucky charm, and it felt like my father's unwavering support was with me all along, much like when he picked me up as a toddler or steadied me while I learned to ride a bike.

The controversy was indeed a storm in a teacup, passing as quickly as it had erupted. Such short-lived artificial storms in teacups have become a common phenomenon in a modern democracy, fueled by the ubiquitous spread of social media activists hungry for attention through controversy.

There were numerous challenges to put the campaign back on track, my priority was to address concerns within the Third Way party. Calming the candidates was essential, as their confidence played a crucial role in regaining support from donors and volunteers. Despite these manageable issues, I hadn't anticipated the unexpected betrayal from Anderson, a development that added a layer of complexity to the situation. I had unrealistically assumed that his high ratings and attention would align him with us in the remaining two debates.

"Big brother. I know you respect people and do not discriminate. Hate has never gotten hold of you even when you were unjustly hurt. Your statements are misunderstood and misrepresented," Zar Wareen attempted to reassure me, recognizing my character as a sibling and the challenges of public perception.

Amid this crisis, my mother remained a steadfast source of support. Her unwavering trust in her upbringing and her confidence in my ability to emerge stronger provided a sense of stability. In the turbulent world of politics, having someone who believed in you unconditionally was a grounding force.

Navigating through the complexities of internal party dynamics and unexpected betrayals, my personal relationships became crucial anchors.

Thirty

Media Moguls

S eated at his writing table, Sher Shah reflected on the whirlwind of events that unfolded following the first debate. As he reflected on the crisis that ensued from his comments on LGBT couples, he marveled at the strategic steps his team had taken to navigate the turbulence. A man who typically sought routine and predictability in his mundane life, Sher Shah was surprised by the unanticipated manner in which he confronted and managed the situation.

As he penned down these past events, Sher Shah felt a certain sense of joy in the act of writing. It was as if he was preparing himself for a peaceful departure from this world. It's curious how, when we enter this world, we arrive crying, as if we are instinctively aware that life will be a challenging journey at times. Open wounds in our hearts make us restless, and departing with them feels like a heavy burden.

Sher Shah found contentment in the knowledge that there

were no lingering wounds within his soul. With this inner peace, he was ready to depart from this world with a profound sense of satisfaction and without any lingering regrets. Above all, it was his paramount goal to finish narrating his life's story before the lights within his physical body dimmed. He hoped to finish it before fate caught up to him.

However, as each day passed, the pain intensified in various organs, and it became increasingly challenging for him to sit for extended periods to write. He possessed a burning desire to complete his narrative swiftly, yet the mounting physical discomfort presented a formidable obstacle.

* * *

August 18, 2066

The handling of the storm after my LGBT couple comments revealed a previously untapped reservoir of resilience and adaptability within me. What had started as an unforeseen challenge had transformed into an opportunity for growth and self-discovery. The crisis prompted me to reassess my values and perceptions, leading to a newfound understanding of the complexities surrounding the issues at hand. In a way, I was being prepared to handle legislation in case voters gave me their trust to be their agent in the US Congress.

I was beginning to recognize that the ability to navigate unexpected challenges was an integral part of leadership. The experience not only reshaped my campaign strategy but also redefined my perspective on the dynamic nature of public life. In the face of adversity, I emerged not only as a candidate but as a person who could adapt, learn, and evolve in pursuit of a greater purpose.

Two days after the tumultuous debate, when the worst of the storm seemed to have passed, James organized a virtual reality meeting for the central committee of the Third Way party. I anticipated their anger based on the messages they had sent to my communication ID, and I was prepared for them to vent their frustrations. I reminded myself to remain patient and not take all this personally.

I sat there for an hour, listening to the committee members' impassioned rants. They labeled me as the party's killer in its early stages, accused me of insensitivity to the impact of my comments on other candidates, and alleged that I secretly held extreme right-wing views while claiming to be a moderate. They believed my statements were slowly poisoning our election prospects.

In my defense, I reminded them that we were a Third Way party, emphasizing our commitment to taking a moderate stance on sensitive social issues. I pointed out that the LGBT community constituted 7.5% of the population, and in a democracy, the majority's choice should be respected. I emphasized that the collective wisdom of people is the hallmark of democracy. I also shared the statement from an interfaith alliance denying the blame on me to be the perpetrator of hate speech and did not deem my remarks as anti-LGBT. I implored the committee to stay united and collectively explore ways to address the situation while devising a mechanism for handling such issues in the future.

After an hour of debate, the committee ultimately decided that James should issue a press statement clarifying that my statements did not represent the party's official position. However, there would be no apology from the party. This last point was a concession I appreciated.

Towards the end of the meeting, some members of the committee suggested my removal from the central committee. While I understood their position, I emphasized that this move would send a negative signal about the unity within the party's leadership. Instead, I proposed that the committee vote on whether I should remain or resign, on the condition that the voting should be done anonymously, rather than through a show of hands.

In the last few months of my election campaign, I learned a fundamental principle of politics - it primarily operates in gray areas of life rather than adhering to clear-cut divisions between black and white. People who appeared to support one side might actually vote differently in private when not judged by others. It was because humans often leaned towards herd mentality, seeking compromise and group acceptance even when they disagreed with a particular path. Politicians were no exception. A politician might say one thing in public to avoid party or public backlash but act differently in private. It was one of the reasons for the lack of trust in politicians, although this attitude was not exclusive to them. I was certain that some committee members were making angry statements to evade public reactions, just as some secretly agreed with my statements but were too afraid to admit it publicly.

James quickly organized an online anonymous vote. As expected, 17 out of 29 committee members voted in favor of my remaining on the committee, securing a simple majority. I was relieved because removal from the committee would adversely affect my election prospects. This was the second mini-election I won before Election Day. It increased my confidence that there was a real possibility I could win the election.

After the meeting, I messaged James, "Next, we need to secure our spot in the two remaining debates. Please arrange a meeting with Anderson."

Within half an hour, James responded, "We have a meeting at the Royal Golf Club at 2:00 PM. I'll pick you up at 1:30."

To my surprise, Anderson appeared to be in high spirits when we met. I couldn't fathom why he would be so cheerful after the storm that had followed the debate.

"The ratings went through the roof. People love controversy, even if they act angry about it," he explained. Human nature is amazing, self-interest supersedes everything else.

"Do you agree with my statements?" I inquired, curious about his stance.

"It doesn't matter whether I agree or disagree. My role is to ensure that all views are represented and heard," Anderson replied, conveniently donning the hat of a professional journalist when it suited him. In theory and ethics, he was right that a journalist should report without bias. However, the reality was different. News channels had assumed ideological positions on most political issues, with some supporting the right and others leaning to the left. It wasn't just politicians who had polarized society; the media shared a portion of the blame.

"But we've been excluded from your next two debates," I got straight to the point. "We delivered the ratings, and you decided to drop us. Is that fair?"

"In the world of media, nothing is set in stone. The channels loved the ratings we achieved, but they had to state support to civil rights organizations to not give them a cause for concern and avoid backlash," Anderson explained and defended.

James chimed in, "What do you suggest we do?"

"Media organizations fear public opinion, and the corporations fear legal action," Anderson became our advisor. We shared a common interest. He loved controversy that could guarantee ratings and we needed access to debates. "Filing a lawsuit, especially one seeking damages, can harm the company's stock price."

Anderson concluded with this advice, "File a petition with the court, seeking a determination on whether your debate statements can be classified as hate speech and pursuing damages from MSBC/CNNBC. It will provide them with a reason to include you in the two remaining debates and relieve pressure on them from civil rights organizations."

Following Anderson's guidance, James asked one of his lawyer friends to draft a petition and file it in the county court. We issued a press release to ensure that the news reached the public, prompting the channels to retract their earlier decision to exclude me from the two remaining debates.

My campaign funds were dwindling, and I needed to secure some of the pledged donations. I asked Ranbir and Ashraf to share the interfaith statement and news of our continued participation in the debates with the donors. I also arranged a virtual meeting to address donors' concerns directly. This approach worked, and our financial position gradually improved.

The final task on my agenda was a heart-to-heart conversation with my children. We gathered for dinner, and during this meal, I offered a heartfelt apology for inadvertently subjecting them to bullying. I explained that bullies often acted out of their insecurities and had weak character traits. I encouraged my children never to be afraid of them and advised them to seek assistance if they ever found themselves unable to handle such situations alone. This conversation helped alleviate their fear and anxiety, though it was clear that the memories of the bullying would take time to fade.

Over the following four weeks, I diligently worked on rebuilding my election campaign. It was essential to formulate a strategy aimed at winning back the voters we had lost in the next debate. Failing to do so would lead to an embarrassing defeat on Election Day. Recognizing the importance of this, I contacted James to arrange a meeting with Aaron for consultation.

Thirty-One

Back to the drawing board

Sher Shah sat at the table, pondering the profound lessons he had learned during the first debate. He couldn't help but recollect the surprise he felt at Anderson's reaction to his comments on the LGBT issue and the subsequent backlash. It was a stark reminder that the misfortune of one person could sometimes translate into gains for another.

Sher Shah's thoughts then drifted to his meeting with Aaron after the first debate as they prepared for the upcoming debates. The reaction he received during that meeting was yet another surprise. With his pen in hand, he began to document the details of that encounter.

* * *

August 20th, 2066

In contemplating the nature of various professions, I reflected on the inherent dichotomy that existed among them. Certain professions, like doctors, lawyers, and police, were built on addressing the miseries and challenges faced by others. It wasn't a matter of fault; rather, it was simply the nature of their work to navigate through and alleviate the difficulties that people encountered.

On the other hand, he considered professions such as artists, architects, engineers, and builders as merchants of happiness. These individuals worked in domains that allowed them to create and contribute to the positive aspects of life, dealing in the currency of smiles and joy. Whether through the creation of beautiful art, the design of inspiring structures, or the construction of functional and aesthetically pleasing spaces, these professionals had the ability to enhance the well-being and happiness of others.

This reflection underscored the diverse roles that different professions played in society, with some focused on addressing challenges and alleviating pain, while others were dedicated to creating joy and enhancing the quality of life. The acknowledgment of this balance highlighted the intricate web of interconnected roles that collectively contributed to the functioning and richness of human experience.

Recognizing the critical juncture in my campaign and the potential pitfalls of the upcoming debate, I acknowledged the need for Aaron's expertise to navigate the narrow channel ahead. The stakes were high, and another misstep could be a significant setback, possibly dealing a death blow to your efforts to regain ground.

In seeking Aaron's help, I understood the importance of

careful planning and effective communication in the realm of political debates. Aaron's experience and guidance could prove instrumental in crafting a message that resonated with the audience, addressing concerns, and steering the conversation in a way that would benefit your campaign.

Navigating the complexities of a political campaign required a team effort, and enlisting Aaron's help underscored the importance of making informed decisions and maximizing our chances of success in the challenging terrain of the next debate. I had the potential to make another mistake on live TV, if not contained by expert advice.

Our meeting with Aaron was scheduled for Friday, August 20th, 2066. The day before our meeting, I received a message from James that read, "It appears Aaron is just as eager to meet with us as we are with him. Our appointment is set for Friday at 2:30 pm at his studio, and I'll pick you up at 2:00 pm."

"Do you think Anderson had a hand in this?"

"We will find out on Friday."

During our ride to Aaron's studio, we discussed the key topics we intended to cover in our meeting. Our primary focus was to create a strategy for generating positive reactions in upcoming debates. We only had two strikes left to achieve that. I couldn't help but feel concerned about my ability to shock people with my unconventional statements, even if I genuinely believed in what I was saying.

Upon our arrival at Aaron's office, he greeted us with a warm smile and exclaimed, "You're a celebrity now! Congratulations on your success."

The reactions of individuals like Anderson and Aaron suggested that both the media and artists thrived on abnormal events and situations. In their view, any form of fame, even if it was controversial, could be leveraged as an asset. I pondered whether some of these actors and actresses intentionally concocted rumors to remain in the media spotlight. I wished I could ask Aaron this question, but the twinkle in his eye hinted that it might hold some truth.

I replied to Aaron's congratulatory remark with a touch of annoyance, "What success, Aaron? I've been through hell since that debate."

Aaron swiftly defended his comment, "Don't get me wrong. Look at the bright side. Just a few days ago, no one knew your name, and your pollster was concerned about your name recognition. Now, you're at the center of the national debate. It's not every day that a person experiences such a meteoric rise to fame."

James chimed in to support Aaron's viewpoint, stating, "Controversy is almost inevitable for a politician. It's just part of the process, and some statements will inevitably rub certain people the wrong way."

I addressed them both, "Alright, but this reputation could cost me the election. How can we turn it in our favor?"

Aaron responded, "Yes, we can turn it around. I have a plan that I'd like to share with you. But keep one thing in mind - another controversy like the first debate will be the end of your election campaign. You've used up all your chances for error. No more shock and awe." With that, he began outlining his strategy for our consideration.

It was evident that Aaron was well-prepared for this discussion, having likely encountered similar situations before. He presented a practical plan to help me project a perspective that would resonate with the public.

His strategy consisted of three key components. First, he

provided me with a list of linguistic terms that held positive resonance among the public. He wanted me to memorize and practice it. He also created three-dimensional video clips of my performance in the first debate to pinpoint areas of improvement in my facial expressions, posture, and hand gestures. Second, he designed a personality survey that Gina would administer to collect data from voters. This survey specifically focused on people's perceptions of my personality based on my performance in the first debate and whether they had a positive or negative view of me. Aaron also developed a plan for focus group discussions with carefully selected voters based on demographic criteria to gain insight into their perception of our election campaign. Third, utilizing the data and feedback from these sources, we agreed to conduct four practice sessions in the two weeks leading up to the second debate.

I felt considerably more confident after hearing Aaron's plan, and the results from my performance in the subsequent two debates exceeded even his expectations.

Thirty-Two

Right to choose

September 13th, 2066

On the day of the second debate, James picked me up at 5:00 pm. This time, Nour chose to stay home as the shock from the first debate still lingered in her memory. She wanted to be with the kids, watching the second debate in the safety and comfort of our home.

As I settled into the car, James, a smirky smile adorning his face, greeted me with a question, "Are you going to surprise us again tonight?"

I responded with a smile, "What if I do surprise you?"

"Please make it a pleasant surprise," clearly enjoying the highs and lows of the roller coaster ride of the election campaign. It was becoming evident to me that this constant high-adrenaline exercise could be quite addictive. Transitioning back to a slow-paced, mundane life was a challenge for those who had been involved in the world of public life.

I playfully teased James, "I'll try, but I can't promise." I knew he relished being on the edge and was addicted to the rush of high-octane moments.

The debate began on time, and I immediately noticed a shift in Roberto's attitude. He seemed to be ignoring me and directing his criticism towards the incumbent Democrat, Kevin. His election strategist had possibly taken note of my comment about him being an ally of the other party. They should have focused their efforts on Kevin from the start, as I wasn't the primary threat to their election prospects. Instead, I could potentially eat into Kevin's support that would benefit them.

The debate proceeded, addressing policy issues one by one, until Anderson asked how to address carbon emissions, which had continued to rise despite three decades of global efforts. It contributed to the increasing environmental temperature. Roberto and Kevin reiterated their parties' longstanding positions, which had remained unchanged for as long as anyone could remember. Republicans downplayed the issue's importance, while Democrats demanded extensive commitments from businesses, making it challenging for them to comply. The economic cost of compliance had made many US corporations noncompetitive. I sensed an opportunity to make an impact.

I seized the moment, asserting, "Kevin is directly responsible for the bad air and noise pollution in the city. He has consistently supported legislation that favors technology companies, especially air taxi service providers, and he's profited greatly from it himself. On the other hand, Roberto continues to deny that climate change is a real issue to appease his Republican Party bosses and loyalists." I targeted both candidates, and it was evident that Anderson was delighted. I could see the ratings climbing in his starry eyes.

But I wasn't finished. I made a promise to the voters on the spot, "I commit to voting in favor of every piece of legislation that aims to improve air, water, and soil pollution. However, I have two grievances. First, the people have consistently re-elected Kevin despite his pro-business stance at the expense of society as a whole." I paused momentarily, as Aaron had advised me to do in our coaching sessions, to make a key policy statement for maximum impact. "Second, on average, each of us uses ten different electronic devices that generate heat in the environment. This increasing heat signature from every citizen contributes to rising overall temperatures. We need to evaluate the use of these devices and consciously reduce their number. I'll also initiate a campaign to secure research grants for reducing electronic device heat emissions and demand that manufacturers adhere to heat emission standards."

Roberto and Kevin in their counter arguments vehemently criticized my proposal, arguing that it would adversely affect our lifestyle and warning of potential economic consequences for manufacturers. They defended their records and expressed concerns about potential job losses due to the high economic costs of regulatory compliance if my proposals were adopted.

Interestingly, the most memorable moment of the debate wasn't related to the climate issue but instead focused on women's abortion rights, which Anderson brought up right after.

"Mr. Shah, we're familiar with the positions of the Republican and Democratic parties. What is your stance on abortion rights and state support for planned parenthood?" Anderson's expression suggested he was seeking a more radical response, aiming to attract more viewers. It seemed he wanted to use me as a shock jock once again.

I responded with a mischievous smile, "Thank you for asking this crucial question, Anderson. Our Constitution promises every citizen the right to life, liberty, and the pursuit of happiness. It is a gender-neutral constitutional right. It does not differentiate between genders; it grants women the same right to choose a path that ensures their life, liberty, and happiness, just like any other citizen. You all know that pregnancy, especially the first one, can be risky. Since the state has promised to help every citizen equally in their pursuit of happiness, it should provide as much support as a woman needs."

Roberto was the first to react, "We cannot support ending a life. People should be more mindful about starting a family rather than terminating an unborn child."

I questioned him, "Do you consider an unborn child to be a citizen of the state, Mr. Roberto? If so, why don't we provide women the right to claim an unborn child on their taxes as credit and accumulate resources for the child's future well-being?"

Kevin had no choice but to support my position, "It's far-fetched to consider an unborn child a full citizen, but we do want women to have the right to choose, and the state should provide support for abortion and continue funding planned parenthood."

My response aimed to take the conversation further, "That's not the point I'm making, Mr. Kevin. It's not just about dollars and cents. I'm asking why we're making politics out of women's bodies and questioning how they manage it. Why haven't we discussed men's responsibilities regarding reproductive control? Why is it that women are always the focus of such debates? Why aren't we paying women equal wages in the job market, even though it has improved over the past few decades? The issue is not just about whether abortion should be allowed or whether the state should bear the cost. The real issue is equal rights for all citizens, regardless of their gender. We live in a male-dominated society, that should change as we approach the twenty-second century."

Roberto emphasized his party's opposition to any efforts to amend the Constitution, defending it as a sacred document that had served the nation well for over three hundred years. Kevin reiterated the Democratic Party's stance in support of women's right to abortion and state assistance.

Anderson was relentless in his pursuit of provocative content, asking me, "Mr. Shah, what solution are you proposing regarding abortion rights?"

I was kind of expecting this question and would have been disappointed if he had not asked me.

"I propose two things. First, we should uphold the constitutional rights granted to all citizens without gender bias. Second, it's not the role of courts to deny women their constitutional rights. To definitively address this issue, we should let women decide whether abortion should be allowed. We should hold a referendum on this matter, with only female citizens casting their votes. Why are men voting on an issue that doesn't primarily concern them?" I delivered the shock and awe Anderson had anticipated. I wasn't sure if my campaign team considered it a positive or negative development for us.

Roberto contended that men had a say in abortion since

they shared equal responsibility for the pregnancy. Kevin, on the other hand, expressed support for some of my demands, which I considered a political victory, as it was likely to help me gain some of his voters. However, both of them rejected my proposal to hold a referendum on abortion rights, exclusively voted on by women.

The remainder of the debate involved discussions of nominal issues and candidates jockeying for screen time. After the debate, James and Gina met me on the stage.

"You won the debate tonight. Everyone will be talking about it tomorrow," James said with excitement.

Gina chimed in, "Our approval ratings have jumped and crossed the levels we had before the first debate. We're the top choice among women voters, who make up nearly 51% of registered voters. We're also leading among younger voters under the age of thirty, although they have a low voter turnout. However, we're lagging among voters 50+ years old, who have a higher voter turnout."

I playfully inquired, "Do you think your sister will have a better opinion of me tonight and vote for me?" I recalled her reaction to my first debate.

Gina responded, "She messaged me, saying she would have voted for you after hearing your comments on abortion if you withdrew your statements about LGBT couples."

"Let's keep working; we have eight more weeks to go," I said, eager to capitalize on the enthusiasm.

On my way home, I received three messages that held personal significance.

Nour's message read, "You did well tonight. I'm proud of you."

My sister, Zar Wareen, messaged, "You should have been a

human rights lawyer, not me, big brother."

My father-in-law's message simply stated, "You won tonight." If nothing else, I had earned respect from my family.

The following day, discussions continued to center around abortion and women's rights, though not to the same extent as we had experienced after the first debate. I remained puzzled as to why my statements about abortion rights did not elicit as strong and charged a response as my comments on a relatively minor controversial topic. The human psyche remained an enigma, an ever-evolving work in progress.

The Third Way party had captured national attention, and candidates were steadily gaining support in most constituencies.

Thirty-Three

A dirty act

ﾟ❀ﾟ

As his terminal cancer continued to progress, Sher Shah found himself too weak to even walk with the assistance of a walking stick. His wife gently brought him to his writing table. Sher Shah recognized the urgency to finish documenting the events of the third debate. With each passing day, he considered himself fortunate, as his doctor had informed him that he was already living on borrowed time.

With a determined spirit, he activated a few buttons on his handheld device to display the photograph taken after the third debate. In the image, Anderson occupied the central position, with Roberto on his right and Kevin on his left. Sher Shah stood beside Roberto, forming a trio of candidates flanking the moderator. This photograph had been captured as a memento at the close of the third debate, and each of the participants had signed a copy, cherishing it as a keepsake.

Sher Shah knew that it was this third debate that would ultimately define his performance on Election Day.

* * *

October 18th, 2066

As we approached the final stages of the election campaign, with just two weeks left until Election Day, our campaign office was abuzz with activity every day. Volunteers, pollsters, and staff members were all diligently carrying out their assigned tasks, including reaching out to voters, answering their questions, managing our social media presence, and conducting frequent surveys to gauge the voters' sentiments. I made sure to stick to our commitment to holding regular core committee meetings every Saturday. Our campaign had successfully raised close to 300,000 aÇ, exceeding our initial budget by 50,000 aÇ. Most of this funding came from voters who believed in our message, giving us a significant boost in our election prospects. We proudly shared this achievement in our press releases, town hall meetings, and social media posts.

My campaign team was growing increasingly confident that we might have a shot at crossing the finish line and winning the election. Despite our relatively short six-month campaign, it felt like we had come a long way both as a team and as individuals. My lack of a political background had turned out to be an asset, attracting those who were disillusioned with the two major parties. James' strategy had proven to be effective.

I wanted to use the third debate to reinforce that we had fresh ideas to solve problems.

Nour, initially hesitant about attending the debates, agreed to accompany me this time. I also extended invitations to my entire core team and close family, including Alex, Ranbir, Ashraf, Jimmy, and my in-laws, Dr. Rabbani and Afshan Rabbani, and my sister.

The day before the third debate, Alex had a question for me. "Do you regret your decision to run for office?"

I responded, "Not at all. This is important work, and I'm grateful that your question prompted me to embark on this journey."

"Do you think the voters will give us their mandate?"

"Why not? All the surveys suggest that people are tired of the two parties and are looking for a third option."

I wanted to assure him and myself. "Don't forget to show up for the third debate tomorrow," I reminded him before leaving, and he confirmed with a smile.

On the morning of the debate, I received a message from Gina, who shared her research findings. "My research and surveys show that we are drawing support away from Kevin. Be careful during today's debate; he'll likely try to undermine you."

I thanked her for the timely warning. During the car ride to the debate, I asked James, "What do you think Kevin's strategy will be to attack us?"

James replied, "His team must have thoroughly researched your background, dating back to your birth. Is there anything we should be concerned about, besides the boiler accident?"

"Nothing I can think of," I assured him.

"Don't worry, then. We started with a mere 5% chance of success, and now we're considered serious contenders. We have nothing to lose," James encouraged me. "Just enjoy the limelight and have fun tonight. But don't do anything foolish," he added, still remembering the debacle of the first debate.

Upon arriving at the debate stage, I noticed an exchange of glances between Anderson and Kevin, hinting at a possible secret understanding. As was customary, Anderson asked us to make opening statements or address a topic of our choice. I began with my concerns about environmental deterioration, rising healthcare costs, the advent of 3D-printed organs that were out of reach of most people, and people's safety concerns regarding air taxis. These were the key issues identified by Gina's research as important to the voters. Roberto highlighted his record and contributions to the farming sector, while Kevin launched a personal attack on me, instigating a confrontation that would last throughout the debate.

Kevin began his introduction by expressing gratitude to the voters for entrusting him with the role of representing them in the U.S. Congress for the past two decades. He took pride in the contributions he believed he had made to the growth and prosperity of the city. He urged voters to focus on the track record and performance of the candidates and advised them to reject those who had demonstrated negligence in their lives.

However, Kevin's attention quickly turned towards me, initiating the attack that Gina had warned me about. He alleged, "Mr. Shah almost cost the life of his colleague who was a member of his team and was terminated for negligence. Legislation is a serious business and requires individuals who are responsible." Kevin revealed his intent to destroy our chances, with a personal attack. While this attack reminded me of the incident that had initially motivated me to enter politics, it no longer had the power to make me feel guilty and remorseful about it. For me, it was a closed chapter and no longer mattered.

Anderson then turned to me and asked if I wanted to respond, his smirk indicating a deeper game at play. It became clear that they had used me as a pawn and were now casting me aside since my purpose was to achieve a higher number of viewers – now it was time to ensure the two parties continued their hold on power. I silently thanked Gina for her warning earlier that morning and Aaron for preparing me to handle this scenario.

I addressed Kevin's attack by defending my actions. "Mr. Johnson is a seasoned politician, and politicians are losing the respect of the people because they often distort facts. There was no negligence on my part or my team's in the boiler accident he is referring to. The whole incident underwent a thorough investigation, led by independent inspectors from the food company and state regulator. My name was cleared by the inspectors and investigators. I had the option to pursue legal recourse for wrongful termination. This incident catalyzed my decision to enter politics. I believe in creating a socially just society where individuals who have been wrongfully blamed or have served time for minor offenses should be allowed to have a second chance. I'm committed to working on legislation that offers people that second chance."

Following my response, Roberto took the floor. "Mr. Johnson should not boast about his voting record or attempt to take credit for the city's prosperity," he asserted. "As we have pointed out in previous debates, he has consistently voted to benefit big business interests. He even voted against the water conservation bill proposed by the Republican Party. Our city's economic strength lies in agriculture, given the rising global demand for food. I am proud that our agricultural reforms at the state congress have transformed this city into a contributor to global food supply, particularly to impoverished nations."

It was evident that Roberto's team had recognized the advantage of targeting Kevin while offering their support to me in the face of his attacks. The dynamics of the debate were shifting, and the battle for voters' trust was intensifying.

During the debate, Anderson posed a question about the concerns raised by economists regarding a potential recession and asked Roberto about the Republican Party's economic plan to prevent it. Roberto's response adhered to the party's long-standing formula: low taxes and a focus on small government. In contrast, Kevin presented the traditional counter-formula of his party, advocating for social security for the people, higher taxes to fund government initiatives, and more regulation of the securities market. Evidently, new or innovative ideas could not be expected from these old-school politicians.

When it was my turn to weigh in on the economic matter, I prefaced my response by emphasizing my background as an engineer, where the fundamental principle is that $1+1$ should equal two. However, I noted that this basic arithmetic principle didn't seem to govern our economy. I expressed my concern about the cyclical boom-and-bust patterns that recurred every few decades, citing the cyclical recession caused by the mortgage and bond market crisis. I laid blame on the concept of interest, which I viewed as an instrument of capitalist greed. In my opinion, interest played a pivotal role in creating income inequality and was responsible for the ever-widening wealth gap.

I elaborated on how the reliance on interest had made the

rich wealthier while leaving the poor even more impoverished. Additionally, I argued that it had contributed to uncontrolled government spending, as capitalists often lent money to the government at low-risk, high-interest rates. I stated that interest was the root cause of most of our social and economic problems.

Kevin immediately challenged my viewpoint, asserting, "Mr. Sher is not an economist, as he has acknowledged, and his stance on interest demonstrates his naivete and lack of experience." He aimed to undermine the credibility of my argument.

Roberto chimed in, aligning with Kevin's perspective. "I agree with Kevin on this point," he said. "Interest has been a crucial tool that allowed low- and middle-income families to become homeowners and afford reliable transportation." Roberto's position was influenced by the interests of the party and their alliance with big business, making it unfeasible to challenge the status quo.

Anderson, attempting to give me another opportunity to clarify my stance, asked if I was suggesting the abolition of interest. I responded by explaining that my intention was not to abolish interest at this stage but to advocate for greater government control over how financial institutions used interest to generate profits while increasing the risk for depositors. I emphasized that the uncontrolled use of interest as a profit-making tool had led to significant issues such as home foreclosures, financial crises, bank closures, job losses, and stock market meltdowns. I proposed that it was possible to regulate and control the excessive and layered use of interest by banks and financial institutions. I accepted the fact that the cryptocurrency American Coin had contained the issue to some extent but it was still prevalent through legal and regulatory loopholes that needed to be closed. Furthermore, I suggested that these institutions could contribute more to the economy and make profits by funding new businesses and job creation rather than using money as a commodity to trade. In the event of my election, I pledged to appeal to voters and encourage Congress to assemble a team of economists to develop plans for the regulated use of interest in profit generation.

The debate highlighted the stark ideological differences among the candidates, as Election Day drew nearer.

As I finished my arguments, Anderson glanced at Roberto and Kevin, but they had no appetite for further discussion on this sensitive topic of regulating big banks. He swiftly transitioned to another subject: the use of microchip implants containing individuals' medical data and vital information for emergencies.

Roberto and Kevin both voiced their endorsement of this idea, albeit using distinct language to set themselves apart. However, my stance differed significantly. I articulated my reservations, emphasizing that storing sensitive information in a machine-readable format might pose a risk to individuals' private data. Consequently, I expressed my opposition to the proposal.

The debate had been proceeding well, and I felt increasingly confident that voters would put their trust in me. However, my confidence wavered when Anderson posed the final question of the night, beginning with me.

The question pertained to crime rates and gun laws, subjects I had not considered as pressing issues due to the apparent reduction in mass shootings attributed to recent gun control laws. I discussed how these laws had made our schools and colleges safer and voiced support for a well-resourced and well-trained police force.

Kevin seized this opportunity to attack me once more, pointing out that my team included a convicted member with a criminal record. This revelation took me by surprise, as I had nearly forgotten that Alex had a prior conviction, even though he had served his time. The camera captured my brief moment of hesitation.

In response to Kevin's accusation, I acknowledged that a member of my team had indeed served time for a minor offense but had demonstrated an unwavering desire to become a responsible citizen. I defended giving people a second chance in life, emphasizing that no one should be punished indefinitely for past mistakes.

The damage had been done, and I had no time to fully recover before Election Day, just two weeks away.

After the debate, when Gina and James approached me, I inquired about the survey results. Gina's data indicated that the final attack on me had been effective. It had taken a toll on our support among women and older voters, who were particularly sensitive to concerns about crime rates. However, our support had increased among younger voters, which provided a glimmer of hope. James was determined to keep fighting and suggested that we should meet soon to discuss our approach for the remaining two weeks of the campaign.

During our journey home, I received a message from Alex expressing regret. He mentioned that he wouldn't have volunteered for my campaign if he had known about the attack using a prior criminal record. I tried to assuage his guilt by explaining that I owed my political journey to him and should have used his story as a testament to the importance of giving people a second chance in life. The responsibility for the situation was as much mine as it was his.

Thirty-Four

Alex & me

~ ∽∾∿∾∽ ~

October 19th, 2066

The day after the third debate, James called for an urgent meeting of the core committee at our campaign office. The meeting commenced with Gina presenting her latest poll results. They revealed that the third debate had significantly affected my standing among voters over the age of 40, although we did gain some support from the 18-35 age group. The challenge lay in the fact that the younger demographic had the lowest turnout on Election Day. Gina presented historical data from the past five decades, which clearly illustrated that younger voters were becoming increasingly disillusioned with the democratic process, leading to a gradual decline in their voter turnout, reaching a low point in 2064 with a 37% turnout.

"James, what's the plan?" I inquired immediately after Gina's presentation.

"We need to share Alex's story and inspire the younger generation to come out and support him," James replied, showing that he had already put thought into it. "Alex and you both are now the candidates in this contest."

"And how do you propose we do that?"

James outlined his plan, which involved arranging interviews for Alex to narrate his story and explain why he joined my election campaign. We would also create a short hologram video to be played near community colleges and Fresno State University and have volunteers stationed at places frequented by younger voters.

"I've never done interviews or videos," Alex admitted with a visible sign of nervousness on his face. "I'm not sure if I can do that."

"Everyone starts somewhere, Alex. We'll ask Aaron to coach you and prepare you," I reassured him.

"I need to think about it," Alex replied hesitantly.

"I understand, Alex. Don't feel pressured. If you can't do it, we'll find another way. But we have limited time, so let us know by tomorrow."

"All of this might increase our support among younger voters, but how do we ensure they turn out in larger numbers to vote on Election Day?" Gina, with her analytical mind, still had doubts.

"We need to do something bold on Election Day to motivate them," James responded. "We have two weeks to devise a strategy for Election Day."

My foray into politics stemmed from a genuine desire to provide second chances for individuals like Alex and myself. However, the twists of fate seemed to have intricately linked my political journey with Alex's. We were entangled in life like the entangled particles. Our connection ran deeper than I had initially anticipated. Uncertainty loomed as I pondered whether Alex would agree to face the media. Being a shy and introverted person, overcoming these inherent traits presented a considerable challenge for him — a challenge I knew well from my own transformational journey into the public eye.

Reflecting on that day, I doubted whether Alex would embrace the proposal; his reserved nature suggested a reluctance to endure the spotlight. If forced to wager, I would have bet on him declining. Yet, reality proved me wrong. The very next day, an early morning message from Alex arrived, altering the course of our shared political destiny.

"Professor, do you think I can do it?" Alex seemed to place the weight of this life-changing decision on my shoulders.

"If I can do it, then you can do it. Aaron will prepare you. But if you still feel you cannot do it, you can say no," I responded, not wanting to pressure him into something he might later regret.

"I'll do it. I suppose I need to share my story as much for myself as for you."

That wasn't the only surprise that day. Around noon, I received a message from James.

"Anderson wants to interview Alex," he informed me.

"Do you think Alex can handle it?" I recalled the conversation I had with Alex earlier in the morning.

"Let Aaron coach him, and then we'll see. I'll agree to Anderson's request with the condition that the interview airs a day before Election Day," James, with his never-say-die attitude, wasn't ready to give up until the very end.

These developments heightened my expectations that we

might finally cross the finish line ahead of my two opponents. I was eager for it all to end, as constant campaigning for the past ten months had taken its toll, and I was becoming exhausted.

Thirty-Five

Anderson & Alex

⟨ oͻo ⟩

November 1st, 2066

The day before the election marked the conclusion of our campaign activities. Nour extended a warm invitation, gathering her parents, my sister, and her husband for a family dinner – a rare occurrence since I began campaigning. It served as a fitting way to unwind before Election Day. Nour, known for her sociable nature, frequently hosted friends and families at our house, making the family dinner a special occasion.

Not only was it an opportunity to relax, but we also had another reason to get together. We decided to watch Alex's interview with Anderson, scheduled for prime time at 8:00 pm. Nour, my favorite cook, spent the entire day preparing a delightful menu featuring my favorite South Asian dishes – haleem, mutton aloo gosht, and beef biryani for the main course, followed by gajjar halwa and Kashmiri tea for dessert.

Gathering at 6:30 pm, the family engaged in lighthearted conversation. The children, including my nephew and niece, joined in the festivities, playing a game of basketball in the backyard before the dinner.

After the delicious meal, we all convened in the living room to watch Alex's crucial interview. The stakes were high, as it had the potential to motivate youth to come out and vote. Despite Aaron's coaching, Alex, still nervous, had sought final tips from me that morning. I emphasized the importance of authenticity and truth, reassuring him that honesty, even if painful, was the key to resolving issues.

The introduction before the interview delved into Alex's background, exploring the sensitive topic of underage drug use. Alex appeared calm in a white t-shirt, dark blue jeans, and workmen boots. His tattoos gave the impression of a kid in trouble. He answered Anderson's questions about his background with sincerity.

"Alex, can you tell us about how you met Congressional candidate Mr. Shah," Anderson asked.

Alex narrated the story of our relationship and how I helped him with math in the correction facility to prepare for college.

"Why did you join his election campaign?"

"I felt it was important to contribute in some ways because he decided to contest because of my questions to him."

"Did he ask you to be part of his campaign?"

"No. It was my decision."

"Did you not think that your background could hurt his campaign?"

"No. I never imagined I could hurt rather than help."

"Do you regret your past life?"

"No."

"Why?"

"Would regretting it change anything?"

"No. But regret is the first step to reform." Anderson was prepared to get the most out of him as an expert journalist.

"Past lives with us. Regretting it becomes a constant reminder. I don't want to remember my past. I want to work on my future."

"Did you ever apologize to the kid to whom you sold drugs?"

"No."

"Why not?"

"I got out of prison a few months ago and the family had moved."

"What are your plans?" Anderson wanted to explore.

"I want to be an engineer like Mr. Sher."

"But Mr. Sher failed to do his job and was terminated for negligence. Is he your role model?"

"Yes, he is my role model. He dares to stand up and fight for justice." Alex surprised me with his statement.

"Thank you, Alex. As you all heard, he has no regrets but aspires to improve his future. He has not contacted the family or the kid to apologize for his past mistake. His role model is a person who failed but stood up to fight back. Stay with us we will be back after a short break." Anderson concluded this interrogation-cum-interview by emphasizing failure more than appreciating qualities.

I felt the interview did not help us and our position did not change.

Alex sent me a message after the interview, "Did I mess up?"

"No, you did great. Thank you for going through it." I did not want him to feel bad about something that was not his responsibility.

"We did not gain anything tonight, I checked with Gina," James messaged.

"It's alright. We will see tomorrow." I was beyond getting worried about these things. It was time for voters to decide whom they chose to be their agent and represent them in US Congress for District 23.

Thirty-Six

The day of reckoning

S her Shah looked at the notebook Nour had obtained from an antique shop. She had only managed to find one, and it had a different style compared to the other three he had used. He preferred symmetry in his possessions, and the dissimilar notebook didn't sit well with him. He checked the number of pages he had filled in the second notebook, finding himself a little over the middle. Today, he intended to write about Election Day.

His body ached at nearly every joint, making it increasingly difficult for him to sit and write for extended periods. He took more breaks, often reclining on his couch, eager to complete his life story before it reached its conclusion. The thought of leaving an unfinished tale behind was disheartening. He remembered that Election Day had been a source of relief, marking another significant milestone in his political journey. It was a day that held the promise of bringing about the societal change that had been almost unimaginable just ten months earlier when he embarked on this political career.

* * *

November 2nd, 2066

Advancements in technology have transformed the voting process, streamlining it for voters, enhancing security for election officials, and expediting result reporting for the media. It became routine for results to be available within an hour of the polls closing at 5:00 pm on Election Day. This modernized system eradicated the issues of paper ballots, hanging chads, or counting errors, as technology efficiently managed the process with minimal human intervention.

Nevertheless, conspiracy theorists persisted in questioning the integrity of the results, often positing that they could be manipulated by ruling elites or tampered with by foreign powers. Despite their persistent claims, these theorists failed to present any credible evidence substantiating their assertions.

Early voting had been abolished after the introduction of election technology by the state secretaries. People voted from the convenience of their homes using their fingerprint and iris identification on their handheld devices. Exit polls were replaced with online polls to gauge voters' preferences. It added a layer of sophistication to predict results because of the rich behavioral data available about each citizen. Pollsters were restricted from publishing their election predictions until the votes closed at 5:00 pm local time.

On Election Day, the county clerk's office would publish a web page accessible from any device with a fingerprint and iris reader. Voters simply had to click on the candidate they wished to vote for. They were required to provide their government-issued communication ID, the last four digits of their state-issued social security, and their birth date to complete the process. After entering this information, they scanned their thumb and permitted the device to read their iris. The system ensured the security and privacy of this information. At the end of the voting process, each voter received a receipt with a unique reference number containing all the details about their vote, including the date, time, and device information.

Voting information was stored on government servers. Candidates had the right to verify the integrity of the election by requesting a copy of the voting record. If more than 5% of votes were found to be inaccurately recorded, a recount was automatically triggered, and if more than 10% were flawed, the election was scrapped. These safeguards had worked and developed credibility for it. This system had been in place for two decades. People began to like convenience and trusted it. Turnout had improved over the years, averaging around 65% for congressional elections.

By law, election campaigns had to conclude at midnight the day before voting began on Tuesday. My seven-member election core committee had organized a results party at our election office, and we instructed everyone to arrive by 4:30 pm to socialize before the results started rolling in at 6:00 pm. The office was adorned with American flags and an abundance of purple balloons. It was a festive atmosphere, regardless of the outcome. James advised me to prepare a victory speech.

The County Clerk's office was set to announce results for each zip code, of which there were 42 in my constituency, starting at 6:00 pm.

I woke up early on Election Day, with plans for a brief mountain hike since there wasn't much I could do aside from casting my vote and helping organize the election watch party at our campaign office. After rising, I promptly logged on to the county clerk's voting mobile app to cast my vote, a process that took scarcely a minute.

At 6:00 am, with a backpack stocked with breakfast and water, I set out for the nearby mountains. My car served as a trusty transport, ferrying me to the rugged terrain where I could ponder the intricacies that had defined my journey. The Sierra Nevada Mountain range was my sanctuary—a haven of serenity and revitalization. Having devoted my all to the election campaign, the pivotal decision now lay in the hands of the voters as they selected their representative for the U.S. Congress.

The hike became more than a physical endeavor; it evolved into a ritual to relax and re-energize my body. Surrounded by the majesty of nature, I found solace in the rhythmic crunch of gravel beneath my hiking boots and the crisp mountain air. The trail became a metaphorical path, each step allowing me to shed the burdens of the campaign, if only momentarily.

As I ascended, the memories of the challenges of the campaign seemed to fade into the distant valleys. The mountains became silent witnesses to my contemplation, offering a perspective only nature could provide. With every stride, I embraced the solitude, finding strength in the quietude of the mountains and preparing myself for the journey ahead, whatever it might bring.

Back at home, I took a shower and dressed up in a dark gray suit with a pastel purple shirt.

We left home at 2:00 pm, Nour and the kids were filled with excitement as we drove together to the election campaign office. My mother was happy that it was finally over. Soon after, my father and mother-in-law arrived, as well as my sister and her husband. The office buzzed with activity, equipped with two displays to watch the results – one showing the county office app that refreshed every thirty seconds to show updated results, and the other tuned into MSBC's reporting on Election Day.

Countrywide results began coming in at 3:00 pm from the East Coast, with Third Way party candidates leading in only 20 out of the 100 contested constituencies. At 4:00 pm, Central American states reported their results, and the Third Way had 40 candidates, with six leading in their constituencies. On the West Coast, where I was contesting, the party had 40 candidates, including myself. The early results from East and Central America somewhat dampened my spirits, and I grew restless and mentally prepared for an outcome that was not in my favor.

As the clock struck 6:00 pm, the county commenced reporting results, beginning with the first zip code we clinched by a mere handful of votes. Roberto secured the second position, while Kevin trailed in third. The initial success prompted a burst of excitement and celebratory high-fives. However, as results from subsequent zip codes were tallied and reported, our fortunes began to shift. Roberto consistently outpaced us, and Kevin lingered in the third position. With each reported result, the voting gap between us and Roberto widened.

In the end, victory belonged to Republican Roberto, marking a return to the red for Fresno after three decades of being a stronghold for the blue, the colors of the two parties. Despite our best efforts to turn the city purple, the endeavor had fallen short. The office bore a visible sense of disappointment, a sentiment echoed in my own surprise at Kevin's third-place finish and our own performance securing the second spot. The outcome underscored the unpredictable nature of politics, leaving us to reflect on the challenges faced and the lessons learned during this hard-fought campaign.

Even today, articulating my emotions remains a challenge. The anticipation of victory and the aspiration to set a precedent for challenging the status quo fueled my hopes. However, as the results poured in, my emotions oscillated between hope and joy, tinged with the bitterness of failure and tempered by a surprising sense of relief. The experience was a complex mixture of sentiments, painting a picture that defied simplistic categorization—it was neither entirely black nor white. The shades of gray at that moment encapsulated the intricate tapestry of my journey, reflecting the nuanced nature of political endeavors where success and setback coexist in a delicate balance.

Following the announcement of the results, I delivered a brief speech with my family and core committee standing by my side. I thanked everyone for their unwavering support and reaffirmed my dedication to working for the betterment of our community, even though I was uncertain about what the future held.

The Third Way party emerged victorious in 35 out of 180 contested constituencies, making significant inroads against the two major parties. My immediate reaction was one of deep disappointment and an overwhelming sense of exhaustion. I spent the following week doing nothing but resting. After that week, I began to analyze the results, particularly the poor performance of Kevin in a Democratic-leaning constituency. The voter turnout had been exceptionally high at around 75%, and while youth votes had increased, older and party-affiliated voters turned out in higher numbers than expected. I also consulted with other Third Way party candidates, and a clearer picture started to emerge.

There were rumors of potential election rigging by government officials appointed by the two major parties, but without credible evidence, it was dismissed as a conspiracy theory. Accusing the established electoral system without concrete proof would be unwise.

A more credible report suggested collusion between the two parties without violating any laws. The Republican and Democratic parties had perceived the Third Way party as a genuine threat. They analyzed all 180 congressional seats where we were contesting and arrived at a deal to divide these constituencies between them. A whisper campaign was launched, urging party voters to vote strategically – supporting Republicans in some areas where surveys suggest they were ahead and Democrats in others.

Kevin became a victim of this organized conspiracy hatched by the two major parties. Democrat voters dumped Kevin to protect party interest and voted for Roberto to deny me the victory. They wanted to preserve the two-party system even if it meant defeating their own candidate. The vote difference between my loss and the percentage of higher turnout among party-affiliated voters was almost the same. I could not do anything about it. There was no written record or concrete evidence to take legal action against them.

I couldn't definitively determine whether I had secured victory or faced defeat in the election, but I could certainly count several triumphs. My family now held me in higher regard, and we had successfully established a political platform capable of challenging the entrenched dominance of the two major parties. Our party had elected thirty-five congressmen, which was a significant influence in shaping legislation. Notably, the Republican Party emerged victorious in a constituency they hadn't won in over three decades, largely due to our campaign diverting Kevin's voters. Most importantly, my ultimate triumph lay in the transformation of Alex, as I had seen him on Election Day with fewer tattoos on his face and neck. He was resurfacing and gradually becoming more visible to the world once more.

After the results were announced, Alex approached me, apologizing, "Sorry, Professor."

"There's nothing to be sorry about. We've only just begun," I assured him although I was hurting as much as one could after a long journey without the satisfaction of reaching a destination.

"Son, you were born during the peak of spring when nobody expected you to survive. Never forget that, and shine like a bright spring sun." The words of my father were once again there to save me from depression and despair

Thirty-Seven

Epilogue

❧

Nour assisted him in the study, supporting him with his waist. He walked with a noticeable limp; his face etched with pain. A fall in the bathroom the previous night had left him injured, but at least his hip remained intact, sparing him from a more dire fate. She thoughtfully laid a thick cushion on the chair to alleviate some of his discomfort. Afterward, she brought him a cup of black tea with milk and sugar, a small comfort in a trying time.

Sher Shah, feeling drained and sensing that his time was drawing near, resolved to write each day to document as much as he could. He picked up the second notebook and noted that it was already two-thirds full. Turning to the third notebook, he placed a sticker marked with a #4. Uncertain about how many more days he would have to write, he decided to begin from its end, considering the whirlwind of events that had unfolded since the elections.

April 25th, 2090

The choice to welcome a child into the world is typically a decision made by parents, influenced by a myriad of motivations. The journey into parenthood is often marked by profound transformation, shaped by personal aspirations, shared goals as life partners, and a pursuit of fulfillment. While the endeavor of raising children carries significant personal meaning, it also frequently acts as a cornerstone that has the power to mend strained marriages and fortify the connections between spouses, nurturing sentiments of tenderness and love.

Parents grapple with the moral dilemma of bringing another human being into existence, knowing full well that life can be fraught with hardships. It is not a catwalk where a person walks pretty, looking glamorous. It has sunny days and dark clouds. It has successes and failures. Wouldn't it be better if parents decide not to have a child to prevent traversing such a perilous journey? Despite these challenges, parents who decide to conceive a child aspire to contribute positively to society, driven possibly to overcome the guilt of having a child for selfish reasons. They have the desire to create and leave a better world for their offspring than the one they inherited. In essence, this seemingly self-interested act of parenthood is grounded in the practical ambition of improving the future for the next generation. A child provides a rationale and motivation for parents to reduce the likelihood of conflicts or wars and cultivate compassion. While this perspective may be perceived as cynical, it reflects the practicality of human experience.

Yet, there is a more hopeful aspect to having children. A child represents hope for a brighter future, a collective effort to improve the human condition. Many great contributors to society in fields such as science, philosophy, sports, entertainment, politics, and the arts may never have lived if their parents had chosen not to have children.

It is not to disparage childless couples; their contributions to society are equally valuable. However, the introduction of a child often reshapes a person's perspective on life.

The realm of politics is an intrinsic component of human experience, much like the presence of religion. Ever since the creation of Adam and Eve, politics has played an influential role in shaping the decisions and relationships of humanity. Throughout history, human societies have consistently encompassed elements of politics that have informed various aspects of life.

Politics transcends the grand stage of the larger society; its influence intricately permeates the very fabric of our families. Within the household, parents adeptly employ a mix of incentives and disciplinary measures as tools to shape and guide their children's behavior toward desired ends. This process is essentially a political act, deftly manipulating emotions to achieve specific outcomes. Simultaneously, sibling relationships harbor elements of political maneuvering, as brothers and sisters engage in a subtle contest, vying for limited resources and seeking favor by employing diverse political strategies to attain individual objectives.

The timeless narrative of the rivalry between Cain and Abel, each seeking divine acceptance for their sacrifices, continues to echo in contemporary times. This age-old tale serves as a poignant reminder that, even within the most intimate family dynamics, politics remains a defining aspect of human existence.

The competition for success in the marketplace of ideas and skills once again tests our political acumen. Pleasing supervisors, fostering collaboration with peers, and overseeing team members all demand the deliberate practice of political skills.

This intrinsic political behavior etched into the human psyche extends well beyond the confines of the family and work life and becomes a defining characteristic of public life. People apply political methodologies they have learned both within their households and from their interactions outside the home to navigate the complexities of broader society. In this sense, politics is an ever-present aspect of human existence, shaping both our personal lives and the world at large.

Navigating the balance between self-interest and a commitment to the greater good is one of the most significant challenges for a politician. Those who successfully rise above personal concerns and prioritize the welfare of others often emerge as leaders who shape the course of history. Conversely, those who struggle to do so may find themselves preoccupied with securing re-election in the next political cycle.

The age-old debate on nature versus nurture in the context of leadership remains a persistent consideration. Undoubtedly, an individual is profoundly influenced by their environment, and distinct genetic traits contribute to setting them apart from others. The interplay between inherent qualities and external factors shapes the character and approach of leaders, determining their ability to transcend self-interest and make a lasting impact on collective well-being.

In the pursuit of a fair and flourishing society, the significance of justice cannot be emphasized enough. Fundamental to this quest are elements of social justice, such as freedom of expression, religion, movement, and association. While individuals might tolerate certain levels of inequality arising from circumstances of birth, the tolerance for injustice is notably limited. Societies actively endeavor to rectify real or perceived injustices, and a just state is one that treats every citizen impartially. In this light, the appointment of unbiased and fair judges is often deemed more crucial than the election of capable politicians in the pursuit of justice and equality.

My existence on this earth for 70 years is a reality that could easily have been otherwise. I survived the life-threatening experience of an umbilical cord twisted around my neck in the womb. There's no room for regret in my heart, but if I were granted the choice, I might have opted not to be born. Throughout my life, I've made an earnest effort to maintain a sense of balance. If I were to summarize my life philosophy, it would revolve around my determination to avoid developing a God complex. I've always been conscious of the limits of my knowledge, recognizing that my insights are inherently subjective, and that the realm of absolute truth remains perpetually beyond my reach.

This awareness of the constraints of my understanding of the universe and life has allowed me to embrace my imperfections and the inevitability of making mistakes, as well as the realization that I don't possess all-encompassing solutions to life's myriad challenges or answers to all its profound questions. Additionally, I've constantly borne in mind that every other human being shares my fallibility and is just as susceptible to making errors. Therefore, I've attempted to approach others with compassion and empathy.

However, the endeavor to avoid developing a God complex is far easier said than done. Observing the world around us, we can't help but notice numerous individuals from various domains—politicians, scientists, artists, athletes, celebrities, and business leaders—who seem to exude a God-like aura. They appear to have forgotten that birth inevitably leads to death, and the vulnerability of our mortal existence remains unresolved. Birth and death are intrinsically connected, inextricably bound together, two facets of the same timeless cycle that no human can escape. It is yin and yang forever embraced in a delicate dance.

A self-actualized life requires maintaining a positive cash flow, ensuring financial independence, and the freedom to fully express oneself. While circumstances may occasionally lead to a temporary negative cash flow, the goal should be to restore it to a positive state.

Ultimately, the purpose of life remains a profound and subjective question, open to interpretation and reflection by everyone. It is this question I want to address before the light in my soul is out.

* * *

Sher Shah began to feel discomfort in his wrist, thanks to the mechanical watch adorning it. The timepiece seemed to be digging into his skin, causing a sharp pang of pain. To alleviate the pain, he removed the watch and gently set it down on the writing table nearby.

Contemplating the profound question about the purpose of life, he recognized the need for careful consideration before providing an answer. To concentrate fully on this significant query, he leaned his head upon his notebook to delve into deep thought.

"Shero, lunch is ready." Nour calling him out could be heard in the room. She called him a few more times.

Nour entered the study with a concerned expression, to invite Sher Shah to join her at the lunch table. However, when she entered the room, she noticed that he had dozed off, his head resting on the notebook before him. She placed her hand on his shoulder to wake him up. There was no response. The mechanical watch, which had inflicted the discomfort, sat motionless on the table, its hands halted at 1:30 pm.

About the Author

An author of four books, Abdul Q. Kundi is a visionary storyteller known for weaving intricate narratives that transcend time and societal norms. With a passion for literature and a unique perspective, Kundi explores the complexities of human experience and the interplay of power, ideology, and resilience. A master of speculative fiction, his works challenge conventional thinking, prompting reflection on societal intricacies. Grounded in a deep understanding of political and social landscapes, Kundi's commitment to authenticity and thorough attention to detail is evident in the rich tapestry of worlds he creates for his storytelling.

Residing in Central Valley, California, Kundi's narratives offer intellectual stimulation and emotional connection in a literary landscape craving fresh perspectives.

You can connect with me on:

- http://abdulqkundi.com
- https://twitter.com/aqkkundi
- https://www.facebook.com/Abdul.Quayyum.Kundi
- https://www.goodreads.com/abdul_q_kundi
- https://www.youtube.com/@AbdulQuayyumKhanKundi
- https://tiktok.com/@abdulqkundi
- https://instagram.com/abdulqkundi

Subscribe to my newsletter:

- https://books2read.com/author/abdul-quayyum-khan-kundi/subscribe/59408

Also by Abdul Kundi

All the below works have focused on understanding human nature and our place in the universe.

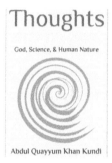

Thoughts: God, Science & Human Nature

https://books2read.com/Thoughts-Kundi

British philosopher Bertrand Russell made a striking observation about dreams. He suggested that if our dreams were coherent night after night, then it would be difficult for us to differentiate between our living and sleeping moments. I am sure you can imagine the effect such a situation would have on our lives. Dreaming is a fascinating aspect of our lives and still largely a mystery. Why do we experience dreams? Do other species dream too?

I have tried to answer it as well as what makes us happy?

Book is available at Amazon, Apple, Google, B&N, Kobo and your favorite bookstore. Ask your library for it.

Islamic Social Contract

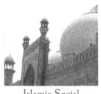

https://books2read.com/Islamic-Social-Contract-Abdul-Q-Kundi

At the dawn of the 21st century two events seem to be dominating to decide the trend for the entirety of it. The first development is the continuing economic recession in the industrialized West. This is producing civic unrest against the established social order and raising questions about the effectiveness of secular democratic institutions. The popular uprising of people to overthrow autocratic rulers in the Muslim majority Middle East and North Africa is the other cataclysmic event demolishing existing order. These two phenomena are still shaping up making it difficult to ascertain their final impact on the political landscape of the world. It is evident, the status quo is not acceptable to the majority of citizens around the world.

Book is available at Amazon, Apple, Google, B&N, Kobo and your favorite bookstore. Ask your library for it.

Lessons from Quran

https://books2read.com/Lessons-from-Quran-Kundi

Philosophers agree that religion presents a higher truth which is beyond the reach of philosophy and science. Reasons alluded to are that science is limited to explaining nature and combination of things. Science is handicapped since it cannot create anything in a vacuum.

Religion struggles to convey an immovable and unchangeable absolute truth which is beyond rational reaches of mind. This creates uncertainties that could have devastating consequences for mankind.

Book is available at Amazon, Apple, Google, B&N, Kobo and your favorite bookstore. Ask your library for it.

Milton Keynes UK
Ingram Content Group UK Ltd.
UKHW010715280324
440307UK00004B/172